VOW OF DECEPTION

RINA KENT

To every one of us who defied logic and fell in love with villains.

AUTHOR NOTE

Hello reader friend,

If you haven't read my books before, you might not know this, but I write darker stories that can be upsetting and disturbing. My books and main characters aren't for the faint of heart.

Vow of Deception is the first book of a trilogy and is not standalone.

Deception Trilogy:
#0 Dark Deception (Free Prequel)
#1 Vow of Deception
#2 Tempted by Deception
#3 Consumed by Deception

Sign up to Rina Kent's Newsletter for news about future releases and an exclusive gift.

My husband. My tormentor.

The most notorious man in the city offers me a job.

Act as his dead wife.

Adrian Volkov isn't the type of person who takes no for an answer.

He commands with an iron fist and all his orders are met.

When he approaches me with the offer, I have two options.

Go to prison or put myself under his wrath.

I choose to have a roof over my head. What's so hard about acting, right?

Wrong.

The moment I step into his wife's shoes, everything spirals out of control.

My only way of survival is through Adrian.

Or is it?

PLAYLIST

Snuff—Slipknot

Demons and Angels—LOWBORN

Darkness in Me—Fight The Fade

I Don't Know What to Say—Bring Me The Horizon

Designer Drugs —FNKHOUSER

Virgin—Manchester Orchestra

Simple Math—Manchester Orchestra

Pale Black Eye—Manchester Orchestra

Warning Sign—Coldplay

Hemorrhage—Red

Crawling—Dream State

Ashes—Claire Guerreso

Survivin'—Bastille

Heavy Rain—Solence

Apprehension—Manchester Orchestra

Mighty—Manchester Orchestra

Flares—The Script

Haunted—Acacia Ridge

In The Shadows—Amy Stroup

Under Your Scars—Godsmack

You can find the complete playlist on Spotify.

PROLOGUE

DEATH CAN COME IN THE FORM OF A doppelgänger.

There's this myth as old as time that says when you meet someone who looks just like you, one of you will die.

Who is the question.

Who would die first? Me or *her*?

According to the myth, the first to see the other one is bound to meet their end. In the same decade. Same year. Perhaps even the same day.

I lift my trembling hands and stare at the blood coating them, intertwining with my fingers and crawling under my nails.

Oh.

I think this means I saw her first. I made eye contact first.

What bad luck. But I guess I've never had the good type. Not when I was born, and certainly not when I was shoved into this life.

My attention remains on the deep crimson covering my

hands like a second skin. It's thick, sticky, and its dark color burns in my head. I rub my palms together to wipe it off, but that doesn't make it better. If anything, the fresh, warm blood smears further, as if it's already chosen my hands as a permanent place of residence.

I screw my eyes shut, dragging in sharp intakes of air. The sound is raspy, guttural, grating on the surface of my lungs with long rusty nails.

That's okay. When I open my eyes, I'll wake up. This isn't real. It's only my wild imagination and my superstition joining forces to torture my mind.

It. Is. Not. Real.

My lids feel like they've been glued together when they part from each other.

The blood is still the same—warm, sticky, and almost black due to the lack of light. I clench my fists, my body turning rigid as a taut whip.

Wake up. Wake the fuck up.

My nails dig into my palms, but nothing I do pulls me out. Nothing stops this nasty cycle.

I lift my head and study my surroundings. Savage trees envelop me like a cocoon. They're so tall that the dark sky is barely visible through the small opening overhead.

Clouds condense over the moon's silver hue, and I shiver. The thin sweater over my cotton dress barely protects me from the chill.

Feeling the cold should be a good sign, but it isn't. It's not a clear indication of whether or not this is real.

The blood on my hands won't disappear and neither will the tremor shooting through my body.

He is after me.

If he finds me, he'll kill me.

I squeeze my eyelids together and count aloud, "Three, two, one."

When I open them again, the trees are the same and so is the chill. The blood is colder now. Thicker. *Stickier.* Like a demon's possessing my mind and is starting with my hands.

No.

I dig my nails into the long scar on my wrist and claw at the skin as hard as I can, intending to remove it and peer under it. To see the blood actually flowing, to differentiate this nightmare from reality.

If there's no pain, then this is not real. It's only another cruel manifestation of my subconscious and another self-punishment. Soon, it'll be all over and I'll wake up, safe and sound.

My skin breaks under the assault of my nails and searing pain explodes on the injury.

My mouth parts and a tear hangs from my lid.

This is real.

This is not a nightmare. I didn't sleep and wake up in hell. I went there with my own two feet.

No.

No…

My dry lips tremble as a few droplets of blood fall from my wound and join the massacre on my hands.

This much blood can only mean one thing.

I took a life.

My demons finally won.

They're silent now, not even attempting to whisper those malicious things, those thoughts that have plagued me day and night. They rose in volume, crashing and clawing at the confines of my head until I heard them.

Until I made their wish come true.

"I'm not a murderer. Not a murder…" I murmur the words to myself. Maybe if I keep doing it, I can undo what happened.

Maybe I can go back and change it.

I stare up at the gloomy, bleak sky, tears clinging to my lids.

"If there's someone out there, please let me go back to change it. I'm not this person. Don't let me be this person. Please…"

Only the howling wind answers me, its sound echoing in the empty forest like vengeful spirits with yellow eyes and gaping mouths.

"P-please…" I beg. "Please stop torturing me with my own self. *Please.*"

I know my pleas have no effect whatsoever, but it's the last hope I can hold on to. The last thread that can save me. Because I desperately need saving right now.

And I don't trust myself to do it anymore. If I try, I'll just make it worse. I'll spiral out of control and slide down the path of no return.

Next thing I know, I'll be my own demons.

I'll be my own downfall.

I'll be the thing I've run away from my entire life.

"Please make it stop." My voice chokes and I sniffle. "Please. I'll do anything."

This time, the wind isn't my answer. The shuffling of footsteps comes from around the trees.

My feet falter and I stop breathing. My demons couldn't have found me this soon.

Though…*wait.* This is reality. My demons don't show up in reality. That means the footsteps belong to someone more dangerous than them.

I spin around and sprint ahead, elbowing the low branches out of my way. The fallen leaves crunch under my flat shoes, but I don't stop to think about the sound I'm making—which gives a clear indication of where I am. That's not important right now. If I'm caught, I'll be killed.

Actually, my fate will be a lot worse than death.

Live. You're a fighter. You were born to live.

Mom's words echo in my head, charging me with a large dose of adrenaline. I have to live and stay that way for both of us.

I *need* to live.

The footsteps grow closer with every passing second until their thudding is right behind me. I don't look back or even try to. Instead, I use the trees as camouflage, dashing between them so fast, my tendons cry out in pain.

If my pattern is irregular, he won't find me. If I'm unpredictable, I'll be able to escape death's clutches.

I was taught to never take the short end of the stick or have less than what I deserve. It's ironic that *he* taught me that but is now coming after me.

So ironic.

The trees clear out and I come to a screeching halt at the top of a cliff. Pebbles escape from under my feet and roll down over the huge boulders and finally to the dark, murky water that's crashing against the rocks. The sound of raging waves echoes in the air like a symphony of death.

The sky is completely cloudy now, casting a gloomy shadow on the angry sea.

As I peer down, a strange yet familiar thought plays at the back of my head.

It would be so easy to end it. So easy.

One step is all it takes. One step and I'll drown my demons with my own hands.

One step and I'll kill them once and for all, so they'll never come out again.

"Do it."

A shudder zaps through my spine at the sinister voice coming from behind me.

He found me.

I whirl around so fast, I lose my footing and swing backward. I reach out to him and grip his arm with both hands, nails digging into my shirt. Blood smears on the light gray cloth as evidence of my desperation to live.

He's motionless, like a cold statue, as I remain suspended

in mid-air. His face is shadowed and I can't see anything except the contours of his jawline and hair.

Since I know he won't make a move to help me, I try to use my hold on his sleeve to pull myself up.

"You ended a life." His calm yet threatening tone stops me in my tracks.

I shake my head violently. "I d-didn't want to."

"It still happened."

"No, please…don't…"

"Die for your sins." He yanks his hand free and I stumble backward and down the cliff.

I open my mouth to shriek, but no sound comes out. The fall isn't as painful as I expected it to be. If anything…it's peaceful.

After taking one last look at the silhouette peering down on me, I close my eyes, letting the tears loose.

It's finally the end.

ONE

Adrian

THE SCENT OF ROSES HAS MORPHED INTO THE stench of death.

I stare down at the blood gushing from her wounds, at the life stubbornly leaving her body without pause or second thoughts.

The red color is marring her fair skin, painting rivulets down her arms and legs and contouring her soft face.

Her eyes are open, but she's not looking at me. Their blue is blank, vanished, already existing someplace else where I don't belong.

I cradle her head in my arms, gently stroking her dark brown hair. Lifting a wet strand, I inhale deeply, searching for what's possibly my last fix of roses. It doesn't matter if they're thorny and would prick me in the process. The method holds no importance to me as long as I get things done.

What greets me is the furthest thing from roses. It's not even death. It's worse.

Nothingness.

Numbness.

A place where she can't and won't feel me. Where she ended everything just so she could seal her heart and her soul.

Just so she could…disappear.

I sweep her hair away from her face and brush my lips over her forehead. "I'll find you again."

People say death is the end.

For me, it's only the beginning.

TWO

Winter

I THINK I'VE STOPPED FEELING.

It's not that I've turned off my emotions, but I'm pretty sure I've lost sense in my hands and feet.

I can almost see the blisters from the cold on my fingers inside my torn gloves and between my toes that are covered with old socks and man shoes that are a size too big, making my feet slouch with every step I take. The frigid air is even moving past the barrier of my four thin sweaters and the coat that's three sizes too big.

Snow season hit hard this year in New York City. I feel like I'm a walking snowman with the weight of the clothes I'm wearing. None of them feel soft or protective enough, but it's better than dying from hypothermia.

It'd be ironic if I died from the cold when my name is Winter.

Is Fate a little too cynical, or what? He must have thought of this moment when he whispered to my mom that she should name me after the coldest, harshest season.

Fate also chose the worst state to throw me in. Not only are the winters here cold, windy, and wet as hell, but the summers are also unbearable with all the humidity.

But who am I to complain? At least here, I can slip through the crowd unnoticed.

As if I don't exist.

Invisibility is a powerful tool. In a city that harbors over eight million residents, it's actually easy for someone like me to go unnoticed.

The cold forces me to stand out more, though. As I walk down the wet streets among the hundreds of thousands of people, I get looks sometimes. They're not always out of pity—oftentimes, they're judgmental. I can hear them say, *You could've done better, young lady.*

But most New Yorkers are so desensitized that they don't give a flying fuck about a nobody like me.

I try not to focus on the people exiting bakeries with takeout, but I can't ignore the divine smells that waft past me. I open my mouth, then close it as if that will get me a taste of the goodies.

If only I could have some hot soup right now or a warm piece of bread.

I swallow the saliva that forms in my mouth at the thought. Whenever I'm starved and don't have access to food, I picture a table full of delicious meals and pretend that I'm feasting on them. But my stomach just believes it for half a minute before it starts growling again.

It's hard to deceive that one.

As hungry as I am, however, what I'd really love is more to drink.

I lift the can of beer that's wrapped in a brown paper bag and down the rest of it. There goes the final drops that were supposed to get me through my day.

It's only the afternoon and I haven't eaten for the last... when was it again? Two days?

Maybe I should go back to the shelter for a meal and a piece of bread...

I dismiss the thought as soon as it comes. I will never return to that place, not even if I have to sleep on the streets. I guess I should search for another shelter where I can spend the rest of the winter or else I'll really freeze to death outside.

My feet come to a halt in front of a framed poster hanging on the side of a building. I don't know why I stop.

I shouldn't.

I don't—usually.

I don't stop and stare, because that would draw attention to me and ruin my chances of having invisibility superpowers.

But for reasons unknown, I halt this time. My empty can is nestled between my gloved fingers, suspended in mid-air as I study the ad.

The poster is for the New York City Ballet, advertising one of their performances. The entirety of it is occupied by a woman wearing a wedding dress and standing on pointe. A veil covers her face, but it's transparent enough to distinguish the sadness, the harshness, the...despair.

'Giselle' is written in script over her head. At the bottom are the names of the director and the prima ballerina, Hannah Max, as well as the other ballerinas participating in the show.

I blink once, and for a second, I can see my reflection in the glass. My coat swallows my small frame and my oversized high-top sneakers resemble clown shoes. My faux fur winter hat covers my ears, and my blonde hair is disheveled and greasy, its ends hidden inside my coat. My hat is pushed back a little, revealing my dark roots. Feeling somehow subconscious, I pull the hood of my coat over my head, allowing it to shadow my face.

Now I look like a serial killer.

Ha. I'd laugh if I could. A serial killer is smart enough to not end up on the streets. They're smart enough to not drown so much in alcohol that sustaining a job becomes impossible.

I blink again and the poster returns to view. Giselle. Ballet. Prima ballerina.

A sudden urge to gouge the woman's eyes out overwhelms me. I inhale, then exhale. I shouldn't have such a strong reaction toward a stranger.

I hate her. I hate Hannah Max and Giselle and ballet.

Spinning around, I leave before I'm tempted to smash the poster to the ground.

I crumple the can and toss it in a nearby trash can. This change of mood isn't good—at all.

It's because of the lack of alcohol in my system. I haven't had enough beer today to get drunk in the daylight. The cold becomes more tolerable when my mind is numb. My thoughts aren't as loud and I don't get murderous feelings over a harmless ballet poster.

I absentmindedly cross the street like I do every day. It's become my routine, and I don't even pay attention to it anymore.

That's my mistake—taking things for granted.

I don't hear the blaring horn until I'm standing in the middle of the street.

My feet stop in place as if heavy stones are keeping them glued to the ground. As I stare at the van's hazard lights and hear its continuous horn, I think my twenty-seven-year-old life from birth until now will pass in front of my eyes. That's what happens at the time of death, right? I should recall it all.

From the moment Mom relocated us from one city to the other, until life threw me into New York.

From the moment I flourished, until the accident that turned me into an incurable alcoholic.

However, none of those memories come. Not even a fragment of them. The only things that invade my head are little toes and fingers. A tiny face and body that the nurse put in my arms before she was taken away for good.

A lump forms in my throat and I tremble like an insignificant leaf in the cold winter streets of New York.

I promised to live for her. Why the hell am I dying now?

I close my eyes. *I'm so sorry, baby girl. So very sorry.*

A large hand grips me by the elbow and yanks me back so hard, I trip over my own feet and stumble. The same hand gently holds me by the arm to keep me standing.

I slowly open my eyes, halfway expecting to find my head under the van. But instead, the horn blasts as it passes me by, the driver screaming through the window, "Watch where you're going, fucking crazy bitch!"

Meeting his gaze, I flip him off with my free hand and keep doing it to make sure he sees it in the rear-view mirror.

As soon as the van disappears around the corner, I start trembling again. The brief wave of adrenaline that hit me when I was being insulted withers away, and now all I can think about is that I could've died.

That I *really* would've let my little girl down.

"Are you all right?"

I whirl around at the sound of the accented voice. For a second, I forgot that someone had pulled me out of that van's path. That if they hadn't, I would be dead right now.

The man, who's Russian, judging by the subtle accent he just spoke with, stands in front of me, his hand still gripping my elbow. It's a gentle touch compared to the brute force he used to pull me back.

He's tall, and while most people are taller than my five-foot-four, he goes way beyond that. Probably six-two or more. He's wearing a black shirt and pants with an open dark gray cashmere coat. It could be the colors, or the length of the coat, which reaches his knees, but he looks elegant, smart, in a lawyer sort of way, and probably worked as a model to pay his college tuition.

His face tells a different story, however. Not that he's not handsome, because he is, with sharp, angular features that fit his model body. He has high cheekbones that cast a shadow on his thick-stubbled jaw.

His eyes are an intense shade of gray that's bordering on black. The color of his clothes could be intensifying their appearance, though. The fact remains that they're too...uncomfortable to look at. You know when something or someone is so beautiful it actually aches inside to look at them? That's this stranger. Peering into his eyes, however bizarre they are, hits me with a feeling of inferiority that I can't shake off.

Although his words conveyed concern, I see none written in his facial expression. No empathy that most people are capable of.

But at the same time, he doesn't seem like the type who'd feign worry. If anything, he'd be like the rest of the passers-by who barely looked in the direction of the near-traffic accident.

I should be feeling grateful, but the only thing I want is to escape from his clutches and his uneasy eyes. His deep, imploring eyes that are decrypting my face, little by little.

Piece by each tiny piece.

"I'm okay," I manage, twisting my elbow free.

His brow furrows, but it's brief, almost unnoticeable, before he goes back to his previous expression, letting me go as gently as he was gripping me. I expect him to turn around and leave so that I can chalk up the entire experience to an unlucky winter afternoon.

But he just stands there, unmoving, unblinking, not making one single step in any direction. Instead, he chooses to watch me, his thick brows drawing over his eyes that I *really* don't want to be staring into, but I find myself dragged into their savage gray anyway.

They're like the harshness of the clouds above and the merciless gust of the wind from every direction. I can pretend they don't exist, but they still make me lose the feeling of my limbs. They give me blisters and pain.

"Are you sure you're all right?" he asks again, and for some reason, it feels like he wants me to tell him I'm not.

But why? And to what end?

I'm just one of thousands of homeless people in this city. A man like him, who's surrounded by an impenetrable air of confidence, hinting that he's in some prominent position, shouldn't have even looked in my direction.

But he did.

And now, he's asking if I'm okay. Being used to invisibility makes me feel fidgety when I'm suddenly visible.

Ever since this Russian stranger gripped me by the arm, there's been an itch under my skin, urging me to jump back to the shadows.

Now.

"Yeah," I blurt. "Thank you."

I'm about to turn and leave when the authority in his voice stops me. "Wait."

My big shoes make a squeaky sound on the concrete when I follow his command. I normally wouldn't. I'm not good at listening to orders, which is why I'm in this state.

But something in his tone gets my attention.

He reaches into his coat and two scenarios burst through my head. The first is that he'll pull out a gun and shoot me in the head for disrespecting him. The second is that he'll treat me like many others and give me money.

That sense of inferiority hits again. While I usually accept change from people to buy my beer, I don't beg for it. The idea of taking this stranger's money makes me feel dirty, less than invisible and more like a speck of dust on his black leather shoes.

I intend to refuse his money, but he only retrieves a handkerchief and places it in my hand. "You have something on your face."

His skin brushes against my gloves for a second, and though the contact is brief, I see it.

A wedding ring on his left finger.

I bunch the piece of cloth in my hand and nod in thanks. I don't know why I expected him to smile or even offer a nod in return.

He doesn't.

His eyes penetrate mine for a few seconds, then he turns around and leaves.

Just like that.

He's erased me from his unlucky afternoon and is now going back to his wife.

Considering the extreme discomfort I felt in his presence, I figured I'd be relieved when he left.

On the contrary, it feels as if my breast bone is digging into the sensitive flesh of my heart.

What the hell?

I stare at the handkerchief he placed in my hand. It has the letters *A.V.* embroidered on it and appears to be handmade. Something of value.

Why would he even give me this?

Something on your face.

There's a lot of shit on my face. A layer of dirt, actually. Since I haven't been in a public restroom for some time. Did he really think a freaking handkerchief would be the solution?

Pissed off at him and at my reaction toward him, I toss the handkerchief in a trash can and storm in the opposite direction.

I need a hot meal and a bed tonight, and if it means meeting the devil again to have them, so be it.

THREE

Winter

I STOP BEFORE ROUNDING THE CORNER TOWARD THE
shelter.

Saying I'll face the devil and actually doing so are two
different things. After all, I clawed at his face, kicked him in the
balls, then shoved him against his desk the last time I saw him.

He might really catch me and force me to spend a day in
the police station.

A low growl escapes my stomach and I wince as it con-
tracts against itself. I can almost feel it opening its mouth and
when it finds nothing, makes this god-awful sound.

I wrap an arm around my middle as if that will magically
appease the ache.

Okay, I'll just try to sneak in some soup and leave. Many
homeless people who don't spend the night here come only for
meals, so my plan shouldn't be weird.

I pull my hood over my head and rub my hands together in
a half-assed attempt to warm them as I round the corner.

Two police cars are parked in front of the shelter with their blue and red lights on. A few news vans are scattered around the shabby building. Reporters and cameramen are everywhere, like bugs searching for a juicy piece of trash to bite down on.

Don't tell me that slimy asshole called the police and the media because of me? I only kicked him. Okay, maybe I clawed at his face and punched him, too, but that was in self-defense. He's the one who called me into his office and was feeling me up where he wasn't supposed to be touching.

I might have little—okay, nothing—but I can protect myself against bastards like him.

But if I tell that to the police or the media, they won't believe me. Why would the respectable director of a homeless shelter, who's also running for mayor, touch an insignificant, dirty person like me?

I really should search for another shelter. But will they let me in if Richard has already blacklisted me?

Was it the clawing, the punching, or the kicking that sealed the deal for him? If it was the latter, so be it. Because kicking him in the balls isn't something I regret in the least.

A pebble hits me upside the head and I wince, turning around. A smile lifts my mouth when I make eye contact with the only person I'd call my friend in this shithole.

"Larry!" I whisper-yell.

"Come here." He motions at me to join him in a small alleyway that's used for tossing trash.

I briskly move to his side and wince at the smell of garbage. Not that Larry and I are the best smelling people around, considering the limited amount of time we get to shower.

Larry's tan skin appears even darker in the shadows. He's a middle-aged man—around mid-fifties, as he told me—and he has the wrinkles around his eyes as proof of the time he's spent on this earth. His features are harsh, angular, and the bone in his nose protrudes due to being broken before.

He's wearing a second-hand hot orange cashmere coat that

he got from some charity. His boots and gloves are navy blue. Obviously, his sense of fashion is definitely better than mine.

We met a few weeks ago at one of the subway stations and he shared his dinner with me. I gave him half of my precious beer and we somehow became best friends. The one thing I love most about Larry's company is that he's not the talkative type. We both daydream in each other's presence, not bothering to ask too many questions. We've found camaraderie in silence. In shutting the door on the world. He knows about my alcohol problem, though, and he told me that he's a veteran.

Larry is the one who brought me to this shithole, saying we'd get free meals and a warm bed. We've stuck around for each other, so when one is sleeping, the other takes guard so no one touches us. When there are no beds available, we sit beside each other, I lay my head on his shoulder, and we sleep like that.

"I've been searching all over for you." He pants. "Where have you been?"

"Around."

"Did you steal some beer again?"

"No!"

"Winter..." he pinches the bridge of his nose as if I'm an insolent child.

"Okay. Only one. I didn't have any change."

"We agreed to never steal."

"Desperate times, Larry. Besides, you know I don't like the sober me. She has issues." Maybe that's why I've been feeling off-balance all afternoon. I have a low alcohol tolerance, but even I need more than a single beer to get drunk.

"Winter..."

"Forget about me." I throw a dismissive hand in the shelter's general direction. "What happened here?"

He thins his lips before releasing them. "I ought to ask you that."

"Me?"

"Yes, you. Why do you think the police and the media are here?"

"Because Richard called them over to demonize me?"

"Not exactly."

"Then what?"

"Richard was found dead in his office this morning."

I pause, a strange sensation gripping me by the throat and confiscating my air supply. When I speak, it's in a strained whisper. "What?"

"The cleaning staff found him in a pool of his own blood and the police are suspecting you did it."

"*Me?*"

"Yeah. I don't know if Richard called them before he died or if the staff and the others witnessed that you were the last person who saw him alive."

My fists clench on either side of me. "I didn't kill him, Larry. I didn't do it."

His brows draw over his wrinkled eyes as he sighs. He has thick skin with some blotches, probably due to staying out in the sun for so many years. "I know."

"Really?"

"Really, Winter. You're a crazy little thing, but you're no murderer."

I smile a little at that. "Who are you calling crazy, old man?"

"I'm no old man, you little shit."

"You act like one, Larry."

He headlocks me, then swiftly pushes me away. Larry has always kept distance between us, as if he's afraid to touch me, and I'm thankful for that. Not because his touch is bad, but because I dislike being touched. That's why I prefer invisibility.

"Anyway, you need to leave before they find you."

"No. I did nothing wrong, and if I hide, that means I'm admitting to a crime I didn't commit."

"So what do you plan, woman? Are you thinking of barging into the midst of those policemen? What are you going to say? Like, 'umm, hey there, officers, I'm the one you think killed Richard, but I actually didn't, so let's just shake hands'?"

"I'll simply tell them what happened."

"No one will believe you, Winter. Your fingerprints are all over his office and you were the last one who saw him alive before you disappeared. You're guilty in their eyes. And if you go in there, they'll lock you up for twenty years. You won't get a good lawyer either, because state-appointed ones are shit."

His words penetrate my brain, slowly making sense, but I want to dismiss them as fast as possible. I want them to be untrue. Because I can't accept that option.

"So what do you suggest I do, Larry? Run away?"

The older man snaps his fingers. "Exactly. Lie low for a while and then we'll figure some way to get you out of this city."

It's the most logical thing to do under the circumstances. It is. But I've always been attached to this merciless city with super glue. Besides, it's where I have memories with my baby girl, and if I leave, it'll be like I'm abandoning a piece of me.

"But…Larry…"

He sighs, jamming both of his hands in his orange coat. "You don't want to leave?"

I shake my head.

"But you might get locked up. You have to."

"I know. Are you…coming with me?"

"Absolutely, woman. We ride together and die together."

"That sounds like some motorcycle club's slogan."

"I stole it. Roll with it." He peeks his head around the corner, his hazel eyes shining with concentration before he focuses on me. "Now, go. Don't stay in open places and avoid cameras. I've got your back."

I wrap my arms around him in a brief hug. "How will we meet again?"

"I have my homeless intel. I'll find you. Just lay low."

After I reluctantly release him, I carefully make my way through the back of the alley.

I glance behind me to cast one last glimpse at Larry, but he's already gone.

♋

Usually, when we're not at a shelter, Larry and I spend the night in the subway station. The benches are our friends and the marginal silence is better than the loud city outside.

So that's where I go first, but soon realize my mistake when I see the news about Richard's death on the station's TV.

Two middle-aged men, who appear to be football fans judging from their blue Giants hats, stop in front of me to watch the news. I shrink backward and blend in with a wall in case anyone here recognizes me.

"What a mess," one of them says, lighting a cigarette, despite the no smoking signs.

"Maybe it's a sign that he wasn't meant to run for mayor," the other replies, shrugging a shoulder.

"Wasn't meant to? Man, have you even been living in this city?"

"Why? What?"

"Richard Green was the prime candidate for mayor." Cigarette Man leans toward his friend and lowers his voice as if he's sharing Central Intelligence Agency secrets. "There are rumors that he was backed by the mafia."

"The mafia?" the other man whisper-yells.

"Keep your voice down, you idiot. You want to get us whacked?"

I scoff at the way he mimics the famous mobster movies, but I find myself moving closer, while still keeping a distance, to get a whiff of their conversation. If Richard was backed by the mafia, then the scary men dressed in dark suits make more sense since they dropped by occasionally and went straight to his office.

"Is it the Italians?" the non-smoker asks.

Cigarette Man blows out a cloud of smoke and I block my nose and mouth with the back of my hand to keep from coughing. "No. The Bratva."

"Russians?"

"That's what the rumors say."

"Are the filthy Russians getting involved in our politics again?"

"Yeah, man. And their mafia is no joke. Heard they kill people like they're flies."

"This is a country of law."

Cigarette Man bursts out laughing, waving his hand to catch his breath from the force of it. "What law, man? Those monsters make the law wherever they go."

"Are you saying Richard's death isn't as simple as the media's painting it out to be?"

"Yes, I am. All that is a diversion." Cigarette Man motions at the line that reads "Richard Green, New York City mayoral candidate, was killed by one of the homeless people in the shelter he directed."

I squint at the TV and frown. My picture should be all over the news with a wanted caption on top. How come they didn't even mention my name? Did the police not give concrete statements to the media yet?

But that doesn't make any sense. My handprints are everywhere in Richard's office, and I'm, without a doubt, their prime suspect. So how come I'm just a homeless person in his shelter? Even my gender isn't mentioned.

"The Russians are scary, dude," Cigarette Man says.

"Worse than the Italians?"

"Right now? Way fucking worse. Their power and

influence run deeper than any other criminal ring." He throws his cigarette on the concrete without extinguishing it as he and his friend rush to catch a train.

I walk to where they stood and kill the cigarette with the sole of my shoe. The topic on the TV has changed to some other world news and I keep staring at the burnt butt. How the fire left a black line on the white exterior. So even after it's gone, the evidence remains.

Just like my life.

I touch the bottom of my abdomen where my scar is tucked neatly under the countless layers of clothes. It still burns as if my fingertips are on fire, bursting through the clothes and flaming my skin.

Another protest of hunger comes from my stomach and I sigh, leaving the station. I need to go to a quieter place because, even though they didn't reveal my identity, they will eventually.

The Giants fans' conversation keeps playing in the back of my head as I sneak from one alley to another, my footsteps light and fast.

When Cigarette Man mentioned the Russians, the only thought that came to mind was the stranger from earlier today. His accent was very Russian, but not really rough like I've heard before. It was smooth, effortless, almost how I'd imagine Russian royalty to speak if they ever learned English.

Could he be a part of the mafia Cigarette Man mentioned?

I internally shake my head. Why would I place him with the mafia just because he has a Russian accent? He could be a Russian businessman, like the thousands who swarm New York all the time.

Or a spy.

A shiver shakes my insides at the thought. I really need to rein in my wild imagination. Besides, in what world is a spy that attractive? Except James Bond, but he's fiction. The Russian stranger drew so much attention, and the weirdest part is that he seemed kind of oblivious to it. Or maybe he was bothered by it, like he didn't want to be the center of attention, but he was forced into that position anyway.

I reach into my pocket and retrieve the handkerchief he gave me. Okay, so I did throw it in the trash, but then I took it out. No idea why. It felt like a waste, I guess.

Running my gloved fingers over the initials, I wonder if his wife made him this and if she'll question him about its whereabouts. Though he seemed to be the type who does the questioning, not the other way around.

Shoving the handkerchief back in my pocket, I push the weird stranger out of my head and take a few turns until I arrive at an underground parking garage Larry and I frequent.

The guard is snoring at the entrance, mumbling about some baseball player being an idiot. It doesn't take much effort to slip past him. Now, all I have to do is leave early in the morning before he wakes up.

The parking garage isn't big or fancy, only fit for around a hundred cars and half the slots aren't occupied. Just one-third of the neon lights work, but even if they all blinded me, it wouldn't make a difference. I've slept in worse places with stronger lighting and louder noises.

The key to staying safe is sleeping with one eye open. Not literally. But basically being a light sleeper so that the slightest movement springs me awake.

When I sit down on the concrete floor between two cars and close my eyes, I'm well aware of the buzzing from the half-broken lights and the swishing of the cars passing by on the streets upstairs. I can even hear the guard's mumbling, though I can't make out his words.

If he stops, I'll know he's awake and I need to be alert. He could call the cops on me, and that's the last thing I want in my current situation—or any situation, actually.

I try to get as comfortable as possible in my position,

although the cold is seeping through my bones from the wall behind me and the floor underneath me.

I try not to pay attention to my growling stomach or the pulsing need to get drunk.

I try to think about where to go from here when I officially become a wanted person.

Soon enough, exhaustion takes its toll on me and I fall into a dreamless sleep.

I don't dream. Ever. It's like my mind has become a blank canvas since the accident.

The mumbling stops and the guard starts talking. My eyes pop open and I stare at the small opening across from me that serves as a window. It's still night, and judging by the lack of cars buzzing about, it's late enough that no other vehicles should come here.

And yet, a black car slowly slides into the parking garage. It's so silent, I wouldn't have heard it if I weren't so attuned to the outside world's noises.

I drag my knees to my chest and wrap my arms around them, then pull the hood of my coat over my head to cover it completely. Only one of my eyes peeks through a narrow gap.

As long as it doesn't park in the spot opposite me, I should be fine. It's more logical to pick one of the countless spots near the entrance.

The sound gets closer and I catch sight of the black car. I shrink in the tight space between a Hyundai and the wall, thanking everything that's holy for my small frame. It helps in my invisibility scheme.

But in doing this, I've blocked my vision of what the car is doing. For long seconds, there's no sound. Not the opening of doors or the beeping of a lock.

Crouching down, I peek under the car and see one pair of men's feet standing right in front of the Hyundai. I place a gloved hand to my mouth to smother any sound I might make.

The rotten smell from whatever shit I've been touching triggers a sense of nausea and makes me want to retch.

I breathe through my mouth while I keep watching his feet. He's wearing brown shoes and he's not moving, like he's waiting for something.

Go away. Go!

I repeat the mantra in my head over and over again as if that will make it happen.

Mom used to tell me that if you believe in something strongly enough, it'll come true.

And just like magic, the brown shoes walk away. I release a breath of relief, but it's cut off when a strong hand yanks me up from behind the car by my hood.

The force is so strong that I'm momentarily suspended mid-air, before a bulky man with scary features says with a Russian accent, "Got her, Boss."

FOUR

Winter

GOT HER, *Boss.*

I don't pause to think what those words could mean. My first and most important role in life is survival. I'm not living for myself. I'm living on behalf of my baby girl. For the life she couldn't have.

The man who's captured me is bulky and as big as a mountain. His expression is stern, harsh, like he was born with a permanent scowl. His hair is short, white-blond, and his light eyes are as cold and merciless as ice.

As soon as he puts me on my feet, I wiggle to slip out of the hold he has on my hood. Twisting and squirming, I grab his hand and try to yank it away, but I might as well be a mouse fighting a cat.

He appears utterly uninterested as he pulls me along, my struggle not deterring him at all. I step on his foot, but he merely grasps my hood tighter as he continues to take me away. My feet drag on the floor and I lose one of my shoes.

"Help!" I scream at the top of my lungs. "Help—" The man

places a stone-like hand on my mouth, cutting off any sound I can make.

Unlike the stench of my rotten gloves, his hand smells of leather and metal. Despite the somewhat tolerable odor, it's still stifling as if I'm being stuffed in a small place where I don't fit.

My limbs shake at that prospect. I attempt to wrench my mind from it, but it's already grown and expanded, tearing through flesh and bones to materialize in front of me.

I'm in a closed space, it's so dark, so very *dark* that I can't see my own hands. The odor of urine fills my nostrils and my own breaths sound like the red-eyed monster from my most terrifying nightmares.

I'm trapped.

I can't get out.

"Let me out..." I whisper with hoarse desperation. "Please let me out..."

"Where is the little monster?"

No!

I scratch at the hand holding me, at the one who will kill me. I won't let them.

I *have* to live.

Before I know it, I'm shoved into the back of the black car. I must've been so caught up in that moment from the past that I didn't pay attention to the distance he'd dragged me. Bulky Blond releases me and slams the door shut.

My fingers are shaking, and the remnants of the flashback of that dark, tight space still beats under my skin like a demon about to rear its ugly head. Usually, after such episodes, I run into an open space and keep running and running until the air burns my lungs and erases the image.

Not now, though.

Now, I need to force my body to be on a high so I can survive.

Survival comes before everything. Before pain. Before mental prisons.

Everything.

I attempt to open the door before Bulky Blond can get in the driver's seat and take me to God knows where.

But he doesn't climb into the car.

Instead, he stands in front of it with his back to me. Another man joins him and when he turns to the side, I catch a passing glimpse of his profile. He's shorter in size and appears younger than Bulky Blond. His physique is also on the leaner side and his suit jacket doesn't cling to his shoulders like that of the larger man. He has long brown hair that's gathered in a low bun and a crooked nose that I'm sure I've seen before, but where?

The moment of hesitation vanishes when Crooked Nose and Bulky Blond both face away from me.

I tug on the handle, but the door doesn't open. "Shit."

Jamming my sock-covered foot against it, I push, then pull until heat rises up my cheeks. I click the button to lower the glass, but it's also locked.

"It's useless. Save your effort."

I flinch, my movements coming to a screeching halt. In my adrenaline-induced haze, I failed to notice that someone else was in the back seat with me.

Still gripping the handle, I slowly turn my head, hoping to hell that what I just heard was a play of my imagination.

That I've thought about him for so long, I've started hallucinating.

I'm not.

My lips part as I'm wrenched into those intense gray eyes from this afternoon. They appear darker, more shadowed, as if the night has cast a spell on them.

I cut off eye contact as soon as I make it, because if I keep staring, my skin will crawl, my head will get dizzy, and I'll feel like vomiting my empty stomach out.

Using my foot on the door, I pull and push on the handle

with all my might. At first, I thought the bulky man could be with the police and that he's picking me up for killing Richard, but there's no way this Russian stranger is a cop.

He doesn't look like one.

Maybe he's a spy, after all. This seems oddly similar to the beginning of some spy movie about an underdog—me—who will be recruited to work in secret for an intelligence agency.

When all the pushing and pulling doesn't bring me any results, I jam my elbow into the glass. A zing of pain shoots through my whole arm, but I won't stop, not until I'm out of this place.

It's starting to feel like that damn closed box. I need *out*.

I'm about to punch the glass with my fist, when the stranger's voice fills the air, "It's bulletproof, so you'll only hurt yourself."

My arm lies limp beside me. I might be willing to sacrifice pain, but I won't do it for no result.

"Are you done?" he asks in that calm, almost serene tone— just like royalty. His voice is velvety, smooth as silk, but still deep and masculine.

I don't look at him and, instead, lunge to the front seat. If I can open the door or go out the window, I'll run and—

Strong hands grip me by the hips and yank me back with effortless ease. I'm now so close to him that his thigh touches mine.

I expect him to let me go now that he has me by his side, but he doesn't. If anything, his hold tightens on my hips, and even though I'm wearing multiple layers of clothes, I can feel the controlling warmth in his hands. It's different from the heat in the car. This is burning, tearing holes through my clothes and aiming at my skin.

This close, I can smell him—or more like, I'm forced to in-hale him with every drag of air. His scent is a mixture of leather and wood. Power and mysteriousness.

He speaks against my ear, his tone dropping in range with the purpose of cementing the words in my bones, "It's useless to fight me, for you'll only get hurt. You're not at my level, so do not cause me trouble or I won't hesitate to throw you to the wolves. I'm giving you my hand, so be grateful, thank your lucky stars, and take it without asking any fucking questions."

My lips have been dry the entire time he's been talking. He's issuing clear threats, but he sounds like a calm lawyer presenting a case in front of a judge.

He has a particular way of speaking. His words are deliberate, sure, and have a commanding edge, without being too much in your face.

"What do you want from me?" I want to kick myself for the small voice. I almost sound scared. Scratch that. I *definitely* sound scared, because holy shit, I am. I just met this man today, and in the span of a few hours, my life has flipped upside down.

Up until now, my only purpose has been to live, but even that sounds impossible at the moment.

"I have an offer for you, Winter."

How do you know my name? I want to ask that, but it'd be useless. He seems like the type of man who knows everything he needs to.

"What offer?"

His lips graze the shell of my ear as he murmurs, "Be my wife."

FIVE

Winter

MY MOM USED TO SAY THAT THE BEST WAY TO DISARM someone is to tell them what they least expect.

I don't know what I thought the Russian stranger would say, but 'Be my wife' certainly was not it.

It takes me a few seconds of staring blankly, caught in a state of shock I can't shake off. He remains calm, composed. Unrailed.

Ever since I met him this afternoon, he's been as sturdy as an oak and as still as a statue. Now, I realize why I kind of wanted him to smile earlier, why I waited for it with bated breath. It would've humanized him a little, and I was desperately and irrationally looking for some human trait in his robotic features.

Now, though? He seems like some sort of a force. A current. A tyranny that's about to sweep away everything in its path before changing lanes to something else.

Be my wife.

His words, though calmly spoken, explode in my head like

the Fourth of July fireworks. They're so loud that they drown my own thoughts in a web of nothingness. They're trapped somewhere beyond reach, in that tiny black box that brings on a shiver whenever I think of it.

The most proper reaction to his ludicrous offer is to actually laugh. But I don't have the sense of humor for that. And I suspect he wouldn't take it well if I somehow burst out laughing in front of him.

He's so serious, it's etched in his features, his mannerisms, and even the way he speaks—as if he's never smiled a day in his life.

Like the act of smiling would be offensive to him.

He and the men outside are not normal. I can see that without having to learn who they actually are. It can be tasted in the air. It instantly shifted after they came into the picture.

Dangerous people need to be dealt with using caution, not force, because the second option will only get me hurt.

"Be your wife?" I repeat, my tone low, but it projects the incredulity I feel.

The Russian stranger releases my hips and I scoot to the other side of the car, putting as much distance between us as possible.

The lack of his touch is like losing warmth in the middle of an icy storm. But I'd rather freeze than be burnt to death by him.

"Correct." He interlocks his fingers in his lap. They're long and manicured, and I can't help but stare at the wedding ring on his left hand.

"You're already married."

His gaze slides to his ring as if he's forgotten it's been there all along. His thick black lashes frame his eyes while he takes a moment, studying it. His expression is weird. When someone thinks about their spouse, they would ordinarily either soften out of adoration or grow grim out of sadness or despair.

He's doing neither.

His lips thin in a motion that suggests he wants to strangle the ring and the one who slid it on his finger.

Before I can read further into his reaction, his attention glides from his hand to me, and the emotions I thought I saw in his steel eyes vanish as if they never existed. "You'll pretend to be my wife."

"Pretend?" I don't know why I keep asking these questions, entertaining him, but the situation is so surreal, it feels like I've been thrust into one of those Christmas tales.

"My wife passed away a few weeks ago, and there's no one who can perform her duties anymore, so you will be her replacement."

"Oh." I don't mean to say that out loud, but it escapes from me anyway.

I stare at him from a different perspective. At his straight, confident posture, at his choice of dark wardrobe, at his black hair and thick stubble, at the shadows caused by his cheek-bones. And, finally, at the dimness in his gray eyes that appear to have been cut from New York's gloomy sky.

Have I felt uncomfortable around him because of this negative energy he projects? Now that I've learned the reason behind that energy is the recent death of his wife, I don't know how to feel.

Still, the unease is lurking under my skin like a clotted blood vessel, blocking the normal flow of oxygen to my heart.

His hands, although resting on his lap, feel like they're pushing up against my soul, applying pressure and trying to burst through.

That's…dangerous. Terrifying, actually.

I might have ended up on the streets, but my instincts are intact and they can at least recognize danger.

This man is the definition of it.

His good looks, strong physique, and effortless

confidence don't fool me. If anything, I view them as his tools of destruction.

"I'm sorry about your wife," I say as calmly as possible. "But I can't help."

"I don't need your insincere apologies. Just do as you are told."

"Didn't you hear what I said? I can't be your wife."

"Yes, you can. In fact, you're the only one who's able to fit that role."

"The only one? Have you *seen* me?"

He taps his fingers against his thighs as his gaze slides from my face to my torso and down to my foot that's missing a shoe. I'm the one who asked if he's seen me, but now that I'm trapped under his scrutiny, the sense of inferiority from this afternoon grips me again.

He must be seeing a monster, a smelly one at that, and while I rarely feel self-conscious about my lifestyle, I do now. The unwelcome sensation slams into me with a harshness that robs me of breath.

I begin to squirm, but stop myself.

"I do see you." He speaks slowly, almost like he has a different meaning behind the words. The tapping of his fingers comes to a halt. "Clearly."

"Then…you must see I'm not fit to be anyone's wife." *Let alone his.*

He reaches into his coat pocket and I expect him to pull a gun out and shoot me in the face for wasting his time. However, he retrieves a black leather wallet, opens it, and slides a picture out.

A small gasp leaves my lips as I stare at the woman in it. It's a solo shot of her in a wedding dress. Her dark brown hair is gathered in an elegant bun, revealing her delicate throat. The dress's neckline falls off her shoulders, accentuating their curves and her collarbone.

Her nose is petite, and the contour of her face is defined

while remaining soft. Light makeup covers her fair skin, enhancing her quiet beauty. Her full lips are painted in a nude color and her eyeshadow is a similar shade.

Her eyes are a turquoise so blue, it's like she's peering into my soul and waiting for it to peer right back.

A small smile pulls at her mouth. It's a mysterious one, almost like she doesn't want to smile, or perhaps she has a different purpose behind it.

But her beauty and elegance aren't the reason for my trembling fingers.

It's *all* of her.

I'm staring at a dark-haired, clean, and well-groomed version of myself. I barely remember the last time I was as clean as she is, but I do remember my reflection in the mirror at the hospital a few weeks ago, and I definitely looked like this woman, only with blonde hair.

"That's why it has to be you."

I startle at the stranger's voice. While I was lost in his wife's picture, I just about forgot that he was there all along.

"But how…?"

"How?" he repeats with a slight furrow in his brow.

"How is this possible? I was an only child, so she…" I chance another look at her. "She can't be my twin or my sister."

"She isn't related to you by blood."

"Then…how do you explain the resemblance?" *Scary one, at that.* She even has my freaking eye color that I've always thought was rare as hell.

"Do you believe in doppelgängers, Winter?"

"Doppelgängers?" I scoff. "Are you joking?"

"Do I look like the type who jokes?" The authoritativeness in his tone causes me to glue myself to the closed car door. Shit. He really is terrifying.

"N-no."

"Correct."

"Are you saying she and I are doppelgängers? How is that possible?"

"It's more common than you think."

"I still…don't believe it."

"It doesn't matter what you believe. It's already happening."

"Already happening?"

"Yes. You will be my wife."

"No. I didn't agree to this."

"Didn't agree to this," he muses, as if my words are somehow comical. "You believe you have that option? Who the fuck do you think you are?"

I inch farther into the door until the handle digs into my side. "I'm a free person."

"Free? How do you define freedom? Is it sleeping in parking garages and begging for food?"

"The way I live is none of your business."

"Don't talk back to me again or you won't like the way I react." He's so calm in issuing his threat, but that doesn't diminish its impact. I wish I could become one with the floorboard or the door—I'm not picky.

He stares at me for a beat too long, making sure his words hit their mark, before he continues, "You'll have a roof over your head, a warm bed to sleep in, and hot meals all day long."

The picture he's painting is tempting, but *he* is not. He's far from tempting. He's so frightening that even sitting beside him is giving me a sense of anxiety. I feel like I need to be in fight-or-flight mode around him. Actually, I'll have to go with flight because the fight option will definitely get me killed.

So while I do want all the things he listed, their price—being with him—isn't something I can afford to pay.

I need to find a way out of this.

"If you're still not convinced, fine."

My head snaps up to meet his blank gaze. "You're letting me go?"

"If you wish."

I narrow my eyes. "Really?"

"Yes, but the police are on standby a few blocks away. As soon as you leave this car, you'll be arrested for the murder of Richard Green."

I gasp. How…how the hell does he know about that?

"I blocked the police and media from divulging your name and picture, but if you'd rather live on the streets, then you won't mind prison. You should thank me, really. They at least give you meals there."

I can feel the car closing in on me, its seats turning into octopus tentacles to choke me.

He's planned everything from the murder to the police to how they never mentioned any detail about me. But he's been playing his cards, one by each one in a methodical, psychopathic way. He never planned to give me any choice to begin with. He came here with the purpose of turning me into his wife, and I can do nothing to escape this fate.

"Why…" I swallow the tears and the clog in my throat. "Why didn't you use that threat from the beginning? Why did you give me hope that I could refuse this?"

"It wasn't my intention to give you hope. And you couldn't have refused me, Winter. You're a nobody. A pest everyone stomps on without looking twice. A nameless, forgettable face no one remembers down the line. Be grateful that I'm giving you this offer. Say thank you and go with it."

I raise my hand and slap him across the face so hard, pain bursts over my palm and shoots down my arm.

A weird type of anger took hold of me at his words, and I needed to relieve it somewhere. This is the only solution my brain came up with.

One that I now realize could cost me my life.

The stranger's eyes darken and a muscle tics under his stubbled jaw.

I fully expect him to strike—or punch—me back, and I squeeze my trembling lips together in preparation for the impact.

However, his hand loops around my nape and he hauls me over so that my face is mere inches away from his. "The last person who dared to touch me is now buried six feet under."

I gulp down the lump in my throat. His words alone are suffocating me and digging my grave. I would've preferred he hit me instead.

"This is the first and last time you do that. Repeat it and you'll meet a worse fate than being buried in a grave."

He releases me with a shove and I stumble back toward the door, my heart beating so loud, I can hear the buzzing in my ears.

"What are you going to do with me?" My voice is small, fearful.

"Whatever I wish."

My teeth chatter for a different reason than the cold weather, but I can't resist the feral need to ask the question, "Are you going to hurt me?"

His attention fixes on me, his eyes turning ashen, blank. "Depends."

"On what?"

"On whether or not you're good at following orders."

I stare up at him with another swallow. I'm not, I'm really not. But I need to start to be, because I don't want to give this man a reason to hurt me.

Not that he'd need one.

"You'll be cleaned up before you come to my house." He gives me a condescending glance, cementing the fact that he does indeed think of me as a pest.

"When will that be?"

"Now."

"N-now?"

"You have an objection?"

I shake my head once. I want to see Larry again, but that will probably put him in danger with these men, so I opt not to do it. I'll have opportunities to come see him once I'm…someone else.

That realization hits me deeper than I would've anticipated.

I'm going to live as someone else.

I won't be Winter Cavanaugh anymore.

My thoughts are reinforced when the Russian says, "From now on, you're Lia Volkov. Wife of Adrian Volkov."

SIX

Adrian

I'VE NEVER BELIEVED IN SECOND CHANCES.

Trusting that someone can change is wishful thinking in ninety-nine percent of cases. It's a waste of time and energy.

However, there's always that pesky one percent. The anomaly. The…deviation of human behavior.

The fact that it's almost impossible to predict or catch such a moment is what makes it special. Desirable, even.

It's a sin waiting to be committed.

An untouched rose about to be plucked so it will wither in a place that's far away from her natural habitat.

And even that one percent can't be trusted. It's not that people change of their own volition. They're forced to by external exertions, by circumstances and tragedies.

In a way, second chances don't really exist. They're a myth told once in a while to appease emotionally fragile people so they can look forward to new days instead of spiraling into depression.

Sooner or later, however, they realize such things don't exist and are hit by a deeper form of depression, a form that will eventually lead to their ruin.

I don't believe in myths. I'm a man of facts. I may twist them in my favor, I may use a distorted version to reach a certain end, but I do not go after illusions.

And yet, there's an exception.

An illusion I *will* pursue.

The woman sitting beside me in the back seat of my car is a myth, herself.

A doppelgänger.

"Do you believe in doppelgängers?" Lia once asked me as we sat down for breakfast.

I raised a brow. "Doppelgängers?"

"Don't give me that look. They're real! It's said that everyone has forty people who look exactly like them. They're scattered all over time and space, so it's extremely rare to find your doppelgänger in the same time and place."

"Lovely."

She narrowed her eyes. "You don't believe me."

"I only said 'lovely'."

"You're being sarcastic."

"Am I?"

"Yes, you are, Adrian!"

"Hmm. How can you be so sure?"

"That's not the point."

"What is, then?"

"Imagine my doppelgänger somewhere in the world right now." She gave me a soft smile. "If you saw her, you wouldn't be able to tell us apart."

"That's impossible."

"It is possible. I hope it happens to you."

"You seem to be the one intent on meeting her. Why don't you wish for it?"

"No, Adrian! We can't meet our doppelgängers. The first one who sees the other will die," she whispered the last words with a spooked tone.

The first one who sees the other will die.

That's exactly what happened. Lia saw this homeless thing and just disappeared as if she'd never existed.

When you don't believe in something and it ends up happening, you blame that something because you can't simply start believing in what you never have.

This woman is that something.

She's the one who took Lia away and thought she could waste her life in the dirty streets without repercussions.

She stares out the window as my senior guard, Kolya, drives the car through the busy streets. My other closest guard, Yan, sits in the passenger seat, keeping an eye on the road, his hand close to his gun on his waistband. They're strong, loyal, and silent men, who speak with actions more than words. Just as I prefer it.

Winter is gripping the door handle with both hands. It can't be because of Kolya's driving, since it's smooth. It can't be because she's mesmerized by New York's night view, because her eyes are unfocused.

It's almost as if she's fantasizing about opening the door and jumping out while the vehicle is speeding down the road.

She's slightly unpredictable, so I wouldn't put that action past her. I can still feel the sting of her slap on my skin, and a part of me is demanding I punish her for that insult.

But all will be well in due course.

For the rest of the ride, she doesn't look at me, probably scared that I'll act on my threats from earlier. She's smart at times but has foolish patterns at others. She still doesn't know who I am or what I do, but she's already figured out that I'm not a man she can afford to mess with. And for that, all her walls are up with wires wrapped around them.

What she doesn't realize is that I can and will destroy those walls until I get what I want.

If there's anything I learned from my fucked-up parents, it's to be like a river with a strong current. Not only will others think twice before they cross me, but I'll also clear out everything in my way, whether it's friends, enemies, or *her*.

We arrive at one of our malls downtown. It's owned by the Bratva's legal front, V Corp, the company that's currently managed by the *Pakhan*'s grandniece, Rai.

I didn't go through her to come here, though, because no one needs to know about this.

Kolya and Yan get out first and stand guard by the side of the car, facing away from me. Winter stares at me from under her lashes, silently questioning what we're doing here.

"Remove the coat," I tell her.

"Why?"

"Stop talking back and do as you're told."

I can see the spark of rebellion in her aqua eyes, the need to question me again. I wait for it, intending to squash it once and for all, but she blinks away that urge and opts to pick her battles.

She unbuttons her coat and slides down the zipper before she removes it and lays it on her lap. I pull the thing from under her fingers and throw it out the window. Kolya catches it and walks with it toward the trash.

Her gaze follows the action, eyes wide, as if I murdered her favorite puppy. "Why did you do that?"

"It smells and makes you look like a beggar."

"I *am* a fucking beggar," she snaps, then clamps her lips together when she realizes her mistake.

"What did I say about talking back? Do you wish for a few years in prison? Is that it?"

"N-no."

"Seems like it."

"I'm sorry. Okay?"

I don't like the tone she speaks to me with. It doesn't sound apologetic at all. If anything, it's a bit sarcastic. This woman is a lot different from my Lia.

Deciding to let it go for now, I study her, tapping my fingers on my thigh. She's wearing baggy jeans and an ugly striped sweater that swallows her tiny frame, making her appear like a runaway pubescent kid. But her clothes don't stink like the urine and vomit from her coat.

Something else smells, though.

"Remove the gloves."

This time, she doesn't ask why and does as she's told. I throw them out the window, too. Black lines of dirt have taken refuge under her ragged nails and a few red blisters mar her fingers due to the cold.

I reach into the console beside the driver's seat and retrieve some wet wipes. She stiffens when I take her hands in mine, her pupils dilating as I clean them off. They're as frail and small as Lia's, and they're pale, almost to a sickening level. Only the red blisters and the green veins peeking from underneath her skin show a break of color.

Reaching into my pocket, I retrieve my wife's wedding ring and slide it into her finger. Her expression widens and she stiffens but she thankfully keeps her mouth shut.

Instead of asking her to remove the hat, I do it myself. She remains still as her greasy blonde—or half-blonde—hair falls to her shoulders. After I throw the filthy scrap of fur out the window to join the other trash, I use the wet wipes to clean her face.

She tries to do it herself, but a single glance from me makes her drop her hands to her lap. I glide the cloth over her forehead, the soft contours of her cheeks, and the ridge of her nose. When I move to her chapped lips, they part slightly. I try meeting her gaze to see what she's thinking, but she's staring at her hands lying limply in her lap.

When my thumb pauses at the lower line of her bottom lip, a dark desire grips hold of me, and I'm tempted to bite it into my mouth and feast on the cracked exterior. To see if she'll scream.

As if sensing my thoughts, Winter trembles, but it's for something a lot different than desire.

Fear. Raw, potent fear.

I release her and she pushes back against the leather seat.

Opening the car door, I step out and take in a long inhale of the night air. I stride to her side and open hers as well. "Get out."

She does, cautiously, and instantly shivers, wrapping her arms around herself. When I remove my coat and drape it around her, she stares up at me with a weird expression, one that says she never expected someone like me would do that.

Kolya shrugs off his jacket and offers it to me, but I shake my head. I'm not cold. If anything, I've been hotter than normal today.

"Follow me," I tell her and she starts to hobble.

When I turn around to inspect the problem, she comes to a halt, her sock-covered foot resting on top of the other.

I wrap my arm around her back, lift her under her knees, and carry her bridal style. She's too thin and bony; it should be a crime.

She stiffens, even though her fingers grip my shirt. "I can walk on my own."

"You're missing a shoe."

"I can manage."

"Or you can stay still."

"You…" She clears her throat, and as if not wanting Kolya and Yan, who are following close behind, to hear, she whispers, "You said I smell."

"Let me worry about that."

She opens her mouth to argue, then seems to think better of it and purses it shut.

Once we're inside one of the department stores and get in one of the elevators, I hit the button and the four of us go to the tenth floor. The mall is closed, but the manager stayed late at my request.

As soon as the doors open, we're greeted by her and three of her most trusted workers, whom Kolya forced to sign an NDA in blood before we went to fetch Winter. The manager, a woman in her fifties who seems to have a painted smile on her lips, nods at our arrival.

Winter misses the gesture because she's completely entranced by the view ahead of us—the designer clothes hanging under the strong white lights, the luxurious sitting areas, and the high-class décor.

Her nails dig into my shirt as if she's considering this place a threat. However, she considers me a threat, too, so the gesture means nothing.

I set her to her feet and she staggers before standing upright. When her huge eyes scan her surroundings, she visibly shrinks at the grandiosity of it all. It takes her about a minute before she finally stares at the manager, acknowledging her smile with a nod.

"I want her as good as new," I say.

Winter's nose scrunches at my words, but she doesn't protest like I expect her to.

"Yes, sir," the manager tells me and directs her smile at Winter again. "Please follow me."

Winter lifts her nose, then does as she's told.

My gaze follows her as she hobbles on her one shoe until she disappears around the corner, but my focus remains on the empty spot she left behind for a second too long.

The clearing of a throat pulls me out of the moment.

"Are you going to stay here, sir?" Kolya asks in Russian. "Yan or I can drive her back."

"It's fine."

I sit on a red leather sofa and pull out my phone. Kolya and Yan stand on either side of me, their hands crossed in front of them. Yan, in particular, isn't a fan of what I've decided, and his scowling features—that rival Kolya's impassive ones—were a constant during the entire ride.

"Relax, would you?" I say in Russian.

They each widen their stance but don't change position. They might be my two closest guards, but they're as different as night and day. Kolya, who's my age, is the more diplomatic one—the talker, the pacifier, who may or may not carry a bomb with him at all times in case those pacifying methods don't work.

Yan is younger, more reckless, less of a thinker and more of a muscle person, who's always ready to snap someone's neck and amputate someone else's arm at the same time. His character is evident in his hair that he keeps long, even though every one of my other men gives him shit about it. He pays them little to no attention because he's also hotheaded and already has strikes against him that he'd need to answer to.

They've been with me since I was young. Kolya and I basically raised Yan, though. They were groomed by my father to be my inner circle. He actually only brought them in to spy on me, but things have long since changed.

Kolya's muscles flex as he retrieves his phone. Yan has always called him a mountain, because of his physique and his personality. My younger guard is lean, which makes him faster, but he's still jealous that no amount of training could make him as big as Kolya.

My second-in-command pockets his phone. "Igor has been trying to reach you, sir."

"Ignore him."

"Mikhail, too."

"Don't pay him any attention. Unless it's the *Pakhan*, I have no one to answer to."

He gives a curt nod as I go through my emails. I periodically change my phone number, and since I recently did so, the elite group of the brotherhood are bugging Kolya on my behalf.

My position in the Bratva is high enough that I get away with disrespecting the other leaders. There are four heads of the brigadiers, Igor and Mikhail being two of them. I'm an *Obshchak*, meaning the only person I answer to is the *Pakhan* himself.

The only other member on my level is the *Sovietnik*, Vladimir, but he's not demanding. We co-exist for the Bratva as we have been for the past twenty years, ever since we were both officially recruited by Nikolai at the age of fifteen.

Or, more like, Vladimir was recruited. I was born into this world. But even though my father was some sort of nobility in the Bratva, I had to put in the extra work to get where I am. I even surpassed his rank, and continue to do so.

Others think I'm doing it for family honor, when, in fact, I'm interested in squashing everything my father did. If I suppress him, no one talks about him.

My session of reading my emails is interrupted by a number flashing on my screen. I don't save names on my phone, even though it's encrypted and I can virtually destroy it the moment it's stolen.

One of the benefits of my parents' tyranny is that they taught me to always be ready. Never take anything or anyone for granted.

So when I recognize the digits on the screen, I stare up at Kolya. "Since when does Kirill have my new number?"

He frowns. "No clue, sir."

I contemplate ignoring him like I did the other two brigadiers, but Kirill doesn't call to chat.

"Volkov," I answer.

"Morozov," he mimics my closed off tone.

"What do you want, Kirill?" I speak in Russian.

"Does this mean I can't check on you after you've been absent from the Bratva's meeting?" he asks in the same language.

"I'm hanging up."

"Jesus Christ. Loosen up a little."

"I'll loosen up in death."

"I doubt it."

"Do you have a point behind your call, Kirill? Because you just wasted time I could've used to find out the best investment route V Corp can take in the upcoming months."

"I'm waiting for a shipment to arrive, so you're not the only busy one, asshole."

"You want help with customs?"

"It's taken care of. That's not the reason behind my call."

"Then what is?"

"Information and rumors that I thought you should be wary of. What should I start with?"

Kirill isn't the type who offers anything out of the goodness of his heart. He's cunning and only gives when he knows he can take twice as much. If I receive anything from him now, he won't hesitate to ask me for things in the future. I could hang up and ignore him, but he has his ways of acquiring crucial details that even I can't get a hold of.

The difference between us is that I'm strategic in a methodical way. He's strategic but in the chaotic sense. He waits for things to happen before he reacts to them, making him the ultimate opportunist.

"Information," I say.

There's a rustling from his end and distant chattering in Russian. I can imagine him and his men waiting at a secluded warehouse in the cold for the shipment to arrive. "Richard Green's murder is being investigated."

"That's nothing new. I know the police have got their noses in it."

"This is not a police investigation. It's Vladimir's. The *Pakhan* ordered him to look into it."

I pause as his words register. I expected Sergei to ask me to investigate it further, not Vladimir.

"I know what you're thinking," Kirill continues. "I had the same thoughts. Why ask Vladimir when you're the one who usually takes care of that stuff? Lucky for you, I'm a fast thinker and came up with two possible scenarios. Do you want to hear?"

"Spill. And stop wasting my time."

"How I keep up with you is a mystery. Anyway, back to my scenarios. One, the *Pakhan* doesn't want to distract you from growing our alliance with the Italians. Two," he pauses for dramatic effect. "He suspects you."

I tap my fingers on the arm of the sofa as the meaning behind his words reaches me loud and clear. If Sergei suspects me, everyone else does, too. So I choose to probe Kirill, "Why would he suspect me?"

"I don't know, let me take a *wild* guess." He speaks slowly, too slowly, drawing out the words in a provocative manner. "Let's see. We were all counting on getting Richard to become mayor so we could get our hands on easy shipments without having to threaten the DEA at every turn, but suddenly, he's dead. Suddenly, the Italians' candidate is now on the road to be mayor. If I were Sergei, I would suspect the one who's getting cozy with the Italians."

Makes sense. At least none of them figured out the actual reason.

"I'd show up more if I were you," Kirill continues. "Your absence only allows the others to speak behind your back."

"The *others*? As in, you're not involved in the backstabbing?"

"What do you think I am? I don't bite the hand that feeds me. Jesus."

"Hanging up."

"You're not going to ask about the rumors?"

"Not interested in rumors."

"It concerns your wife."

My fingers stop tapping for a second before I resume. If I show Kirill even an ounce of interest, he'll latch on to it like a mad dog.

He's an opportunist—a ruthless one at that.

"Still not interested." I sound bored, even to my own ears.

"Listen anyway and answer with yes or no." The Russian noises get quieter as he speaks. "Mikhail told us that his wife saw Lia going into Sergei's mansion all alone at night. Some say she's betraying you by telling all your secrets to either Sergei or Rai. Some say she's having an affair with someone there. Is any of that true?"

My jaw tenses. "No."

"*Really?*" he drawls the word.

"You think I'd let her breathe another second if that were the case?"

"Right. You wouldn't." He pauses as noises erupt from the other end of the line. "My shipment is here."

The beeping sound is the only thing I hear after he hangs up.

I remove the phone from my ear, tightening my hold on it until my knuckles turn white.

"Kolya. Yan. I need you to uncover all the rumors circulating about Lia. Start with digging into what Mikhail's wife is spouting and move from there. Don't leave any fucking thing out."

"Yes, sir," Kolya says.

I fix Yan with a stare when I don't hear his confirmation. "You have a problem?"

He stares right back, his light eyes clashing with mine. "Aside from the problem you created, *sir?*"

"Yan!" Kolya glares at him because of his show of insubordinate behavior.

I dismiss my senior guard with a hand. "Let him continue. You seem to have a lot to say. Let's hear it, Yan."

He doesn't even smooth his glare. "This is wrong and you know it, sir. Stop this madness."

Kolya punches him in the face. "Shut up."

The punch is so strong that Yan staggers backward, clutching his jaw and staring at Kolya with hurt mixed with anger. He thinks Kolya hit him to cause pain, but Yan is an idiot sometimes. He fails to realize that the ever so diplomatic Kolya went out of his way and punched him because that will lessen my reaction toward his insolence.

But even Kolya's gesture won't save Yan.

I stand up and my second-in-command tries to get in my way. "He won't repeat it, sir."

"Nice try, Kolya." I tap his arm as I bypass him toward Yan and grab him by the shoulder.

My guard stands upright, a red bruise already forming on his cheek. I speak calmly, not letting my emotions get the best of me, even though he has many strikes to count. "Whose guard are you, Yan?"

"Yours."

"Correct. Then why are you acting otherwise?"

"I didn't mean to."

"How long have you known me?"

"Since I was three."

"You're twenty-five now, so that's twenty-two years. That's such a long time, don't you think?"

"Yes."

"It'd be a pity to end them with your head chopped the fuck off." I grab him by the nape, peering into his eyes. "Kolya and I brought you up and made a man out of you. Don't make me regret it."

"But, Boss—"

"Shut the fuck up, Yan," Kolya grits out from beside me, and that manages to silence the younger guard.

I release Yan, and Kolya grabs his nape and forces him to nod in apology.

Ignoring his sullen presence, I concentrate on work. I spend the next two hours or so opening emails and combing through the information my various hackers have sent my way. Some are insignificant, but others are saved until I can ensure their integrity.

The entire time, my focus is scattered by what Kirill said. Though the first part—that *Pakhan* suspects me—should get my attention, it's the latter half that's on my mind.

The motherfucking rumors.

I'll eradicate each and every one of them until the truth is mixed with lies. I'm good enough at exercising that tactic to the point that even those closest to me are fooled.

Like Yan.

A movement in front of me makes me lift my head.

"She's ready, sir." The manager smiles with utter pride, as if she's made a swan out of an ugly duckling.

But that's not the case. She was always a swan, only hidden.

Winter steps from behind the manager to stand in front of me.

As I requested, her hair is dark brown. It's tied in a bun and her face is radiant, though a bit thin.

A simple beige dress reaches her knees, molding against the curve of her breasts and hips. Black heels cover her feet. She's wearing the same makeup from the wedding picture I showed her earlier.

The only difference is that she's not smiling.

Almost like she's already stepping into my wife's shoes.

As she should.

Winter is no longer Winter. She's Lia.

She took my wife's life, and her punishment is spending the rest of her existence being Lia's replacement.

I'll bring my Lia out of this woman, even if it's the last thing I do.

SEVEN

Winter

I REMAIN AS STILL AS A CORPSE UNDER THE STRANGER'S scrutiny.

Adrian. The stranger's name is Adrian Volkov and I'm supposed to be his wife now.

The staff took me to a special massage room, undressed me, and placed me in a bubble bath full of roses, which is now my scent. After being the definition of trash, I currently feel like a rose plucked from a field.

And not in an *I'll go to a better place* way, but in an *I'll probably wither and perish* way.

The girls did all sorts of things to my body. They dyed my hair, waxed me, did my nails and my makeup. Then they put me in a straight brown dress that's a bit bigger than my thin frame. The heels are a perfect size, although they're uncomfortable and I can barely stand in them, let alone walk.

The entire time that they were turning me left and right, doing this and that, I felt like a doll. The type that's played with and tossed aside once the fun is over. Already, I felt like I was losing my will.

I didn't want to change my hair color. As hideous as it was, the blonde was something I had chosen. When I said that, the manager, who introduced herself as Emily, said she was following Mr. Volkov's order and neither of us had a say in anything.

I chose not to make her job even harder, considering that she and the rest of her staff stayed late just for my sake. Adrian might feel normal doing that to other people, but I'm not like him. I dislike being the source of others' discomfort—it's a shitty place to be.

Adrian seems more and more like a sociopath, so I doubt he cares who might suffer because of his demands. As long as he gets what he wants, to hell with everyone else.

So even though Emily and her staff were attentive, I felt my skin crawling. No amount of rose baths or luxurious clothes would've made me feel comfortable.

It's like I've been thrust into an alternate reality and have been living on thick, murky air ever since this afternoon. Ever since I was trapped in his gray eyes. Ever since I made the mistake of existing in his space. And now, I'm starting to think it'll be impossible to find a way out.

But even if I did, where would I go? To jail?

Surely, the discomfort of being here is better than jail.

Or so I'd like to believe.

The moment I looked in the mirror after Emily and the others finished, I saw a reflection of the woman in the wedding picture Adrian showed me.

Lia.

I'd become her and a tear nearly escaped my eyes at that thought.

Is there anything crueler than erasing one's identity? Than wiping away the essence of their being as if it never existed?

Because that's what I feel right now as I stand in front of him. I'm not Winter in his eyes. I'm already Lia, and he intends to cement that fact into the very marrow of my bones going forward.

He won't be able to succeed.

I'm Winter Cavanaugh and I'm living on behalf of myself and my baby girl. No one will be able to erase those facts from my head, not even a frightening man like Adrian.

Bulky Blond and Crooked Nose are on either side of him. The bulky one doesn't look at me, but Crooked Nose stares for a second before diverting his attention to his hands that are clasped in front of him.

There's a red bruise on his cheek that I hadn't noticed earlier and I don't know why I dislike the sight of it. I don't know this man, and I'm sure that if his boss told him to execute me, he'd do it in a heartbeat.

Adrian stands, startling me from my thoughts. He's tall, dark, and handsome while sitting. But when he stands, towering over my short frame, I feel the need to bolt out of my skin.

He motions at me with his finger to turn around. I do, my cheeks flaming with pent-up anger. I know he thinks I'm of a lower class, but does he really consider me his pet or something?

"Is it to your liking, sir?" Emily asks, hopefully, expectedly, like his approval is the bane of her existence.

He nods once as I stop, facing him. Emily grins wide as if she has just pleased the king of the jungle and he'll throw a reward her way.

"Here's your coat, Mrs. Volkov." She offers it to me and I put it on, thankful that it hides the deep-cut sleeveless dress. I might have small breasts, but their curves were showing.

Adrian grabs me by the elbow and leads me to the elevators. Bulky Blond and Crooked Nose follow after us but keep a distance. Emily and the rest of her staff stand in front of the transparent glass of the elevator as a show of respect.

Adrian must be someone important if he has guards following him everywhere and staff standing by as he leaves.

I don't think he's a spy, but he seems more dangerous than a simple businessman. I peek a glance at him. He's still gripping me by the elbow, his touch gentle but firm. I know because when I attempt to remove my arm, he tightens his hold, forbidding any movements.

His message is clear: I'm to go along with whatever he pleases. I signed my fate to him the moment he coerced me into this.

Or maybe it was when he first saw me and decided I'd be his wife.

When was that exactly? When he saved me from the passing van? Or was it when he asked me to clean my face as if the smudges on his wife's lookalike features offended him? Or did he perhaps see me in the shelter and has followed me since then?

The entire time Emily and the others transformed me into Lia, I kept thinking about how he found me in the parking garage. I didn't sense anyone following me, and I have an acute awareness of my surroundings, considering my homeless status.

Ex-homeless now.

Any of my fellow homeless people would feel flattered by this opportunity, but my stomach has been knotting in and out of itself ever since Bulky Blond grabbed me by the hood and thrust me in his boss's direction.

When we exit the elevator, Bulky Blond hurries to the car and opens the back door. That's when I notice Adrian is only wearing a shirt and pants. "Your coat is upstairs. Should we go get it?"

"No."

"But it's freezing."

He stares at me for a beat. "Are you warm?"

"Yeah, but I'm already wearing a coat."

"It's fine then." He flattens a palm at the small of my back and places his other hand on top of the car to stop my head from bumping against it as he guides me inside.

My fingers tremble and I clasp them on my lap as I'm surrounded by the smell of leather from the seats. What is this feeling? No one should be this chivalrous yet terrifyingly dangerous at the same time.

But I have to remember that he's not seeing me right now. He's seeing Lia *in* me. I don't know why that makes me want to reach out and…what? Remove myself from her skin? Would that even be possible anymore?

As soon as Adrian joins me and the guards take their seats up front, my stomach growls. The sound is so loud that Bulky Blond and Crooked Nose freeze.

I purse my lips, but I can feel the blood rising up my cheeks. *Damn it.* I've never been embarrassed about my hunger until this very moment.

Adrian's calm gaze slides to me, unaffected—bored, even. I wonder if he ever gets mad, then immediately push that thought out of my mind. He's terrifying in his calm mode, and I don't want to imagine how he is when he's angry.

"What do you want to eat?" he asks.

"I'm okay."

He taps an index finger against his thigh before stopping. "You're obviously hungry. Food comes with the deal, and, therefore, you don't have to feel self-conscious asking for it."

That's right. It's one of the main reasons I agreed to this in the first place.

"Anything." My voice is just above a whisper.

"Anything isn't food. Pick something."

"I don't care as long as it's…food."

"What if I get you fried cockroaches?"

My nose scrunches as I stare at him.

He raises a brow at my reaction. "You said *anything*."

"Not that."

"Then specify. If you don't express yourself, you'll get nothing from me."

Wow. Is he always this…infuriating?

"A sandwich," I snap and clamp my lips shut, hoping he didn't catch it.

If he disapproves of my tone, he says nothing and, instead, addresses Crooked Nose in a foreign language that I assume is Russian.

He looks slightly different as he speaks in it, but not exactly in a better way. More like authoritative and non-negotiable. He gives off that vibe with his subtle Russian accent, too, but it's clearer with his mother tongue. It could be because I don't speak the language, though.

Crooked Nose nods, then steps out. After ten minutes of utter silence, he comes back with a takeout bag. My mouth waters at the smell of hot bread and fresh vegetables. I wish Larry were here with me; he usually steals sandwiches for me and I share, but he always says he's full. He doesn't like me stealing alcohol, but he's fine with stealing food. That old man has a warped sense of morality.

However, none of the sandwiches he's brought me have ever smelled this divine. Like it's right out of an oven.

My stomach growls again, and this time, I don't try to hide it.

Crooked Nose hands the bag to Adrian, not me. Neither he nor Bulky Blond look in my direction.

Adrian opens the bag and hands me the sandwich. I don't even pause to see what's inside it. I bite straight into it, filling my mouth in one go. It melts on my tongue and I don't properly chew before gulping it down.

I'm about to take another bite when it's pulled from my fingers.

"W-what—" I stare incredulously at the perpetrator, Adrian, who snatched my sandwich. Please don't tell me he bought me food just to take it away.

"Eat slower or you'll get indigestion." He tears off a piece and places it in front of my mouth. I try to take it from him, but he shakes his head.

I really don't care about the method as long as I eat right now, so I open wide and let him put it in my mouth. As soon as it's inside, I swallow it in one go.

"Slower," he repeats, more firmly this time. "Chew first."

It's then I realize that we're actually moving. I've been so focused on the sandwich that I lost all awareness of my surroundings.

Except for Adrian.

One way or another, he's been present ever since I first met him. He's a quiet force that slowly creeps under my skin and leaves me panting for more—or less. Either way, he's there, under my skin, and it's impossible to breathe without feeling his presence.

It's baffling to think I've lived twenty-seven years and have never experienced such intensity. Such…raw, quiet display of power.

I've always thought those in power ensured it by brute methods, that they killed or schemed. That they were loud and barked orders—like Richard. Adrian is the complete opposite of that notion—he's silent, calm, but exudes an authority so raw, it's even more terrifying than those with loud power.

When Adrian gives me another piece of the sandwich, I chew, letting the spicy taste explode in my mouth. It's rich and exquisite and might very well be the most delicious meal I've had in…ever.

I don't protest as he continues to feed me, his fingers brushing against my lips with each bite. He has really masculine fingers—long, lean, and calloused enough to cause a weird sensation whenever they meet my skin—no matter how brief the contact.

He's patient, not attempting to hurry the process, as if he has all the time in the world to feed me. He fixes me with a disapproving stare, pausing when I don't chew long enough or when I do it fast, and that's my cue to slow down or he'll take my meal away.

By the time the sandwich is finished, I'm full. Not bloated like when Larry decides to go kamikaze and steal three sandwiches, but I'm full enough that I swallow the final bite with a sigh. I close my eyes to commit the taste to memory in case it's the last delicious meal I have for months.

It would be perfect if some alcohol came with it, too. I can feel the headache starting at the back of my skull, and I can't afford to be sober for too long.

When I open my eyes, I find Adrian watching me intently. His forefinger taps on his thigh in a quiet rhythm as if it's participating in his observation.

I'm about to break eye contact—because it's still as unnerving as hell—when his next gesture stops me. I couldn't look away even if I wanted to.

Adrian plunges his index and middle finger into his mouth, sucking on the tips that are a bit greasy from how he fed me. The way his lips wrap around his skin sends a weird sensation through me. I want it to stop, but at the same time, I don't know if I'll like it if it stops.

He pops his fingers out and finishes by licking his thumb before he uses a paper napkin.

I force my gaze away to stare through the window. The city's endless buildings fly by us, but I can only see the way he thrust his fingers into his mouth as if he…was thrusting them somewhere else and—

My very inappropriate thoughts are interrupted when the car stops in front of a black metal gate that's as tall and as high as one at a palace.

It slowly opens with a loud creak that can be heard from inside the car. Bulky Blond drives inside before it's fully open.

I stare behind us and, sure enough, the gate is now closing.

Is this where Adrian lives?

I wasn't exactly focused on the road on the way here, but we drove far enough to be somewhere on the outskirts of the city.

I let my gaze slide ahead, thinking that I should engrave the details in my brain in case I need to use them later. But for what and to go where? The moment that black gate closes, I feel as if I'm trapped in a labyrinth. The fact that Bulky Blond keeps driving on and on down the driveway might have something to do with it, but that's not the only reason I feel like I've stepped into a place I shouldn't have.

The only thing I can make out are shadows of trees that look like ghosts at the threshold of a rich prince's gate, waiting to take his life for his cruelty. Wasn't there a story like that once upon a time? A prince who refused to feed the poor was cursed by a witch to become a beast.

The car finally stops in front of a gigantic mansion.

No. It's more like a castle from medieval times, but built in modern times.

The moon is the only light projecting down on it, and it's barely enough since it's partially hidden behind the clouds.

An eerie shadow falls on the dark building with its two-story architecture and its imposing size that sits on a large piece of land.

When people see a grandiose building, they either react with awe or intimidation, or both. Me, on the other hand?

I feel like fleeing.

Like I should sprint toward the black gate and climb it to escape.

Adrian and his guards get out of the car first. I'm not in a hurry. I can even spend the night here. It's warm and the leather seats are more comfortable than anything I've slept on.

Adrian, however, has other plans. He opens the door and extends his palm to me. I'm tempted to refuse it, but that would only start an unwanted battle. I'm so exhausted from this day's events, and all I want to do is crawl into a corner and sleep.

So I take his hand with a resounding sigh. He pulls me out and places a palm at the small of my back. The gesture of possessiveness, of staking his claim, doesn't escape me, but I don't dwell on it much either, because he's not doing it to me.

He's doing it to his wife.

As long as I don't consider myself his wife and can separate reality from the role I'm playing, everything will be fine.

And most importantly, I'll survive.

I allow him to lead me to a double metal door with a passcode bar on top. He runs his fingertip over the sensor and the door opens with a beep.

He gently pushes me ahead of him and I nearly stumble from the atrocious heels hurting my feet. Adrian wraps an arm around my waist, keeping me steady. As soon as I make sure I can stand, I attempt to wiggle away.

His presence still gives me a weird feeling. The creeps mixed with fear and…something else I'd rather not identify.

"Stop trying to push away from me, Lia."

"I'm not Lia," I whisper.

"Yes, you are, and you'll start acting like it."

"I can't just act like another woman."

He pauses, his finger tapping once against his thigh. "Did you just talk back to me?"

"No." My voice is small. I really don't want to induce his wrath right now. Or ever, for that matter.

He doesn't seem convinced, but he says ever so calmly, "Your presence here is for one reason only—to be Lia. You'll learn to act like it. In fact, you'll *be* her."

Yeah, right.

But I don't voice that thought, because judging by his brief show of anger just now, that would only get me in trouble.

I expect Bulky Blond and Crooked Nose to follow us, but they don't. The door closes behind us with a click and an automatic light comes on overhead in a vast reception area with pure white walls, dark wood flooring, and a round chandelier hanging from the ceiling.

There's a simple white table in the middle of the floor, surrounded by cream-colored high-back chairs. A wide, sweeping staircase with white railings leads upstairs. The hall is elegant and hints at a minimalist, refined taste, but there's something wrong.

There are no family pictures, no paintings. Nothing.

It's as if no humans live in this house. It's clean but impersonal.

I'm still studying my surroundings when a soft thudding sound comes from upstairs. I freeze, fingers sinking into my palm. Maybe my premonition about this house is coming true, after all, and I'll be attacked.

But then I recognize the sound. It's not threatening; if anything, it seems like…

My thoughts trail off when the footsteps grow nearer and a small human appears at the top of the stairs. He comes down, holding the spindles with each step, his tiny fingers wrapping around them like a vise. He looks no older than five, give or take.

There's no doubt who the little boy is.

He's the spitting image of Adrian with his dark hair and gray eyes. Only, his are lighter and bigger.

My suspicions are confirmed when he hops down the last two steps, yelling, "Papa!"

As he runs toward us, head focused on his feet as if not to lose sight of his steps, my heels falter. A harsh, unyielding weight pushes against my ribcage as if intending to crush the bones and pierce through my heart.

The sight of the boy brings back memories I've kept buried for so long.

Tiny hands and feet.

A little face.

The smell of a baby.

"Slow down, Jeremy," Adrian says from beside me, but I'm hearing him as if I'm underwater.

The boy, Jeremy, lifts his head and stops mid-run. His huge gray eyes meet mine and they widen even more as he whispers, "Mommy...?"

I don't know if it's the word or the way he looks at me as he says it, like he's found the world after he lost it, but tears I haven't shed in too long burst from my eyes.

They stream hard and fast down my cheeks, soaking my skin and ripping a sob out of my throat.

"Lia?" Adrian grips me by my shoulders, lowering his head so he can look at my face. My vision is so blurry, I can't see him. That's when I realize that I'm shaking and my limbs can't carry me anymore.

"Lia!"

"I'm *not* Lia," I whisper as the darkness whisks me away.

EIGHT

Adrian

LIA'S BODY FALLS LIMP IN MY ARMS, HER LIDS CLOSED and sweat covers her temples. I hold her small frame against me by her waist as her legs lose all strength.

Placing my arm under her knees, I lift her up as I did earlier. Her head lolls in an awkward position before it lands on my shoulder. Her lips twitch and her face turns so pale, her veins peek more visibly through her skin.

"Mommy…?"

I stare down at Jeremy, who's holding a toy soldier and fighting back tears. He's supposed to be in his bed this late, yet here he is. He must've tricked his nanny so that he could come down and meet me. He's been doing that a lot the past few weeks, wanting to see me and throwing tantrums so I'll pay him attention.

I know exactly why he's acting like this. After losing his mother, he didn't want to lose me, too. He sometimes sneaks into my bedroom merely to make sure I'm there.

"She just fell asleep, Malysh," I say with an American

accent. The Russian accent is for certain situations and the American is for others.

Being brought up by a half-American mother and a pure Russian father, the accents come naturally to me.

Jeremy, however, has spent most of his time with Lia, who only speaks English, and, therefore, he gets confused when I talk to him in Russian. While that will change in the future, I won't force him to understand now. It's the worst time to add to his stress.

"Your mom just fell asleep."

"Really?" He sniffles.

"Correct."

"But…but you said she was spending a long time on a trip. Does this mean the trip is over, Papa?"

"It is, Malysh."

"And she'll be here every day?" His voice breaks as hope soars in his huge eyes.

My attention slides to her motionless body before I focus back on my son. "Every day."

"Promise, Papa?"

"Promise."

"You always keep your word."

"I do. She'll see you tomorrow, all right?"

He turns his head away, huffing. "I won't see her."

"Are you still mad at her?"

"Aren't you, Papa?" He sniffles and wipes his tears with the back of his hand. "She left without saying goodbye."

"But she's here now."

"I still won't see her." He stomps up the stairs, his small body emanating more energy than a kid twice his age.

He definitely has his mother's temper.

Still carrying Lia, I approach the entrance and I click the intercom that connects with Kolya's radio. "Come inside and make sure Jeremy goes to sleep."

"Yes, sir."

I take her upstairs two steps at a time and head to the master bedroom. When I place her on the high platform bed, I allow her head to fall softly on the pillow.

She doesn't stir as I slowly remove her shoes and put them at the foot of the bed. A few cuts cover her ankles and the soles of her feet are rough to the touch. They're also cold, so I lay them on the bed and pull the duvet up to cover them. When I maneuver her to remove her coat, she still doesn't show any reaction.

I hold her hands in mine and stare at the blisters that shouldn't be on her skin. They're freezing, too, as if her brain still thinks she's sleeping on the streets, in dirty, cold parking garages.

Lifting her palms to my mouth, I blow on them until they're warm enough, then slide them under the covers. I'm about to make her more comfortable when a knock sounds on the door.

I pull the duvet to her chin and take one last look at her face. "I'll be right back, Lenochka."

After stepping out, I slowly close the door behind me, making sure not to make a sound.

Kolya is standing in the hall, his frame blocking my view and his brow furrowed.

"Is Jeremy asleep?"

"Yes, but he was stressed." He pauses.

"If you have something to say, say it, Kolya. I don't have all night."

"He seemed scared after he told me that…well, his mommy fell asleep while standing."

At least he believes she fell asleep.

"Sir."

"What?"

"May I speak freely?"

I raise a brow. "When haven't you?"

"This isn't right."

"This?"

"All of this." He motions with his head at the closed bedroom door. "Her here. Now."

"Is Yan bitching to you?"

"No."

"You don't have to protect him, Kolya. You're spoiling him."

"This isn't about Yan and you're well aware of that.

"Let me worry about things here while you keep an eye on what's happening in the rest of the brotherhood. We cannot be left behind."

"We won't, but she…"

"Stop talking about her, Kolya. It's done. She's here and that's that."

"She fainted, sir."

"How would you know that?"

"People don't just fall asleep standing. I'm not Jeremy."

"She'll be fine."

"What if she—"

"Kolya," I cut him off, my voice hardening. "Drop it."

"This could backfire."

"I said to stop fucking talking about her."

He gives me a disapproving stare, one that says, 'you're fucked up and I regret being by your side for thirty years,' but he knows not to test me in circumstances like these, so he nods and leaves.

I unbutton my shirt on my way back to my room.

This will be a long fucking night.

NINE

Winter

"Lenochka."

I mumble in my sleep, my head feeling heavy and painful, as if a hammer is rummaging through it.

My breath is cut off.

I gasp, only to be met by something…soft? My eyes snap open and I find myself on my stomach, my face nestled against a pillow.

Long fingers undo the zipper of my dress and slide the cloth down my body.

For a second, I'm so disoriented, I don't even know where I am, let alone what's happening. I shouldn't be sleeping on a bed, and not just any bed; this one is warm, soft, I pick up the scent of mysterious wood and rich leather.

Reality kicks back in with a tumbling force that keeps me gasping for air. I came with Adrian to his house. After I saw his son, I had a visceral recollection of my daughter and then… what?

What happened after that? Where am I?

More importantly, what's going on right now?

Air clashes against my bare skin, forming goosebumps. The dress is gone and I'm only wearing a strapless bra and the lace panties Emily gave me earlier.

My shoulders snap into a rigid line as sweat covers my brow. I'm terrified to look behind me and see the look in his eyes right now. If I do, I'll be trapped and driven to the point of no return. However, abstaining from looking at him doesn't diminish from his sheer presence or the overwhelming heat he emanates. It radiates off my skin like flames licking it—or death kissing it.

My mind flashes in all directions as the reality of what's happening settles at the bottom of my stomach with a thud.

Adrian couldn't be so cruel as to do this, right?

What am I thinking? Of course he is. Everything he's done thus far to have me under his thumb only proves the lengths he'll go to in order to get what he wants.

Maybe…maybe if I pretend to be asleep, he'll stop. Maybe he only meant to remove my dress.

Even as I think that, I know I'm merely fooling myself. He's not the type who can be stopped. I know that, I saw it in his eyes and I'm currently feeling it with his firm touch.

"What are you doing?" My voice is slow, broken, and so damn terrified.

"Don't talk." He's speaking with an American accent. There's no Russian accent present now.

He clicks the strap of my bra open and I stiffen as he pulls it out from underneath me, leaving me half-naked. My breasts meet the soft mattress, but it feels like cold metal, one that's ready to cut through my nipples.

"Adrian, please…" I whisper as a tear rolls down my cheek. "Don't do this."

"Do what?"

"Whatever you're doing. I'm scared."

"You like being scared."

"N-no…"

"Yes, you do. You like begging too, Lenochka, so beg me."

His fingers latch onto the waistband of my panties, and a sob catches in my throat. "Please…please…don't…"

He yanks the underwear down my legs in one go and I yelp, a loud sob echoing in the air.

His large hands that I noticed earlier today—kept thinking about, even—grab me by the hips in a ruthless grip as he plunges inside me from behind.

My hoarse scream pierces the silence as his cock tears through me. It's harsh, merciless, and meant to punish.

He doesn't give me time to adjust and thrusts with an increasing rhythm. My walls burn from the discomfort, the power, the violation.

My cries and sobs echo in the air as I beg and wail. But my body doesn't move. Not even a little. I don't try to claw at him, to buck, or squirm.

I don't try anything.

If I do, he'll hurt me. He'll hit me. He'll make me bleed.

So I remain like a doll being used and abused without a fight.

I attempt to escape inside my head, but his thrusts forbid me to. There's an animalistic power behind them, something that's meant to keep me in the here and now, to make me feel every second of what's happening.

Forbidding me from going anywhere else is crueler than the brutal act itself.

Monstrous, even.

My head falls on the pillow to muffle my screams, my tears, everything. My fingers dig into the mattress and my toes stiffen, but nothing erases the chagrin or the mixed feelings going through me all at once.

I pray for it to stop, but it goes on and on. He doesn't finish. Doesn't release me from my agony.

And soon enough, I find myself in my head again. I close my eyes and try to think of the most beautiful place I've been to. A green garden with colorful roses and singing birds.

But then the sky darkens and all the flowers leak a crimson liquid that looks like…blood.

I gasp, eyes shooting open when he pulls out of me and flips me over to face him.

Adrian is naked, his muscled chest coated with a sheen of sweat over the fine hairs. He has double sleeves of tattoos, but I'm unable to make them out in the darkness.

Even his face is shadowed as if he's the Grim Reaper coming to take my life. "Where the fuck did you go, Lenochka? Keep your attention on me when I'm fucking you."

"Please…Adrian…please…" My voice cracks with every word. "Please…stop…"

He plunges inside me again and my head rolls back from the force of it. My sobs and tears come out chopped as his thrusts break them apart.

Then I'm making strange sounds—they're longer, high-pitched, and they aren't sobs. My body tightens with something different than discomfort as sharp tingles assault the bottom of my stomach.

"You're strangling my dick, Lenochka," he rasps. "Are you going to come?"

I shake my head frantically, but even as I do, a wave of heat explodes under my skin and I scream for a different reason altogether.

I wish I was facing the pillow so I could muffle my voice, but since that's not possible, I use my hand, biting down on it with all my might.

The sensations going through me are like being released from that black box. I'm tripping over my own feet, sprinting toward the open air as it hits my lungs with a blast.

The orgasm is strong, harsh, and nothing like I've felt

before. My whole body is trembling and my insides are a mess of tingles and tremors.

I expect Adrian to finish, but he goes on and on, like a machine with no off button. My body glides across the mattress and the headboard hits the wall with each of his movements. He lifts my leg up in the air and pounds into me with renewed energy, as if he just started. His fingers dig into my skin and he pinches my nipple so hard, I see neon stars in the darkness.

The same wave from earlier hits me again, and this time, I don't even have the energy to scream.

I'm so high above, I don't think I'll ever return.

But I do.

My body's limp on the mattress as the aftereffect of the orgasm causes my limbs to shake.

Adrian is still not finished.

"Please…" I sob. "I can't take it anymore…*please*."

"You can. Your cunt was made for me, Lenochka."

"Adrian…stop."

"No."

"Stop!" I scream and my eyes flutter open.

I'm on my stomach on the bed, face down. Sweat covers me under my clothes and the sheets.

I'm wearing the dress Emily picked for me and…my fingers are inside my panties, thrusting in and out of my pussy.

My *soaked* pussy.

My other hand is pinching my nipple underneath my bra.

I startle and sit up, removing my hands as if I've been caught masturbating in a public square. My mouth hangs open at the sight of the juices coating the fingers that were between my legs.

Lifting my dress, I'm mortified by the view. My inner thighs are sticky and my panties are most definitely ruined. Not only that, but my nipples ache, throbbing against the material of my bra.

Was…all of that a dream?

No. I don't dream—let alone about being raped.

And yet, I'm all alone in the room and my clothes are intact. I was even covered by a duvet. Not to mention the evidence that's staring at me on my fingers.

Why the hell was I touching myself to that type of nightmare?

I scoot back against the headboard, pulling my legs to my chest and wait for…what? A sign that I don't have the sort of depraved mind that fills me with those types of nightmares?

Keep it together, Winter. It was just a nightmare. It's not real.

I carefully step off the bed and peek under it. I hold my breath, expecting some sort of monster to jump me.

No sense of relief engulfs me when I find no one.

Because I know, I just know that real monsters are more dangerous. They appear human, too, before they release their beastly selves on the world.

Like in my nightmare.

The room I'm in has the king-size bed that I woke up on with a metal headboard, decorated with golden motifs. A matching dresser with a large mirror is right across from it and I nearly scare myself shitless when I pass by it and sense my shadow.

I head to the only door in sight and pray it's a bathroom. I need to wash up, to remove all the stickiness clinging to my body.

As soon as I open it, I freeze in the doorway.

Adrian is inside a bathtub that's full of water. His eyes are closed, head lolled to the side, and his arms are crossed over his chest.

For a second, I don't know if he's actually sleeping or…dead.

I want to turn around and leave. Better yet, I want my care-free life from the streets back. After the cruel dream I just had, the last thing I want is to talk to Adrian.

But he could be dead—or will be if he keeps sleeping in a bathtub.

My footsteps are careful, slow as I approach him. I touch his shoulder and freeze.

Bite marks.

My hand has a bite mark from when I bit on it from the nightmare.

Was it really a nightmare?

Before I can think on that, a strong hand catches my wrist and pulls me over. I shriek as I lose my balance.

"You're finally awake, Lenochka."

TEN

Winter

MY MOUTH OPENS AS MY KNEE HITS THE EDGE OF the tub.

Being this close, I'm taken hostage by him— and it's not only due to his grip on my wrist. He's naked, and while the water covers most of his body, it's transparent and every inch of him is exposed.

His shoulders are broad, framing defined biceps. Black tattoos are inked along the length of his taut arm that's holding me. His other hand rests close to his tapered waist that leads to a rock-hard abdomen.

Not sure if it's because of the water, but his thighs appear powerful and hard like in those commercials for football players. I force myself to gaze somewhere else and not at his half-erect cock.

How is it possible for someone to exude such physical perfection? His beauty isn't loud like a movie star's or a model's. It's quiet, just like his personality. Lethal, too, because if his eyes were a knife, I'd be bleeding in this bathtub right now.

I frown at that image. Bleeding…

Adrian cuts off my train of thought when he lifts my hand to his nose and a muscle moves beneath his jaw as he sucks in a long breath. "Were you touching yourself, Lia?"

"No…" My voice is strangled, hushed, and a bit hoarse, as if I'm still trapped in that nightmare.

"Don't lie to me." His tone is calm but threatening. "I smell your cunt on these fingers."

"I said no."

"That's your first strike. Lie to me again and I'll punish you."

Memories from the nightmare strangle me by the throat and suffocate every ounce of air from my surroundings.

He'll strip me bare and fuck me now. He'll take me like an animal and leave me without anything. He'll confiscate my power and my will.

His hold on my wrist is firm and heats my flesh like a thousand flames, intending to burn me from underneath my skin.

My lips tremble and I dig my nails into the ceramic edge of the tub to keep myself in a bent position. "Please…don't…don't…"

Adrian releases my hand and I stumble until my back hits the glass door of the shower. I remain there, both palms flattened on the cold surface and my bare feet curling against the tiles.

"What is wrong?" He's speaking with the Russian accent, not the American one from my nightmare.

"N-nothing."

He stands up all wet and…naked.

He's completely naked.

Although I caught a glimpse of him in the bathtub, nothing could've prepared me for this view. His thighs are muscled and taller than I predicted. Fine hairs form a trail on his taut chest and down to…

I snap my gaze up before I start ogling his cock. In my attempt to study anything but him, I'm caught off guard by his tattoos. I saw one earlier, but I didn't see the other. Both his arms are marked. Full sleeves of black ink intertwine over his arms like a labyrinth.

Just like in the nightmare.

While I could've hallucinated about biting my hand, this can't be made up. I've never seen Adrian unclothed, so there's no way I'd guess he has inked arms.

I reach for the nearest thing I can find, which happens to be a ceramic soap bottle, and point it in his direction. "Stay away from me!"

"Lia," Adrian says the name softly.

"I'm not Lia! I'm Winter!"

"Calm down." He continues approaching me, stalking toward me with silent footsteps that I can barely hear.

"I said stay away from me!" I shriek, my voice turning hysterical.

He stops, raising one hand. "Fine. I'm staying away, so put that down."

I shake my head frantically, nails sinking into the solid ceramic. "I'm leaving. I'm not spending another minute in this godforsaken place or with you!"

A shadow passes over his features, thunderous and quiet, almost as if he's…angry. Why the hell would he be? I'm the one who's angry. I'm the one who was forced out of my safe cocoon to be here.

"Give me that bottle, Lia."

"No! And stop calling me Lia!"

My hands flail about and I hear the crack before I see it. The bottle hits the wall and crashes against it. White liquid soap drips down my hand and onto the ground, and then a trail of blood follows.

A broken ceramic piece has sunk into my skin. A sting of

pain explodes on my flesh before blood flows from my palm. I release what remains of the bottle, letting it crash to the ground.

"Fuck!" Adrian hurries toward me, plucks the piece out, leaving a small gash that burns when soap mixes with the wound.

Adrian throws the bloodied ceramic piece in the sink and wipes the soap away. His brow furrows over his darkened eyes and his lips thin into a line.

I squirm against him. "Let me go, you monster! Let me go!"

"*Stop*," he orders and I flinch, going limp.

The word, although singular, is so authoritative that my muscles have locked together at hearing it.

Adrian grabs a beige towel, runs it under the sink, and presses it to my palm. He releases a breath when the blood doesn't soak it for long. As if he's worried about me. As if my well-being means shit in his agenda.

Why is he acting like this? I just can't understand why he's not the callous devil he should be.

His attention doesn't break from my palm as he speaks, "I don't know why you're behaving like this all of a sudden, but why don't you tell me?"

"Are you trying to pretend that you don't know?"

"Know what?"

I purse my lips. A second ago, I was so certain it wasn't a nightmare, but now, I'm not so sure. However, the bite mark and the tattoos couldn't have been a figment of my imagination.

"You raped me just now." My voice starts low, then grows in volume. "You forced yourself on me, even when I begged you to stop!"

Adrian's hand pauses at my wound and he meets my gaze with his darker ones. For the first time since I met him, I really, *really* wish I could see behind those eyes. Just to know what's happening in there. What type of thoughts go into his abnormal brain?

"I didn't rape you," he says ever so casually.

"You expect me to believe that?"

"You should."

"I know what I felt." It was too vivid of a nightmare, too... real. So real that I can still feel his thrusts in me.

"If I wanted to fuck you, I wouldn't need to rape you for it." He glides the towel over my hand. "What made you think that I did it?"

"I just told you, I felt it."

"Felt it how?" His voice is too calm for this conversation. Too infuriating. I want to reach into his armor and yank him out—that is, if there's anything to yank out. Sometimes, he seems like a shell.

A nothingness that can't be touched or altered.

"What type of question is that? I just felt it. Besides, I bit my hand when you raped me and look!" I show him the teeth marks on my non-injured palm. "How do you explain this?"

"You could've bitten your hand while you were sleeping."

"That's not possible, because I sleep completely still. Besides"—I motion at his ink—"I saw your tattoos when I never have before this moment."

"You could be projecting seeing them now to the past."

"That doesn't make any sense! You think I'm an idiot?"

"And you think I'm under the obligation to explain myself to you?" His voice loses all casualness, lowering, hardening, *stifling*. "I don't need to force myself on you and, therefore, I didn't rape you. It must've been a nightmare."

"It couldn't have been a nightmare. I don't dream."

"You probably just started."

"Don't try to make me seem crazy. I'm not."

He stops gliding the towel over the wound. "Are you sore?"

His question catches me off guard and I pause as my legs clench together.

"Are you, Lia? Because if, as you said, I raped you, you wouldn't be able to move."

"I…"

"What?"

"…Am not." Aside from the soaked panties, there's no discomfort whatsoever between my legs or in my muscles. Considering it's been a long time since I had sex, I would be sore.

"There. Your answer." He tosses the towel in the sink and reaches into the cabinet, retrieving a first aid kit.

His shoulder muscles strain with the motion and his tattoos expand. I want to study them, to see if there's a symbol I recognize, but his full nakedness doesn't help me in my quest to focus.

I really don't want to be ogling him right now.

Forcing my gaze away, I concentrate on an invisible dot on the opposite wall. A sense of relief slowly creeps over me at the thought that it was indeed a nightmare.

I don't care if it was my first, or that it somehow matched so close to reality. Maybe that's what happens when you don't dream; your very first one is a visceral, horrifying experience.

The reason I desperately want it to be a nightmare isn't only because of mental damage. It's the fact that I didn't fight. The fact that I *orgasmed*. The fact that I was touching myself to that disgusting act.

Pushing those thoughts away, I try to breathe, even partially, considering that Adrian's still here and his presence always steals some of my air, if not all.

He gets a Band-Aid and puts it on the small cut in my palm. "Don't ever do that again."

"That?"

"The bottle. You should've given it to me when I told you to."

"I wasn't exactly thinking straight," I mutter dismissively. But if I thought that would propel him to let it go, I'm far from right.

Adrian's eyes darken and the air thickens in response to his mood. He towers over me until I have to tilt my head back to look at him as he repeats slowly, "You weren't *thinking*."

"I…wasn't."

"You'll think before you act from now on."

"Okay."

"Not okay. Say it."

"I will think." *Jeez. What is wrong with him?*

"Go shower and change. We have breakfast in half an hour."

I didn't even realize it was morning yet since the curtains in the bedroom are closed. "Okay."

He narrows his eyes. "Drop that word."

"Why?"

"And stop talking back to me."

"I'm merely asking why."

"Because it doesn't suit you."

"More like it doesn't suit your wife," I mumble.

"What did you just say?"

"Nothing," I blurt at the severity in his tone. This man is really not to be messed around with.

Using the towel, he picks up the pieces of broken ceramic, one by one, but instead of tossing them in the trash, he takes them with him on his way out.

I try to look away, but I'm unable to stop staring at his firm ass and long legs. I've never witnessed such a perfect physique before, but it's not only about that. It's the way he carries himself and the sheer confidence he exudes, even while naked.

It's a vulnerable position for most people, but Adrian's acting as if he's dressed in a sharp suit. It takes a lot of mental discipline to give off such a vibe.

That's both fascinating and dangerous.

A man like Adrian should really come with a hazard warning, and not just because of his tenacious self-assurance, but because of all of him.

It takes me a few seconds to shake my head and stop ogling him.

As soon as he leaves, I lock the bathroom door before I strip and take a quick shower. I trust no one, and Adrian is at the top of that list.

When I'm finished, I wrap myself in a robe, cover my hair with a towel, then crack the bathroom door open. After I make sure no one is there, I step into the bedroom and notice another door in the corner that leads to a walk-in closet.

I carefully go inside and startle when an automatic white light flicks on. I stop to study endless rows of clothes, accessories, and shoes. On the left, there are countless suits and shirts, mostly black, gray, and dark blue.

Adrian clearly doesn't prefer flashy clothes, and that's understandable. He's striking enough without them, and these types of colors suit his mysterious character.

On the right, the colors are lighter, more varied, but they're…boring. Just like the dress I wore yesterday, most of what I assume is Lia's wardrobe is composed of suit skirts in muted colors like beige, caramel, and gray. Her dresses are straight and knee-length. There's not a single pair of jeans, a denim jacket, or anything that doesn't look like it's mimicking the Queen of England's style.

It feels weird to rummage through a dead woman's clothes, but I do so anyway because I really don't want to wear another dress and killer heels today.

After what seems like hours of searching at the back of the closet, I find cute jean shorts and a pink tank top that reads 'Special.' Although I would usually go for the heaviest, warmest clothes with the weather, Adrian's house is hot, so I can wear these inside. I put them on and use a pink scarf as a belt for the shorts since they're a bit bigger. Lia and I don't perfectly match in size, after all.

One less item on the creepy scale.

I don't find any sneakers, so I settle on pink flats. I use a scarf that's similar to my belt to gather my hair into a long ponytail.

Staring in the mirror, I smile, satisfied with the result. However, my smile soon disappears when I recall that when I was pregnant, I bought matching mother-daughter clothes like these so we could dress alike.

I never got the chance to.

Refusing to get caught up in memories of her, I step out of the room and stare to my left, then my right, trying to determine where the dining room is located. I assume it's downstairs and take the steps unhurriedly. Or more like, warily.

Even in daylight, this place still gives me the chills. Actually, scratch that. It doesn't only *give* me the chills, they keep mounting with every minute I spend within these walls.

I stop at the bottom of the stairs, wondering where to go from here.

"Mrs. Volkov?"

At first, I don't recognize the name, but then I turn around, realizing it's Lia's and, therefore, mine.

A middle-aged woman, who appears to be in her late fifties, stares at me with a blank expression. She's tall, way taller than me. Her blonde hair with white streaks is gathered into a tight bun and she has a square face that, coupled with her rigid expression, makes her look like that high school teacher we all had, whose class no one dared to breathe in.

She gives me a once-over as if I'm not respecting the school's dress code.

"Yes?" I don't sound convincing, but I'm also not sure how to act. If I ask her where the dining room is, won't that immediately cast me as an imposter?

"What are you doing here?" Her accent is Russian, though subtle.

"I'm searching for Adrian." At least that sounded a bit plausible.

"Follow me." She turns and strides to the left, not waiting for me to follow.

I have no choice but to do so, so I go after her down a long hall. She opens a set of double doors and motions at me to go inside.

I do, conscious of every footstep I take.

A breath leaves me when I find Adrian sitting with the little boy from yesterday—Jeremy.

I'm pretty sure my relief has to do with the child, not the father. Despite my reaction at seeing Jeremy for the first time, it had nothing to do with him and everything to do with myself and the past that's still wrapped around my throat like a noose.

Adrian is dressed in black pants and a dark blue shirt. Grim, non-flashy, and so much him. He lifts his head as soon as I come in, but I quickly avert my gaze, not wanting to be trapped in those ashen grays first thing in the morning.

The rigid teacher walks to an empty seat on his left and points at it. "Your breakfast is ready, Mrs. Volkov."

I hate that name, the fact that I'm an extension of Adrian. That his last name is mine.

But at the mention of the word 'breakfast,' I don't have time to ponder it. When was the last time I had dinner, then breakfast like a normal person?

Probably a week ago when Larry brought us sandwiches. And they didn't smell as divine as the bacon and eggs on the table. I miss Larry and wish I could take him some of what's here.

As soon as I sit down, I'm aware of three pairs of eyes watching me like I'm an alien. What? I didn't even start eating yet, and I was planning to do it slowly, not like the pig I was last night.

I slowly raise my head to find Adrian's darkening eyes holding me hostage.

"What is it?" I whisper.

"What are you wearing?"

I stare down at myself and realize what they're all looking at. "Clothes."

"I know they're clothes." He lowers his voice, and I assume it's because he doesn't want Jeremy to hear how much of a dick his father is. "But those are not your clothes."

"Yes, they are. I found them in the closet." Opting to change the subject, I take a piece of bread and smile at Jeremy, who's dragging his spoon through the jelly on his plate. "Do you want a sandwich instead?"

I didn't know what I expected as a response, but a scowl certainly wasn't it. He glares up at me, hand tightening around his spoon. Aren't I supposed to be his mother? Maybe I'm his stepmother?

"I'm not talking to you." He pouts.

"Jeremy," Adrian scolds.

"She left, Papa! She'll do it again." He dangles his little feet down before he hops off his chair. "I'm full."

And with that, he turns to leave.

"Jeremy!" I call his name, but he's already running out of the dining room.

I ignore my breakfast and stand up to follow him. I don't care if he's not my child, the pain in his face was so raw.

No kid deserves to feel strong emotions like that. I know better than anyone, considering my own childhood.

Adrian clasps a hand around my wrist, keeping me in place. "Don't follow him."

"But—"

He tugs on my arm and I gasp when I'm forced to meet his gaze as he says, "You have me to answer to first."

ELEVEN

Winter

I CAN'T BELIEVE THIS MAN. HIS SON WAS OBVIOUSLY hurt, and all he's focused on is whom I answer to?

Just what type of oppressive man is he?

I try to twist my hand free of his, but he uses his hold to haul me onto the chair. "Sit down."

"Jeremy needs me."

"Needs you?" he repeats with veiled menace. "Who the fuck do you think you are?"

"Your wife. You made me into her, remember?"

"And you think that magically makes you his mother?"

Right. I'm not. Why the hell am I so angry? Adrian is his father and he doesn't seem to give a damn, so I shouldn't be worked up over this.

And yet I am.

Hot flames bubble in my veins at the way Adrian dismissed his son so casually. People like him don't deserve children—or anyone, really.

He goes back to cutting his eggs like nothing happened, his

fingers handling the knife with infinite ease. Pursing my lips, I opt to have breakfast, too. After all, this is the reason I'm here.

To eat.

I fix a double sandwich of butter and jelly, using three slices of toast, then take a generous bite. An involuntary sigh leaves my lips as the food settles in my stomach.

It's not until I take a sip of the coffee, with milk, as I prefer it, that I notice both Adrian and his stern teacher watching me. Their gazes are intent, unblinking, as if I'm some sort of an animal at the zoo.

Did I do something against etiquette or something? I made sure to eat slowly.

My fake husband takes a sip of his own coffee—black like his soul—and continues to watch me over the mug. He has a killer stare, I swear. Without uttering a single word, he manages to push me to the edge of my seat.

"This is Ogla." Adrian motions at the stern teacher with his head. "You can ask her anything about how you used to act. She knows you've lost your memories."

I'm about to tell him I haven't lost my memories, that I'm only playing a role, but then I figure out the angle he's going for. If he tells everyone I've lost my memories, he and I can get away with many things when I act out of character from how Lia used to.

He's smart, but so are most assholes.

The stern teacher, Ogla, gives me a sharp nod that I return with an unsure one.

He continues to watch me eat in that unnerving manner. I force myself to chew slower, but his stare is what will give me indigestion.

"You are allowed to go around the property except for the guest house."

He has a guest house? It was dark last night, so I couldn't have seen it even if I'd tried.

Now that he mentions it and has specifically told me not to go there, my attention is piqued. Curiosity is morbid, like a hungry animal demanding a piece of meat. It would've been better if he didn't warn me in the first place.

"You're not to leave the house."

"I'm not your prisoner, Adrian."

He raises a brow. "You are what I say you are. Titles hold little to no value and it's up to you how you use them. If you prefer to call yourself a princess over a prisoner, by all means, do. The fact remains that you're not allowed to step a foot outside unless escorted *and* with my permission."

Did he just say escorted? "What exactly did you say you do again?"

"I didn't say what I do."

"Well, you should, because I'm not fully grasping these insane measures."

He narrows his eyes on me and Ogla stares at me hard, as if I'm a petulant child whose hands she wants to smack.

"What?" I say to them both, then take a sip from my coffee. "I'm asking a genuine question. If you don't want me to know, fine, but if you're somehow a spy and I act against etiquette, you can only blame yourself."

Adrian calmly places his cup of coffee on the table. "Leave, Ogla."

I stiffen at his deceptive quietness. Maybe what I said was also considered talking back. I wasn't snarky, though. I'm pretty sure I wasn't.

Ogla glares at me, and even with her attitude, I'm ready to beg her to stay. I don't want to be left alone with Adrian right now.

The door closes behind her with a finality that echoes in my chest.

The air shifts, thickening with unspoken words and tension that can be cut with a knife.

I remain completely motionless, my fingers wrapped around the cup of coffee, but I don't dare to take a sip.

Adrian's frame becomes larger than life. He's still sitting, yet I can almost feel his shadow looming over me like doom. "What did I say about talking back to me?"

"I didn't mean to," I blurt. "I was only asking."

He stands and my spine jerks upright as he looms over me. I keep staring at the unfinished toast I left on the table, hoping that I will somehow become it or the cup of coffee or any of the utensils, just so I can escape his scrutiny.

Adrian slides both his fingers under my chin and lifts it up. I want to look away, and not solely because of the general discomfort his eyes give me. Now, they're more concentrated, harsher, as if he's been collecting all his disapproval with me from the moment we met until now.

"You do not disrespect me in front of the staff. You do not disrespect me. Period."

"Okay."

"I said to lose that fucking word."

"Fine. All right."

"Is that sarcasm?"

"No?"

"Why was that a question?"

"I don't know." All I'm certain about right now is that I want him to let me go.

The more his skin is on mine, the harder I think about the nightmare. The way his body violated mine and how I didn't fight.

The frustration is so deep that I want to make up for it now, in real life, but even I know that if I attempt to hurt him, I'll pay the price.

His fingers travel from my chin to my neck, eliciting shivers and goosebumps. I expect him to choke me or something, but he grips me by the shoulder, his gray eyes darkening just like in the nightmare. "Bend over."

"W-why?"

"I said if you talk back, you'll be punished."

My lips part at that word. *Punished.* A war explodes in my chest and my thighs shake as I try to bargain, "But I didn't mean it."

"I don't care. You defy me, you're punished. It's as simple as that."

"I won't do it again. I promise."

"Unless you know your punishment, you'll continue to do it."

"Just give me a chance."

"I have been lenient since last night, Lia, but you keep defying me and pushing against me."

"No, I don't."

"There, a mere example. You don't seem to understand the reality of the situation, and I'm happy to engrave it deep in your bones."

His tone, though quiet, chills me to the deepest corner of my soul. "Adrian…please…"

"Every minute you waste of my time will be extracted from your flesh." He grabs me by the shoulder, forcing me to stand up. I release the cup of coffee with a pained sound.

My legs shake as he pushes the chair away, its creaking sound on the floor mimicking the scratching sound on the walls of my heart.

Instead of waiting for me to do as he's commanded, Adrian flips the tablecloth that holds all the plates and moves it away with one merciless tug. Dishes clank together and the cups of coffee spill on the material and drip on the ground.

"Adrian…" I say, in an attempt of one final plea. "*Please.*"

"It's too early to beg, Lia. Save it for when you actually need it." He palms the middle of my back and pushes me down against the table. My cheek meets the cold wooden surface, and I try not to start hyperventilating here and now.

I hate how my body is in a completely alert mode. How a weird zap is tingling at the bottom of my stomach, clenching it, *awakening* it.

Adrian, however, is sure, confident, each of his movements holding a purpose that's designed to be met. He reaches to my front and undoes my scarf belt, then my button.

I briefly close my eyes as the cloth slides down my legs and bunches around my ankles. I try to forget what he's seeing, my position—bent over with my ass in the air and in his full view.

It's not difficult when his hand meets my backside.

The first slap reverberates in the air, harsh and ugly. Even though I'm still wearing panties, my ass cheek catches on fire.

On the second slap, my entire body reels forward on the wooden surface. I grip the edge of the table with rigid fingers as the flaming pain increases.

His hand is hard, merciless, with the sole purpose of punishing me, of cementing his authority under my skin.

But in that display of authority, as calm and commanding as it is, he shows me a part of him I haven't witnessed before.

Control.

He thrives on it. In fact, he's punishing me to ensure that I don't challenge it—or him. And with each slap against my ass, he's etching it into my whole being.

I wish I didn't react to it. Better yet, I wish I viewed it like I did in the nightmare—as a violation. Instead, a shock of sensations explodes on my skin with each of his ministrations. It's like something has been dormant and he's probing it, awakening it.

My body's reaction to his touch scares me more than his punishment. More than the nightmare.

More than anything I've experienced before.

Adrian grips my ponytail by the ribbon I used to tie it in and yanks me up by it. "Who gave you permission to dress like this?"

I purse my lips shut, but it's not only because I refuse to talk to him, it's also to mute the strange tightness coursing through my legs, my stomach, and even to my damn nipples.

It has to be because of the anxiety and fear. I refuse to believe it's due to anything else.

Adrian slaps my ass again and a needy sound slips from my mouth. I trap my lip under my teeth so hard that I taste metal by the fifth slap.

I'm ready to bloody my lips and cut my tongue instead of showing him what type of effect he's having on me. He won't get the satisfaction of seeing me fall.

No one will.

Not even if my insides are clawing and revolting to release more sounds.

"You will know your place." *Slap.* "You will not cross me." *Slap.* "Is that clear?"

"Yes…yes…please stop." I sob, but it's for something different from pain.

My inner thighs are hot, tingly, getting stimulated by each slap. I don't like this and would do anything to have it end.

He pauses. "You'll do as you're told?"

"Yes…" My voice is breathy—sultry, even.

When he doesn't slap my ass again, I think he'll let me go, but then two of his fingers glide against my folds over the cloth of my panties.

My head snaps back to stare at him at the same time as a wicked smirk paints his lips. It makes him appear like a villain who just found his next target. "So this is why you wanted me to stop. Did you like being punished? Did you get off on it?"

I shake my head frantically, refuting the evidence that he's sliding his fingers over.

He leans over until his lips meet the shell of my ear. "Your soaked cunt says otherwise."

"No…" I continue shaking my head, not wanting to

believe that I'm the sort of person who's turned on by this type of depravity.

I'm vanilla and always will be.

"Stop denying it, Lenochka."

That nickname again. I don't know what it means, but I hate it. I don't want him to call me by it. I don't want him to use me as if I'm really his wife.

I'm not. I'm only playing a damn role so I can survive.

"No," I say, clearer this time.

He continues stroking my folds over the cloth and I close my eyes, waiting for the sensation to vanish, but with every brush, my skin heats to an alarming level. The handprints he left on my ass are burning hotter than when he was slapping me, adding to my agony.

"You can be stubborn all you want, but you can't deny yourself, Lenochka." He slips his hand under the front of my panties and his thumb finds the bare skin that his people waxed clean.

He goes straight to the swollen nub of my clit, as if he knows exactly where it is without looking. He flicks it once and my back arches off the table. Coupled with his expert, measured rubs at my folds and the stimulation of my ass, I feel like I'll go up in flames.

With his hands alone, he's pushing me off a steep edge. I can feel those noises attempting to break free and bite my lip harder, tasting metal.

But this time, I can't control the explosion that ignites in my core and bursts through my whole body.

It creeps out of me slowly, but when it engulfs me, I'm a goner. Completely and with no way out.

I continue biting my lip, even as I shake with the violent pleasure he's wrenched out of me.

I continue biting my lip, even when the feeling gets so intense that I want to scream out loud. Even when muting myself feels like I'm robbing my own pleasure. My desire. My terrifying lust.

A tremor still grips me well after Adrian removes his hand from my panties. He doesn't release my hair, though, and remains like that long enough that my ass cools a little.

I want to steal a glance at him, to see how the devil looks after he gets what he wants. But I don't get the chance to argue against that thought as he flips me around. My back meets the table, and I think he'll fuck me or something, but he just keeps staring at me in that unsettling expressionless manner.

I can't believe I'm thinking this, but I prefer the way his eyes darken over this. At least then I can tell he's somehow displeased. But now? He seems like a tall, sturdy wall, impossible to climb or destroy.

The more he watches me, the harsher my breathing becomes. I hate being under his scrutiny. Or under his roof. I hate being under his anything.

He runs the tip of his finger over my bottom lip and forces me to release it from beneath my teeth. I forgot I was still muffling my voice even after I came down from my orgasm.

He caresses the broken skin, but it's far from a doting gesture. It's deceptive, secretly coarse and callous. "Hide all you like, but I'll eventually bring you out."

Good luck finding what's not there in the first place.

Adrian Volkov might have thought he hit the jackpot by finding his dead wife's lookalike, but what he doesn't know is that he fell upon a shell.

And inside this shell, there's nothing for him to bring out.

TWELVE

Winter

I REMAIN SLUMPED AGAINST THE TABLE LONG AFTER Adrian leaves. I didn't look at him, because if I had, I would've been creeped out by the total darkness in his eyes.

My shorts are still bunched around my ankles because I didn't have the energy to pull them up. My dignity is somewhere on the floor, too, as I stay here, hugging the table even after the click of the door has echoed in the silent dining room.

I don't want to think about what just happened or how embarrassingly I reacted to it, but that doesn't mean I can't feel it. The handprints, the flames on my ass. The damn tingling in my core.

Slowly closing my eyes, I suck in a deep breath and straighten. The movement shifts the tingling, and it's like my world is set on fire. I'm careful in pulling up my shorts, but my ass is burning. The friction causes me to moan. I don't bother hiding it now since he's not here and won't be able to hear me.

This is so messed up.

I need a drink. *Or two.*

I've been sober for way too long and that's probably why I'm reacting this way. If I'm half-drunk, as usual—or better yet, completely drunk—I'll return to my robotic self, who barely feels anything.

Larry never approved of my drinking habits and I miss him, but I can't see him, so this calls for more drinks.

I search the wooden cabinets on the sides of the room, but I find nothing. They probably keep alcohol in the kitchen.

After leaving the dining room, I follow the path Ogla showed me earlier until I find myself in the entryway. I go in the opposite direction, assuming that's where the kitchen will be.

Sure enough, I find it. The space is large and way cleaner than any cooking space I've seen before. The white counters are shining and the stainless-steel kitchen tools occupy a portion of the counter, waiting to be used.

I'm nervous about touching anything in case I ruin something. But my need for a drink overrules that feeling. There's a constant ache at the front of my head that will only ebb with alcohol.

I start with the fridge. There's water, fruits, vegetables, and bottles of juice. But there's no sign of any beer. So I move on to the cabinets, checking them one by one. I find cereals, probably for Jeremy, spices, some utensils, but there's still no trace of alcohol.

My search turns more panicked as I open and close every cabinet, rummaging through them frantically.

"Are you looking for something, Mrs. Volkov?"

I flinch, jerking back, but my hand remains on the handle of the cabinet as I face Ogla. She stands at the entrance, expression closed off as usual.

"I...umm...do you know where the beer is?"

"We don't have beer."

Adrian seems like the type of snob who doesn't drink beer, so that makes sense. I try again. "Whiskey?"

"No."

"Wine?"

"No."

"Do you have any alcoholic beverages here?"

"No."

"How is that possible? Doesn't Adrian drink?"

"Not in the house, Mrs. Volkov."

I want to ask her why the hell he doesn't, but her closed off tone and face deter me from it. I doubt she'd answer if I asked, anyway.

The lack of alcohol is hurting my head. It's even worse than a few seconds ago. Every addict like me holds on to the promise of the next hit, a sip, something to alleviate the ache. Contrary to common belief, we do endure, but only because our brains are attuned to the idea of instant gratification after a certain wait time. Now that my brain has figured out there will be no alcohol, it's actively trying to split my head open, and so I give in to its demands.

"I'll go to the grocery store to buy some beer. Can I tell them to put it on Adrian's tab?" I ask Ogla ever so casually, attempting to get past her.

She raises an arm, blocking my exit. "Mr. Volkov gave clear instructions that you're not to leave the property."

The asshole did mention that.

"It won't take long," I bargain.

"No."

"You're not the boss of me, Ogla. I can push you away and go."

"I wouldn't recommend that, Mrs. Volkov. You'll be stopped by the guards outside with less gentle methods."

He has more guards outside? I thought Bulky Blond and Crooked Nose were the only ones, and I'd assumed they followed him wherever he went.

"So you go," I say hopefully.

She shakes her head once.

"One of the guards can go, then?"

"No alcohol is allowed in the house. You'll have to get used to it."

I can't just get used to it. I've been drunk for most of my life. Okay, that's an exaggeration, but I've always been kind of drunk and that's how I've managed to stay out of my head. That's how I've numbed my feelings.

If I'm sober, all my emotions will be unfiltered and raw, like everything I experienced this morning. Come to think of it, I probably had the nightmare because I didn't sleep drunk. I don't want to find out what will happen if I stay like this.

I'm not ready to experience it.

I wish I could get in touch with Larry so he could smuggle me some beer. But that would be as hard as searching for a specific ant in an ant farm. Larry has always been the one to do the finding, not the other way around. Besides, I have no clue where this mansion is located and how far it is from the city.

And if I attempt to escape, Adrian will turn me in without a second thought.

Ogla is still watching me as if expecting me to bargain again, but I already know she's a lost cause. I have no doubt that she'll report everything I say or do to Adrian, so I have to be smart about dealing with her.

I stare back at her, meeting her quiet maliciousness with contemplation. Adrian said that I can ask her about anything 'I don't remember.' Hmph. Manipulative bastard.

"Hey, Ogla."

"Yes?"

"What does Adrian do exactly?"

She pauses as if she didn't expect that question, then says, "Why do you want to know?"

"He said to ask you for anything and I believe this belongs

in that category. I'm sure I knew all about his work before I lost my memories, so you're just going to have to refresh them for me."

I expect her to shrug me off, but she says, "Mr. Volkov is part of the Russian mafia."

He's not a spy, after all, but that's not a shock. He can pass for a mobster, even though his style and features are sophisticated.

The conversation I overheard from the Giants fans about the Bratva rushes back again and I swallow. They said they were dangerous people who didn't hesitate to kill. Not that I should be surprised that Adrian is a killer, but this information puts everything into real—and terrifying—perspective.

He's one of those dangerous people. It's not only the vibe he gives. His entire existence is set to elicit fear in the hearts of anyone who talks about him or his organization.

"Part of?" I ask, opting to continue probing Ogla. I need to have an accurate assessment of my situation so I'll be able to deal with it.

"Yes."

"What does part of mean?"

"It means he's a member."

Trying to get information from this woman feels like pulling teeth, but I rein in my exasperation. "He seems higher up, having guards and living in a mansion."

"He is."

"How much higher up?"

"Right under the *Pakhan*."

I heard that term once. "Is that the leader of the mafia?"

"The leader of the brotherhood, yes. Mr. Volkov is the brains behind most of the operations."

Again, I should be surprised, but I'm not. Adrian seems like the type of bastard who strategizes from the background to inflict more damage with fewer casualties.

But now that I know he's *that* higher up, I don't know why I'm suddenly nervous. A thousand thoughts occupy my mind and the most prominent of all is that I shouldn't be here. The second one is that I've landed myself in trouble.

However, it's not like I had a choice. It was either become a mafia man's wife or rot in jail.

Though, the more time I spend in Adrian's company, the more seriously I entertain the jail idea.

"If you've finished your breakfast, you need to study," Ogla pulls my attention to the present.

"Study?"

"Follow me."

I do, not sure where she's going with this. She leads me to a sitting area and motions at the coffee table, on which there is an iPad and a phone.

"That will be your phone. My number is three on speed dial. Kolya is two."

"Kolya?"

"He's Mr. Volkov's second-in-command."

"Oh, is he Bulky Blond or Crooked Nose?"

She pauses, probably at the terms I've used. "The bulkier one."

"What's Crooked Nose's name?"

"Yan. He's four on speed dial."

"Let me guess. Adrian is one?"

"Yes, but you're not to call him unless it's a matter of life or death and you can't reach any of us."

"I won't be calling him at all, thank you very much," I mutter.

She narrows her eyes but doesn't comment on my tone, so I ask, "Is the iPad for my entertainment?"

"It's for studying."

"Studying what?"

"The brotherhood. You're Mr. Volkov's wife, and while he

doesn't take you out frequently, you have to make a few appearances per year by his side. For that, you need to know about the structure, the hierarchy, and learn the names of everyone in the brotherhood and its closest circle."

"But why? I thought he'd tell everyone I've lost my memories."

"That's out of the question, Mrs. Volkov. You need to act as you did before."

"But you guys know. You and Kolya and Yan."

"We're loyal to Mr. Volkov. People on the outside aren't." She tips her chin toward the iPad. "You're expected to learn that within a week. If you have any questions, ask me."

She then turns and leaves, her heels clicking on the wooden flooring. I flop on the sofa and wince when my ass burns, the feel of Adrian's hand on me barging back to the forefront of my mind. The way he touched me so firmly, surely, with no hesitation whatsoever. He provoked a part of me I didn't think existed, a part that intrigued and scared me at the same time. Fear is definitely more present, though.

I gather the iPad in my hands and flip it open to find a document that's hundreds of pages long. Holy hell. Who took the time to write this? I was never much of a reader, so this will be like pulling teeth.

But hey, at least there are pictures underneath every name.

I'm about to start when I recall something far more important than all this.

Jeremy.

I was too preoccupied with my craving for alcohol earlier—still am—that I forgot about him. I abandon the iPad and shove the phone in my pocket before I head upstairs, where I assume his room is. I go in the direction of Adrian's bedroom, thinking he and Lia would've put their child near them.

After trying a few doors, I don't find Jeremy's room. It takes me several more attempts at the opposite side of the hall before I spot a young woman shutting a door. She's blonde with her hair cut short, not in a provocative way, but more in a book nerd kind of way. Freckles line her cheeks and nose and she has honey-colored skin. She carries a tray of cereals that appear to be untouched and doesn't notice me as she goes down the hall. Are there other stairs over there? I'll explore them later.

I creep to the room she left and stop in front of it to suck in a breath before opening the door.

Sure enough, Jeremy is sitting on the floor, surrounded by countless toys. His hair falls over his forehead in desperate need of a cut. His eyes are a shade of gray that seems mysterious, even for a kid. He looks so much like Adrian, it's a little disturbing.

Although he's playing, there's no expression of joy. Only concentration and sadness, like there's something inside him that's missing and he's trying to fill it by playing.

"Hey, Jeremy," I say softly.

His eyes snap up, fingers freezing on a toy soldier, but then he lifts it and throws it against my chest. It hits my breastbone before it drops to the ground.

"Get out!"

Aggressive, it is.

But somehow, I can see past his aggressiveness and to the reason he's acting this way.

The look in his eyes says it all. It's part of why I felt out of sorts and fainted after the first time I met him. I share that look, but on the opposite side.

He misses his mother and I miss my baby girl.

We're both two incomplete pieces who might have been brought together by fate.

Or his asshole father.

When I don't attempt to leave, he throws another soldier at me. "I said, leave."

I close the door and approach him slowly so as not to

trigger any negative reaction. When he doesn't throw anything else at me, I crouch in front of him, bringing myself level with him as I soften my voice. "Are you sad that I left before, Jeremy?"

"No." His lips tremble around the word as he grabs a soldier in each hand.

"I was, though." My own voice shakes as I see my daughter through his innocent eyes. "I missed you so much that I couldn't survive in the world without you. It became so bleak and boring. All I wanted to do was to find you."

"Then why didn't you?" he whispers, peeking at me from beneath his lashes.

"Because I have to live for both of us. I couldn't die, baby."

"You were going to die?" His voice holds so much fear, I internally kick myself in the butt for it.

"No, of course not."

"Really?"

"Really. I'm here, aren't I?"

He head-butts the two soldiers together and stares at them as he murmurs, "Are you going to leave again?"

"Absolutely not." I meant it as a lie, but the words come from my mouth like the truest thing I've ever said.

Before I can think on that, Jeremy lunges at me in a tight hug. His arms wrap around my waist with a force that pushes me down on my butt.

I can feel him sniffle against my chest. "I m-missed you, Mommy. Please don't leave me."

"Never." The words escape my mouth with so much conviction that it leaves me breathless. I hug him close and kiss the top of his head, taking my time to smell him. He's like a little marshmallow, soft and beautiful.

"Don't become a ghost either," he whimpers.

"A ghost?"

He nods in my chest without lifting his head. "You were a ghost the other day. I don't like Ghost Mommy. She was scary."

THIRTEEN

Adrian

OUR MEETINGS TO DISCUSS BROTHERHOOD business are the least of my concerns now.

Or most of the time, really.

I have my role to play, and it's behind the scenes. The decisions the *Pakhan* makes are directly influenced by my opinion that's backed up with my intel.

My rise in the brotherhood's ranks to become one of its most indispensable pillars didn't happen by sheer luck. I didn't come this far due to using force like Damien or by manipulation like Kirill.

It was by logic.

I realized early on that to keep rising in the Bratva, I needed systems in place. Trusted men—Kolya and Yan, though the latter is pushing it. Hackers. Informants within every organization possible.

While those elements were in place during my father's time, they weren't utilized to their full capability. I changed that and made them the strongest part of the brotherhood.

Power isn't barking orders and raising guns. It's not declaring wars and commanding hits in a show of masculinity.

True power simmers underneath, hushed in low tones and feared in public.

That's what I've become. The one whose shadow everyone feels, even when I'm not present, whether in the brotherhood or outside of it.

They might not like me—and many don't—but they fear me. Due to my systems, they don't know whether I have footage of them in compromising positions. At an unauthorized meeting with a cartel boss in South America. On a yacht sailing in the Mediterranean Sea that they embezzled from their organization. At the mayor's house, fucking him and his wife when they should've been merely keeping an eye on them.

It's easy to watch everyone from the confines of my home. The system I spent a long time building works seamlessly, without me having to interject in its course anymore.

Once my enemies—and so-called brothers—know I'm powerful enough to crush them, they don't dare cross me. Some of them still try to wipe me away now and again, but thanks to my system, the hackers, and Kolya, they fail.

They got close once. Only *once*. And I'll figure out the reason my system failed in that instance if it's the last thing I do.

Due to my invisible role in the brotherhood, I don't particularly need to attend the meetings. Something that the other members of the elite group keep reproaching me about. But the previous *Pakhan*, Nikolai, and the current one, his brother, Sergei, have always exempted me of the chore of being present. They're smart enough to recognize that I'm better off putting my system into use and bringing them results.

Or, at least, I thought Sergei did.

While he's been acceptant of my way of doing things, his recent suspicions of me are troublesome. Now, I have to prove my loyalty all over again, but I can't be obvious about it, because that will raise his alarms even more.

We're at his mansion that's situated on the outskirts of Brooklyn. This house has been used as the brotherhood's compound in New York for decades. When my father brought me here as a kid, I thought it was a monster, but way less monstrous than our own house.

I sit on Sergei's right at the meeting table, cradling a glass of cognac I haven't been drinking from. The *Pakhan* is in his sixties and has been hiding his cancer from the brotherhood. I'd already figured it out soon after he did.

Yes, I even have spies on my own *Pakhan*. People overflow with secrets and it's those secrets that keep me one step ahead of them. The men here use guns as their weapons. Mine is information. It's deadlier, faster, and more efficient.

The reason I haven't brought Sergei down using his weakness—the cancer—is because that will cause a power shift. While I don't give a fuck about instigating chaos, I'm not in the mood to deal with it at a time like this.

Only the higher-ups in the brotherhood are allowed to attend breakfast at the *Pakhan*'s house. Out of respect, the number of guards present is limited to our senior soldiers. Kolya stands behind me as sure and as strong as a mountain. Yan remains outside.

The other four kings occupy the rest of the seats. Igor and Mikhail are from Sergei's time, so they're ancient and would rather speak Russian than English. The other two, Kirill and Damien, have lived in America long enough to speak in barely accented English.

I'm in the middle. A Russian bastard of sorts.

Two other members join us. The first is Rai, Sergei's grandniece, the previous *Pakhan*'s granddaughter, and the only woman who has enough balls to barge into a brotherhood meeting.

She's now a regular, even though she's three months pregnant. Her belly is starting to show, but that doesn't deter her from coming in here like she has every right to.

She doesn't. And if she were any other woman, she would've been banished, but her relation to the previous and the current *Pakhan* keep most of the men here from effectively kicking her out.

It might also have to do with her husband, who's sitting by her side. He's a hitman—a sniper, at that—and everyone knows not to provoke him, especially when it comes to her.

The reason I want to shoot her between the eyes isn't due to her being a woman, or because she's been actively trying to eliminate my spies from V Corp, the brotherhood's legitimate front in which she's the executive director. It's because she meddled in something she shouldn't have.

She's the reason I lost Lia, and I won't stop until I know why.

As Sergei talks about our recent clash with the Irish and a possible truce with their new younger leader, I keep staring at the empty chair on his left. Vladimir's.

He doesn't miss meetings. I do. So his absence not only confirms Kirill's words, but it also means that Vladimir is going above and beyond for this.

"What do you think, Adrian?" Sergei asks me.

"The Irish won't accept an alliance this soon after our recent dispute. We killed many of their men and that doesn't go away by a mere change of leadership. We should give them time," I say, as if I've been listening to everything they've been talking about. I excel in the art of deception. I have since I was a kid.

My parents made sure of it.

After a nod from Sergei, the meeting goes on about some strategies that I let filter past me. I'm waiting for a chance to ask about Vladimir without being obvious about it.

While my system is efficient, Vladimir knows about it and, therefore, he's able to evade it. Not entirely, but even that small gap is enough to distort my course of action. I can't make any decisions before I know what he's up to. Otherwise, they'd be ineffective stabs in the dark that could—and would—backfire against me.

As soon as Kirill mentions something about a drug ship-ment aid, I take a sip of my drink and speak casually, "Shouldn't Vladimir help?"

"Vladimir is busy with something else," Sergei says with a dismissive hand. "Damien, you help."

"But that's boring, *Pakhan*," the latter whines like a kid who can't play with his toys—aka guns.

"Are you telling me no?"

"Of course not. I'm happy to be of service." He sighs and re-trieves a cigarette, then mutters under his breath to Kirill, "Fucker."

Kirill merely smirks as he adjusts his black-framed glasses with his middle finger.

"What is Vladimir busy with?" I ask flat out, to which Kirill raises a brow. He knows I don't prefer direct conflict unless it's absolutely necessary.

"You'll all know when I allow it." Sergei stands, signaling the end of the meeting. "We'll talk more on Igor's birthday that I'll be hosting in his honor. Everyone is invited."

"Yes, *Pakhan*." All the others agree.

Instead of leaving, Sergei faces me, fixating on me with a solemn expression. "Bring Lia, too."

"She's been unwell," I say calmly, even though a part of me is inching to an ignition point.

"She can't be too unwell to attend the birthday of Igor by the invitation of the *Pakhan* himself." He figuratively twists my arm with his purposeful words.

"Yes, Adrian." Rai joins her granduncle, speaking in perfect American. "Bring Lia. We have a *lot* of catching up to do."

I don't miss the way she says 'a lot.' I could bring my gun out, shoot her and her granduncle in the face, and torture her guards for answers. But that would get me killed by the rest of the men here or their guards, and I can't die just yet.

"Make sure she'll be there," Sergei orders in a tone that doesn't allow for negotiations.

"Yes, *Pakhan*," I say nonchalantly, almost as if I'm completely fine with the prospect of bringing Lia when she's not ready at all.

Sergei leaves, followed by everyone else except for Kirill, who deliberately stays behind. It's only the two of us, Kolya, and his senior guard, Aleksander, who's tall but slim and has the face of a woman or a pubescent teenage boy.

Kirill readjusts his black-framed glasses, his lips moving in a sardonic smile. "Asking about dear Vladimir was reckless, Adrian. I don't know you to be reckless."

"Sometimes, the best defense is a good offense."

"And sometimes, straight out offense makes you show all your cards."

"You don't need to worry, Morozov. I have more cards to reveal."

His lips tilt in an ugly smirk. "Don't threaten me when I can be your ally, Adrian."

I rise and Kolya moves on standby beside me. "I don't need allies."

"That's what you say now, but there will be a day where you will change your mind."

"Doubt it."

"You want to bet?"

"Try again in ten years, Morozov."

He chuckles. "Save my number, Volkov. You might need it." His voice echoes after me as I head to the entrance.

As soon as I'm in the car and Yan drives out of the property, I tell Kolya, "I want eyes on Kirill."

"We already have someone who's following him."

"I want someone else. Make it three people if need be."

"Yes, sir."

"Aleksander, too. Follow him."

"Consider it done."

"What happened?" Yan meets my gaze through the rear-view mirror, then slides it to Kolya before focusing back on the road.

I tap my finger against my thigh. "Kirill knows something, or else he wouldn't be acting smug."

Silence falls on the car before Yan says in a low voice, "Do you think he knows about Mrs. Volkov?"

"I'm not sure, but whatever he knows needs to be known to me as well. Is that understood?"

"Yes, sir," they both say.

ود

I spend most of my day in my office at V Corp checking financial reports to keep my head from spiraling into unwanted directions. But at the same time, I come up with solutions. That's what I do when I'm overcome by work. I think and allow my mind to go into overdrive.

I try to corner Rai, but apparently, she has a doctor's appointment today and went home early.

There will be another day and she will answer to me no matter what methods I have to use.

I lose track of time and only realize it's ten in the evening when Kolya informs me of the fact. I've been so focused on finding a solution that would allow Lia to skip Igor's birthday that I forgot about her.

That's incorrect.

It's not that I forgot about her. I merely tried to push her out of my immediate thoughts, because if I keep her there, I won't get anything done.

Especially after the way she came all over my fingers after a few spankings. She unraveled wholly, without restraint, as if she's been waiting for my touch all this time.

The sight of blood on her lips won't leave my mind, the way she muffled her voice still gets on my last nerve.

It'll change.

She will change.

Kolya, Yan, and I reach home around ten-thirty. I don't bother finding Ogla, because now that I'm not actively trying to keep Lia out of my thoughts, she's the only thing that's occupying my brain.

I go to our bedroom and freeze in the doorway. She's not there. After searching in the bathroom, I come up empty-handed.

For a second, I remain rooted there on the spot, thinking of where she could have gone. She couldn't have left the property, because Ogla or my guards would've informed me of the fact. I know that, but the possibility is tugging on the vacant place in my chest.

She's here. I know she is. I can feel her presence in the walls of the house, can see it without having to try hard.

I stride to Jeremy's room, and when I open the door, the sight before me leaves me open-mouthed. Lia is sleeping on my son's bed, holding him to her chest.

His tiny fingers are wrapped around her waist and a small smile grazes his sleepy face.

The room is all sorts of chaotic, as if an army of children played here. His toy soldiers are scattered on the floor, surrounded by a dozen drawings and colorful scarfs.

Did she spend the entire day with Jeremy?

My gaze slides to them again, to the way her jean shorts ride up her bare thighs and how her top hugs her waist, revealing her belly button.

The whole look is unusual, but that didn't stop my dick from hardening this morning—or from starting to right now.

I hear soft footsteps at my back and I don't bother to turn around as Ogla stops behind me.

"She came in here after you left, sir."

"What did they do?"

"They played, then they drew, and then they…"

My focus slides to her for a brief second. "What?"

She clears her throat. "She blasted god-awful loud music and made Jeremy dance with her as she wrapped all sorts of scarfs around them."

My lips twitch. "How did Jeremy behave?"

"He was laughing and smiling all day and didn't want to leave her side."

"Anything else?"

"She didn't learn anything from the iPad you left her, sir."

Why am I not surprised?

"Are you going to visit Mrs. Volkov, sir?" Ogla asks.

I give her a quizzical glance.

"Not this one. The other one." Her voice lowers. "Something weird happened to her and it needs your attention."

FOURTEEN

Winter

A CREAKING NOISE STARTLES ME AWAKE.

I place a protective hand around Jeremy, but thankfully, he doesn't stir.

I study my surroundings in search of the sound. The room is empty, aside from me and Jeremy, but the creaking continues, louder this time, magnifying to a terrifying intensity before blaring classical music blasts from outside.

My gaze snaps to Jeremy, who's still peacefully sleeping, his tiny hand strung around my waist. He didn't want to let me go, afraid the ghost would take me away.

Not sure what he meant by that, but kids his age have wild imaginations, so it could be anything. Jeremy is especially bright and catches on to things fast. Whenever I teach him something, his brain absorbs it quickly, and soon enough, he mimics me.

An overpowering giddiness takes hold of me whenever he calls me Mommy. I certainly don't deserve it, but it's the best thing that's happened to me since I stepped into Lia's shoes.

With Jeremy's attachment to me, I can pretend my existence actually has a purpose, after all.

The classical music is louder now, distressed, almost like it's the climax of a scene. Who the hell would blast music in the middle of the night with a child sleeping?

Gently removing Jeremy's fingers, I cover him with the duvet and slowly inch to the edge of the mattress. On my way to the door, I step on some of his toys, but thankfully, it doesn't hurt the way it did when I stepped on them when I was carrying him to bed earlier.

I quietly open the door, then close it behind me when I'm outside. The music is deafening now, almost like I'm in an opera house. An eerie feeling grabs me by my nape like marionette strings as I descend the stairs. I clutch the handrail for balance, because it feels like whoever is gripping the strings will push me to my death.

The music is coming from the sitting room Ogla led me to this morning. I halt at the entrance when I find out the reason behind the music.

A woman.

She's standing in the middle of the room, wearing a wedding dress that stops below her knees. It's identical to the one I saw in that Giselle poster. Ballet shoes cover her feet, the ribbons wrapped around her calves.

She's standing on pointe, her back arched at a sublime angle. A veil covers her face, and I can't see it because she's turned away from me.

Who is she? And why the hell is she dancing in the middle of Adrian's sitting room? Don't tell me this is his mistress or something.

She twirls around to the music on one leg, her other taut in the air. That must hurt. Staying on pointe for that long is pure torture and strains your muscles and tendons; that's why it's supposed to be done in short intervals.

I try to approach her so I can see her or stop her, but she leaps away—jumping, twirling, and arching her back. Then she's running from one side of the room to the other, clutching her head and meeting the distressed music with an act of pure madness.

My feet freeze in place as I watch her insanity unfold with her dance moves.

It's Giselle.

The music climbs to a crescendo as she falls on the ground before leaping up on pointe again, swaying from side to side.

Blotches of blood explode on her feet, soaking the ivory satin ballerina shoes.

I gasp. "Hey, stop!"

She doesn't. Her movements turn frantic, severe, and out of control. Blood mars both her feet, but it's like she doesn't feel the pain as she stands on pointe over and over again.

"Stop…" I sob over the loud music. "Stop it!"

She twirls away from me, her head tilting in irregular positions before it moves back into place.

Blood splashes on her fair skin and leaves stains all over the carpet.

I want to run to her, hold her, and make her put an end to this, but my feet won't move. The marionette strings are keeping me in place and I'm unable to reach behind me and cut them.

"Stop it!" My voice is hysterical, on the verge of something even I don't recognize.

She comes to a halt on pointe and turns to face me while still in that position.

My lips part at seeing her.

It's me.

Or a close replica to me, anyway.

The face under the veil is the spitting image of mine. Bloody tears stream down her cheeks, leaving patches of red on her veil and her dress.

"Did *you* stop?" she whispers.

A sickening crack of bones echoes in the air and her legs give out from underneath her.

"Nooooo!" I shriek.

I sprint toward her, but I'm yanked back by the marionette strings attached to my nape.

My eyes shoot open and I gasp with a sob.

For a second, I think I'm going to find myself in the midst of the blood, or that I'll witness the break in her legs—the protruding bones or the bloodied, broken skin.

Instead, I'm in Jeremy's bed, arms wrapped around his small body as he snuggles into me.

No music blares outside and nothing disturbs the peace.

A long breath leaves my lungs as I murmur, "It wasn't real. None of it was."

"What wasn't?"

I squeal at the calm voice coming from behind me and slowly turn my head, my fingers still shaking, but I don't release Jeremy. Ever since I hugged him this morning, I've been having this morbid need to protect him, thinking that if I fail to do so, it'll be like losing my baby girl all over again.

Adrian sits in the dimly-lit room. Only the light from the phone that's nestled between his long fingers is a break in the black. It could be because of the shadow the screen projects on his face, but he appears scarier now. No light present in his darkness. No escape. No reprieve.

He's like a dark lord sitting on his throne.

A devil.

A monster.

A *villain*.

The innate need to run that I've felt ever since I stepped foot in this house—hell, since I first met him—strikes me again.

"You didn't answer my question, Lia," he reminds me ever so casually. Or what appears as casual, because it's feigned. I can almost hear his actual tone, which is closed off, harsh, and is sucking on the essence of my soul.

Everything about him is sharp and has an edge. The top buttons of his shirt are undone, revealing a hint of his powerful chest. He's half-relaxing in his seat with his long legs crossed at the ankles. *Half*, because his posture is still upright and he looks like he's ready to pounce any second if he feels the need to.

How long has he been sitting in the shadows, anyway?

And why the hell am I having one nightmare after another ever since he brought me here?

"Lia." The single word holds more warning than should be possible.

"You don't need to know." I slowly sit up, gently peeling Jeremy's fingers from around my waist. He mumbles something in his sleep, and I brush his dark hair as I tuck him under the covers that are decorated with spaceships and stars.

"That's two punishments."

My head jerks up to face Adrian. "But…for what?"

"One for not learning the list Ogla gave you and the second for now."

I knew Ogla was his damn spy. "But I didn't talk back just now."

"Defying me is equivalent to talking back. Not answering my questions warrants punishment, too."

"Maybe you should make me a fucking list like the mafia one so I can learn it and magically tiptoe around it."

"And that's three."

"You can't be fucking serious."

"Perfectly am. Four."

"I'm not allowed to talk at all?" I snap.

"Not in that tone, no. Five."

"Just stop it, already, and admit that you're a sick bastard who gets off on spanking me."

"Six."

I open my mouth to say something, but soon seal it shut, realizing that whatever I say will only worsen my state.

Damn him.

He rattles me so much that I keep playing into his hands and digging myself into a hole with him. The visceral nightmare I just experienced isn't helping either. Ever since I woke up, I've been jumpy and disoriented, having little to no control over my reactions.

"Go on, Lia." Adrian's calm yet threatening tone resonates in the air. "I'm very interested to see how far the number can go up."

When I remain silent through the sheer force of my self-control, a small smirk tugs on his lips. "Now, tell me what you thought wasn't real."

"A nightmare," I say quietly, because if I speak any louder, I'll be snapping at him. He's provoking me so he can get the number of my punishments higher, and I won't give him that satisfaction.

His finger taps against his thigh once. "What type of nightmare?"

"None of your business."

"And that's seven."

"*What?*"

"Eight."

"Am I not even allowed to keep my nightmares to myself?"

"Not since you stepped into my house, no." He drops the phone to his lap, places both of his elbows on his knees and leans forward, interlacing his fingers under his chin.

Even though it's dark, I can almost see the blackness of his eyes. It's not only something visual, but it can also be tasted in the air, leaving a sharp tang on my tongue.

"You don't seem to grasp the situation, so let me explain it to you for the last time, Lia. You're my wife, my property, my *thing*. That means you walk the line I trace and make the decisions I allow. If I say you leave your will at the door, you do. If I say you will walk blindly into a well, you will. In my house, my word is law and my decisions are final. If you feel the need to defy me, by all means, do. I'll enjoy every second of whipping you into submission."

My jaw aches, and I realize it's because I've been clenching it tight during the entire time he spoke. I've never felt the need to bolt out of my skin like I do in this very moment. I want to fly out of here, to go somewhere, anywhere, where his presence isn't squeezing my throat with imaginary hands.

But the sane part of my brain knows that I have no choice, that I can't handle life in prison, no matter how tough I think I am. Being with him isn't a choice, it's the only means of survival I have.

Isn't fate cruel? Why is my safety linked to one of the most dangerous men alive?

Adrian rises, and I scoot farther into Jeremy's side, as if a child will be able to help me in this situation.

"Get up," he orders.

"Why?"

"Nine. With every second you don't stand, the count will increase."

"I'm just asking," I try not to snap, but end up doing it, anyway.

"Ten. At this rate, you will have a *long* night, Lia."

I don't miss the hint of sadism when he says 'long.' The bastard really gets off on the thought of punishing me.

He's a freaking deviant.

I scramble to my feet because I *really* don't want the count to get to eleven.

"Follow me." Adrian heads to the door without waiting for me.

I chance a glance at Jeremy's peaceful sleeping face, hoping I can somehow become one with his mattress or his covers.

My hesitation doesn't last long as I follow in Adrian's footsteps and quietly close Jeremy's door behind me.

My legs shake with every step I take. Sweat gathers on my

brow, and my knuckles turn white from constantly clenching them into fists.

People say they know fear. Like when their car almost crashes or when they witness a gory scene on the streets, but that's not true fear. The actual horror is the unknown.

Ignorance about one's fate is the worst type of terror.

It tangles around my ribcage like wires, attempting to break the bones and prick my heart in the process.

The darkness isn't scary; what's inside it is. And right now, that darkness is filled with Adrian's quiet but lethal presence.

My gaze remains focused on his back, on the rippling of his muscles beneath his shirt and the ink peeking from underneath his half-rolled sleeves. His strides are steady, as if this fucked-up situation is normal.

As if picking up a homeless woman and forcing her into his wife's role is something completely acceptable. Does the man ever feel? Does he have a beating organ like the one thudding inside me or is he a different species whose heart only pumps blood into his veins?

If he cared about his wife so much, how could he exchange her with a fake so easily?

But maybe he used her as he's using me. Men like him don't form attachments and are heartless monsters who only know how to take.

As Adrian steps into the bedroom and closes the door behind us, I wish fear was the only feeling inhabiting me. I wish the clenching of my stomach was because of a hit of adrenaline and not because of some other demented sensation I don't want to put a name on.

Because I know he didn't call me here just to sleep. I know that some savage plan is being concocted in his screwed-up head right now.

My need to bolt slowly dims, replaced by a strange type of acceptance.

It'll pass, just like everything else in my life.

As long as he doesn't see my reaction, he won't get to me.

Adrian unbuckles his belt and I stare, transfixed, trapped in a daze, as he wraps it around his hand, a blank expression on his face. "Get on your knees."

FIFTEEN

Winter

MY WILD GAZE FLITS FROM HIS VACANT EYES TO the belt looped around his hand.

He must be kidding.

But he isn't.

Adrian said he's not the joking type, and I believe him.

I've been squirming all day long from the feel of the handprints he left on my ass, so I wholeheartedly believe he's going to whip me with his belt right now.

"Please, don't…" I don't want to resort to begging, and as soon as I say the words, I know it's a waste of my energy. I know that someone like him isn't deterred by pleas or tears. If anything, he gets off on it. Just like he gets off on punishing me.

So when he speaks his next words, I'm jolted out of my skin with surprise. "What are you willing to do instead?"

"Anything," I blurt.

"I'll fuck you against the wall."

"Fine…" I hesitate for a second, a little apprehensive about his intensity. I saw his size, I know it'll hurt like hell, and a man like Adrian seems as if he likes it rough.

However, agreeing to that is the better choice. Fucking or being whipped. Yeah, it doesn't take a genius to decide.

"And you won't bite your lip. You won't suffocate your moans as your cunt strangles my dick."

"No," I snap.

He tilts his head to the side as if I'm some sort of problem and he's contemplating whether he wants to solve it or eradicate it once and for all. "No?"

"You just get to fuck me; you don't get to tell me how I react to it." My silence is my only defense mechanism against him, my last piece of armor, and if I let him take that, too, then I'm well and truly screwed. My identity will be erased and I'll merely be a washed-out version of his wife.

"I decline then."

"W-what?"

"Either you come completely undone or you take your punishment."

I glare at him, my fists burning with pain from how tightly I'm clenching them. My nails dig so hard into my palms, I'm surprised I don't draw blood.

Sucking a long gulp into my lungs, I lower myself to my knees.

As I do so, I notice a shadow of disappointment and something else crossing his face.

Fuck him. He won't break me.

My name is Winter Cavanaugh. I'm not Lia Volkov and I'm no way in hell this madman's wife.

I chant that in my head in preparation for what's to come. To say I'm not scared would be a lie, but my dignity keeps me upright.

"It's unfortunate that you chose the high road with me. Very unfortunate." The smoothness in his voice sends chills down my spine.

"You have your conditions and I have mine."

"Holding on to your conditions will only heighten your suffering. Understand this, Lia. I'm not to be crossed or defied. The harder you push me, the more ruthless I become. The greater you challenge me, the harsher I react. You do *not* want me to react, and you certainly do not want to see my inhuman side. I've been showing you mercy, so be grateful for it."

"Mercy?" I mean to scoff, but my lips tremble due to the assault of his words. "In what world are your actions a show of mercy?"

"Believe me, they are."

"You might think of them as such, you might consider yourself some sort of a twisted, gracious god, but you're not. You're cruel and callous. You're brutal and sadistic. You're perverted, too, because you get off on inflicting pain. Your calm and quiet demeanor doesn't fool me, and neither does your warped sense of *benevolence*. Your sole purpose is to hurt and take as you see fit. So don't stand there, holding a fucking *belt*, and say that you're showing mercy."

I'm breathing heavily after my outburst, and I'm fully prepared for the number of punishments to go up, because that's what sick bastards like Adrian do; they use any chance to turn the circumstances against you.

It'd be worth it.

For the first time since I stepped on his radar, I've given him a piece of my mind.

A cold object touches my cheek—the belt. He taps it gently against my skin—dotingly, even—but his expression remains the same, impassive and unreachable.

"If I'm perverted for liking to inflict pain, what does it make you if you enjoy it?"

My cheeks redden, both at his statement and especially at his veiled admittance. That he *does* enjoy inflicting pain. That I wasn't wrong for recognizing his need for control. But I push those to the back of my head as I lift my chin. "I do *not* enjoy it."

"You came all over my fingers this morning after a mere spanking. What do you think will happen when I whip you?"

"*Nothing.*"

"Do you truly believe that or are you hoping for it? If it's the latter, I recommend that you abandon such hopes, because you'll learn the hard way that I was indeed lenient. That I was giving you leeway and that you lost those privileges by resisting me."

"Just get it over with."

"You'll come to regret your impatience when your skin is red, Lia."

The coolly-spoken threat covers me with goosebumps and to my doom, not all of them are due to dread.

Adrian picks me up in his arms and I gasp as he carries me to the bed. I'm momentarily distracted by how small I am in his hold, how he could easily crush me into irredeemable pieces without effort.

He drops me on the mattress, face down, and it dips under our weight. Did he change his mind?

I lift myself on all fours, but I don't get to celebrate the thought before he flattens his palm on the small of my back, keeping me in place. My heart jolts and picks up in speed when his hand leaves my back and brushes against my hair.

Unlike his earlier demeanor, his touch is gentle, or pretending to be, anyway. His fingers sink into my strands, and I realize with horror that I'm leaning into his palm.

I try to buck against him, but he stiffens his fingers in my hair so they're gripping my skull, communicating without a word that I'm not to fight him.

I couldn't even if I wanted to.

I'm frozen in place, caught hook, line, and sinker in the depths of his chilling calm. It's on the surface, a façade, and I'm learning the hard way that there are multiple layers to him. The more I peel away, the deeper and darker it becomes. Each one is more alarming than the one before.

"Last chance, Lia." He strokes my hair like a doting lover.

I stare at the metal headboard with its exotic golden motifs, refusing to look at him. "Last chance to allow you to break me? Never."

"As you wish, Lenochka."

My muscles lock whenever he calls me that, and I have no idea whether it's in a good or a bad manner. Just like most things he does to my body, whether it's the way he touches or handles me. I want to convince myself that I hate them, that I can't stand them or *him*. However, a morbid thing inside me beats out of control whenever he puts his hands on me. Whenever he's anywhere near me. I want to think that I'm drawn in by how different he is, how silent yet lethal, but it runs darker and sharper than I'd like to admit.

Adrian unhurriedly removes the scarf that's been holding my hair. He then pulls both of my wrists up and ties them to a metal nook near the headboard that seems to be designed for this purpose.

Did he do this to his wife before, too?

Chasing that thought away, I test the knot, but it doesn't budge. It isn't tight enough to cause pain or cut off my circulation, but it'll prevent me from moving or freeing my hands.

A sudden panic expands in my ribcage like wildfire, eating away at everything in its wake. He can hurt me and I won't be able to defend myself.

"You don't have to tie me." The emotion is apparent in my tone, and I hate it. I *hate* that I'm allowing him to see me like this.

"So will you do as I asked? Will you offer yourself completely?"

"No!"

"Then we will do it my way."

"Adrian…"

"Yes?" I can feel him positioning himself behind me, and that fills me with both horror and a sickening type of anticipation that I've only experienced once, when he bent me over on the table this morning.

"Is there any way you'll stop this?"

"Not unless you take my other option, no."

"Are you ever satiated? If I give you more, will that even be enough for you? You took everything from me, *everything*. Why are you demanding more?"

His heat radiates against my back, even though he's not touching me, and that does weird things to me—things that make me clench my thighs. "I didn't take everything from you, Lia. You want to believe that because it's easy to blame others for your mistakes, but that doesn't make it true."

"You brought me here and took me from my life."

"Correction: I saved you from it."

"First, you think you're merciful, and now, you believe you're a savior? You need a wake-up call!"

His fingers sneak over my collarbone and I stiffen as they trace up to my chin, propping it up as his lips find my ear and whisper in hot, dark words, "Maybe *you* do."

My lungs burn and it's then that I realize I haven't been breathing since he caught hold of me. His fingers are caring, but couldn't be any more brutal.

"Tell me to fuck you," he rasps.

"Fuck me," I murmur. "But you won't be hearing *anything*."

I realize my defiance has tapped an invisible red line when his fingernails dig into my skin for the briefest of seconds before he releases me.

"I was generous enough to give you two chances, but you chose poorly. As I already mentioned, defying me will only result in breaking the stubbornness out of you. Challenging me is like swimming against the tides, you'll eventually tire and will be swept away by the current. Understand this, I make the challenges, not the other way around. It's time you learn that."

His impassive voice should have no effect on me, but it locks my muscles into a rigid line.

He lowers my shorts down my thighs, and even though it's similar to what he did this morning, it feels entirely different, tenfold heightened. His hands are like lava from an active volcano, or maybe that's my skin.

His finger curls into the band of my underwear. "You're still wearing the ones from this morning. Did you like walking around all day, remembering how your cunt came undone from my fingers?"

My cheeks flame despite myself as I blurt, "Of course not. I didn't find time to change."

"You didn't find time to change."

"I really didn't."

"Did I say anything?"

"Your tone says it all. You think I'm lying."

"Are you?" He traces my soft entrance and I jolt at the contact. "Is that why you're already wet, hmm?"

I screw my eyes shut as he rids me of my panties and glides his fingers over my slick folds, fondling them, assessing them with utmost care.

"I haven't begun to touch you, and yet, your body is burning with anticipation for the punishment. For someone who was acting high and mighty just a few minutes ago, it seems that the promise of punishment was enough to provoke your deepest, darkest secrets. Do you recognize what that is, Lenochka?"

I shake my head violently but stops when he brushes my hair to the side so his lips can find my ear again. With my eyes closed, everything is heightened—his callous touch, his warm breath, and his scent—that dangerous mix of woods and leather.

"You're a masochist to my sadism, Lia."

"Shut up!"

"And that's eleven. Open your eyes or it'll be twelve."

I slowly do, staring at my bound hands, feeling the helplessness in my bones. And yet, a certain type of freedom overwhelms me. Something I've only ever felt when I was drunk, roaming the streets with no purpose other than to stay alive.

"Now count or it will go up."

I don't know what he means until the belt whistles in the air before coming down on my ass. A scream bubbles in my throat as searing pain explodes on my skin. If I thought his hand hurt, his belt is in a league of its own. The welt it leaves on my flesh aches and burns, bringing stinging tears to my eyes.

I want to shout, to express the physical agony, but I refuse to show him my pain as well as pleasure. I bite down on my lip.

"Do you want the count to go up, Lia, hmm?"

"One." My voice trembles around the word.

It's barely out before the belt hits again. I jolt, trapping my lip so hard that I nearly break the barely-healed skin from this morning. It takes me a few seconds to mutter, "T-two…"

"I wonder, how long do you think you can seal yourself off from me? Is it worth it?" *Slap. Slap.*

"Three…four." I'm sobbing now, my tears wetting the pillow as my teeth break the skin. Blood coats my lips, forcing me to taste metal, but I don't scream. Not even once. I don't beg him to stop either, because that will only steal away my dignity.

"Have it your way." His voice is so calm, and yet so dark that a shiver for something a lot different from the pain takes my body hostage.

By the seventh strike, I think I'll stop feeling my ass altogether, but that's not the case.

Far from it.

And it's with horror that I come to terms with the reason behind the change.

Adrian brushes his fingers over the welts and I hiss, but the sound is about to turn into something else when he gently glides his thumb over the hurt skin, mixing the pain with a softness I never thought he was capable of.

A softness that confiscates my air and pauses my anguished sobs.

Something in me jostles and quivers with the need for friction.

Wait. What?

"What are you doing?" My voice is as shaky as my insides, full of tears and confusion—both at his behavior and mine.

"Shhh." He dips a finger inside me and I buck off the bed at the harsh intrusion.

It's like getting ripped from one phase of being and thrust into another.

"Ahhh—" I muffle my own voice by biting down on the pillow. *Shit.* A euphoric mixture of sensations rise and land inside me with a thud so resonant that I hear the vibration in my ear.

His belt comes into contact with my ass three times in a row and I scream into the pillow. The mixture of the agony and whatever is happening in my pussy turns me into a crying mess. I want it to end, but at the same time, I'm barely stopping myself from pushing against his hand to alleviate the ache inside me.

"That's not counting, now, is it?"

For a moment, my screwed-up brain tells me to stop counting, to let the count rise up, to see how far I can go before I collapse.

But my brain is totally unreliable right now.

It's succumbing to my body's needs and losing all logic.

I release the pillow, leaving a smear of blood and tears on it as I whimper, "E-eight… Nine… T-ten."

Adrian adds another finger and I feel myself disintegrating, decimating in the path of his destruction. My walls clench around his fingers and I cry with relief when he thrusts them in, giving me the friction I've needed since the first time his belt came on my ass.

I try to wiggle and squirm, but the binds keep me strapped in place with no room to move. I'm completely helpless in his hands, a marionette that he can do whatever he wishes with. And for a second, I surrender to that fate as he hits me for the last time.

"Eleven!" I scream as my orgasm powers through me at the same time as the sting. My heart lunges in my throat and I think I'm actually going to stop breathing and die in the throes of pleasure and pain.

It's dark ecstasy, a demented bliss that plays on the edge of insanity. But every part of me craves it, falls for it without any thought.

I bite the pillow to muffle my moans, the defiance in me burning as bright as the orgasm.

Something cold and taut wraps around my throat, and I gasp when I realize it's the belt. Adrian lifts me up using it. My back arches, but I tighten my teeth on the pillow, bringing it up with me.

His lips draw shivers down to my soul as he whispers against the shell of my ear in low words, "Let it go."

I shake my head frantically.

"Let it the fuck go, Lia."

I meet his vacant eyes with my daring ones and shake my head again.

Adrian yanks the pillow away and removes the belt as he flips me over. Pain explodes in my behind as it hits the mattress.

My bound hands twist before they're settled in an easy position above my head. Now that I'm no longer biting down on the pillow, I can feel some other sounds trying to escape. I attack my lips again, uncaring about the blood that keeps oozing into my mouth.

Adrian pulls my legs apart and carves his way between them. He's so large and strong that I feel like he's able to rip me in half with each motion.

Every movement against the mattress causes overwhelming friction on my ass. I wish that was all. I wish the pain and resentment were all I felt right now. I wish there wasn't a zap of pleasure shooting its way from the burning welts and straight to my pussy. The remaining tingles from my orgasm sharpen to an unbearable level.

I need something. I don't know what, but that orgasm wasn't enough.

Adrian undoes his pants and I hold my breath as he frees his cock. It was a magnificent sight when half-erect the other time, but now that it's fully hard with angry veins visible at the surface, I'm scared.

But to my horror, I'm not only scared. A morbid sense of anticipation seeps into my ribcage and nestles between my bones.

Knowing that he got hard by whipping me, that he got off on causing me pain, should be degrading—blasphemous, even—but it's not.

Adrian grips his engorged cock and fists it not so gently, as if he's angry with it—or perhaps it's me he's angry with.

His muscles flex under his shirt with the movement, and his inked forearms appear ethereal, firm, and ready to inflict as much pleasure as pain.

A drop of pre-cum drips down his shaft and I bite my lip harder, unable to look away from it or from him.

My heart aches and my thighs clench.

I think I'm broken. Because right now, I'm having thoughts I shouldn't, under any circumstances, entertain for this man.

Thoughts that will end in my ruin.

"Do you want me to fuck you, Lia?" His voice is raspy, full of unhinged darkness and lust. They seem to go hand in hand for him. Like he can't feel any pleasure if it's not as deranged as his screwed-up head.

I'm not like him. I tell myself that I'm normal. *I'm fucking vanilla.* And yet, I don't shake my head. I know I should; I should tell him to screw off, that I never want him to fuck me.

But I don't.

I'm still trapped by the sight of him jerking himself off. How his muscles and tattoos contract with the motion. How his eyes gleam and flicker from gray to a darker color. I want to know if his expression will stay the same while he's inside me.

I need to know if I'll have an effect on him like I did while he punished me, and if that effect will be more violent.

So I open my legs wider in a form of invitation, one I know I will regret come morning. But I'm already here, and I have nowhere to go. He made it clear since the beginning that he'd eventually fuck me, so what's the point in delaying the inevitable?

"You want me to ram into that tight cunt of yours until you scream?"

I want to look away, because I'm almost sure he can read the embarrassment from my burning cheeks, but I force myself to continue staring at him.

"You will let me fuck you raw, won't you? You'll let me stuff you with my cum like a good wife."

I'm not your wife.

I want to scream, but I don't, because that will definitely ruin the moment, and my pussy is clenching for another release.

This is so fucked up. I'm practically begging the man who welted my ass with his belt to fuck me right after he brought me to orgasm.

"Release your lip," he orders, his fisting movements getting faster.

I shake my head once.

Still gripping his cock, Adrian loops the belt around my

throat and lifts me up so I'm suspended mid-air with my hands bound to the bedpost behind me.

I expected the position to be uncomfortable, but it's surprisingly not.

"Open your mouth."

I don't, shaking my head once. Adrian grips my tank top and rips it down the middle. I gasp as he yanks the bra up, exposing my breasts. I want to turn away so that I don't have to witness him staring at them. They're small and I've always thought they were the most unflattering part about me.

Adrian, however, keeps studying them as if they're pieces of art from a museum. My teeth loosen a little from my lip at the look in his eyes.

Holy shit.

I know he thinks he's looking at his wife, and not me, but how lucky can a woman be to have a man look at her that way? Like he'll destroy the world as long as she stays safe?

My nipples peak under his scrutiny, hardening to the point they ache, and then something hot covers them.

His cum.

It paints my breasts and drips down my stomach and to my throbbing pussy.

I almost cry with disappointment at realizing he did this so he wouldn't have to fuck me.

As if my thoughts are written all over my face, Adrian wipes the blood from the corner of my lip. "If you carry on with this behavior, you'll never get my cock, Lenochka."

I close my eyes to keep from crying in frustration, both at myself and him. Why the hell am I so disappointed that he didn't fuck me?

I shouldn't. I *hate* him.

Adrian releases my hands and they fall limp on either side of me. He disappears into the bathroom, and my eyes start to droop, exhaustion getting the better of me. Then I make out his silhouette reappearing beside me. He's all tucked in his pants as if nothing happened.

A first aid kit dangles from his right hand and a wet cloth from his left. He gently removes my shredded top and bra before he wipes his cum off my chest. I want to release a sound—I don't know what, but I trap it inside.

After he's finished, he turns me over, and I sigh in contentment as the pressure eases off my ass. He applies something cold to it, and I hiss when it burns.

"It'll go away in a second."

I mumble something that sounds like a protest, but then I'm drifting off as he continues rubbing it over my ass in soothing circles.

His fingers are long, slightly calloused, and feel way too good. They shouldn't. They *really* shouldn't.

I think I fall asleep, because suddenly, I hear a phone ringing and I feel Adrian's fingers stroking my hair as he says, "What did she do now?"

And then followed by a sigh. "I'll be right there."

Don't go. I scream in my head. *She's not me. Don't go to her.*

But his fingers leave my hair and the mattress dips. Even though I don't see the emptiness, I feel it in the darkest corners of my heart.

I'm all on my own.

A tear cascades down my cheek, and I have no clue why or who's the 'she' I internally told him not to go to.

SIXTEEN

Winter

"YOU HAVE ONE MISSION. PULL THE FUCKING TRIGGER."

No.

"Mommy?"

I open my eyes, heart hammering so loudly, all I hear is its beat. Jeremy is perching over me, his little hand pulling on my nightgown.

Wait. A nightgown. I thought I fell asleep naked. When did I put this on?

"Mommy?" Jeremy calls again, his tiny chin trembling.

"Hey, baby. Morning."

"M-morning." He sniffles, wiping his eyes with the back of his hand.

I run my thumb over his tears. "Why are you crying?"

"Cuz you weren't there when I woke up this morning. I thought you were gone again."

"I told you I won't leave. You don't believe me?"

His gray eyes blur with tears. "But you always disappear, Mommy."

I do? I mean, Lia does? Why would she? Actually, having had a taste of Adrian, I know exactly why she would. He's not the type of man anyone would stay with willingly.

He's the devil incarnate. A hateful asshole whose only purpose is to sweep away anyone in his path.

But even so, Jeremy is her son. She shouldn't have left him with that type of man. Neither of them deserves the blessing that is Jeremy.

Softening my voice, I smile at him. "I won't do it again, my little angel."

"Really?"

"Absolutely not, so stop crying." I wipe his cheeks with the pads of my fingers.

"You said you'd sleep with me, Mommy."

"Your father had other plans. Talk it out with him." It takes everything in me not to say *your asshole father*.

I wiggle to a sitting position and pain explodes all over my ass and my inner thighs. I wince, grabbing the bedpost for balance.

I'm sore like I've never been before and he didn't even fuck me—and wouldn't, per his words.

My insides burn with the reminder of Adrian's merciless lashes and the depraved type of pleasure that his fingers ripped out of me.

It didn't matter how much I resisted, how much I wanted to hate it. He bent me to his will to the point that I actually craved it. I wanted it like I've never wanted anything.

But now I wish I can incinerate last night and everything that came with it from my memories.

"Are you hurt, Mommy?"

I smile. "A little."

"I'll kiss it better."

I laugh, then give him my cheek. "Go ahead."

He smooches me, his small hands wrapping around my

neck. I can't help feeling the need to hug him, so I pick him up and sit him on my lap, ignoring the sting of pain on my ass.

"Do you love cuddling, Jer?"

"What does cuddling mean?"

Oh, the poor baby has such horrible parents. I pull him to me underneath the blanket and hold him close, stroking his hair away from his eyes. "This is called cuddling."

He grins. "Are you gonna cuddling with me every day?"

"Every single day and then…" I trail off, tickling his tummy. "I'm going to attack you."

He breaks down in uncontrollable giggles. "No, Mommy, nooo!"

"You're done for, Jer."

"Mommy!" He snorts out laughing while trying to protect his stomach.

His joy is infectious and I break down in laughter with him. And just like that, my day is off to the best start possible.

Except for the pain in my ass and the other one at the back of my head. I might've ignored my need for alcohol yesterday, but I don't think I can go on another day like this.

After I shower and help Jeremy with his, we dress in matching colors. Black pants and green flannel shirts. I use a scarf as a belt. I don't find any other tank tops—after the savage tore the only one available. So I put on a short-sleeved shirt and twist it at the bottom, then gather it in a knot so that it's showing my belly button. I'm wearing heels today because I feel like I need the height to go with the cut of the pants.

Jeremy puts on his white-framed sunglasses and I find similar ones in my drawer. It doesn't matter that we're indoors. I take several selfies with the little angel because we believe we're the coolest mother-son duo. Jeremy poses and smiles like a professional model, giggling uncontrollably whenever I try to tickle his tummy.

After our photoshoot, we abandon our sunglasses and I

play a Spanish pop song on my phone in his room. Jeremy's eyes bug out as I take his hand and start dancing with him.

He moves his hips a little and when I twirl him, he gasps in the midst of his laughter.

"You do it, Mommy!" he exclaims.

"Do what?" I shout over the music.

"Twirl like the beautiful girl." He motions at a ballerina in a snow globe that's resting on his nightstand.

My smile falls as I study her, the way she's standing on pointe as snow surrounds her. The first image that comes to mind is broken legs, protruding bones, and blood.

Lots of fucking blood.

"Mommy?" Jeremy stops dancing and I realize it's because I've come to a halt.

I rip my gaze from the snow globe and smile at him. "Yes?"

"Don't worry. You're more beautiful than her."

The innocence of this angel.

"I am?"

"You're the prettiest ever."

"Thank you, my angel." I brush his hair. "Are you hungry?"

"Yup!"

"Let's go then."

I turn off the music and hold his hand in mine as we go downstairs.

As soon as we're in the dining room, the mood shifts. Ogla is waiting for us with scowls and obvious disregard for our clothes. But the one I've dreaded seeing the most and have kept pushing to the back of my head since I woke up isn't here.

"Where's Adrian?" I ask before I can stop myself.

"Working in his office." She pauses for good measure. "He's not to be disturbed."

I sure as hell wouldn't disturb him. If anything, I'm relieved I don't have to face him this morning and can have a peaceful breakfast with Jeremy.

Or *mostly* peaceful since Ogla keeps watching us on his behalf like a hawk.

I ignore her as I sit beside Jeremy. My ass burns and I close my eyes so that the ache passes. It doesn't, though. Every shift provokes the welts, and to my horror, it starts a tingle in my core.

Damn it.

I ignore the state between my thighs and focus on feeding Jeremy and myself.

It feels almost surreal that I've had breakfast two days in a row and that I haven't skipped a meal since that sandwich I ate in Adrian's car. It seems like so long ago, even though it's been less than forty-eight hours.

But I guess so much has happened in such a short space of time that I've mechanically fallen into the routine. The main thing that I'm not used to is the lack of alcohol. No matter how much I fill my stomach, my temples throb, demanding liquor.

There's one more thing I'm not used to. The sting in my ass. It's like needles, uncomfortable as hell, but my mind keeps playing last night like it's the latest, most thrilling movie I've ever seen. All the details are engraved in my memories like a sacred script. Including the part where I actually told Adrian to not go to her. That must've been another nightmare.

This place has been made by Satan himself—aka Adrian. Ever since I stepped inside, I've had one terrifying nightmare after another.

After breakfast, I take Jeremy to play in the garden. Something for which Ogla twists her lips, and I remind her ever so casually that Adrian said I have access to any part of the house.

I'm already cooped up here as it is. I want to at least smell some fresh air.

It's cold today, even though the sky isn't completely gray, so

I make sure Jeremy and I are suited up in our coats before we step outside.

A few guards dressed in black army fatigues and jackets are scattered all over the property every few yards. Some of them have gigantic rifles hung over their shoulders or chests, and their faces are solemn, closed off and without any emotion. Just like their dictator boss.

I tighten my hold on Jeremy's hand, afraid they'll somehow hurt him, but he seems oblivious to them. He must've gotten used to their presence over the years. How sad is it for a small kid to grow up in the midst of dangerous people and weapons like this?

He leads me into a built-in wooden gazebo beneath a large tree. There's a table in the middle and two long benches on either side. Endless soldiers and toys are already waiting for him there.

I drop the iPad Ogla shoved into my hand this morning to learn about the Bratva and blah blah onto the table. I'll throw a look at it later, because I sure as hell don't want to give Adrian one more reason to punish me.

As soon as we settle in, a guard gets into position close behind us. Please tell me he won't be watching over us with a rifle dangling from his shoulder.

I lift my head and instantly feel a sense of familiarity. Crooked Nose—Yan—stands at the entrance of the gazebo, and although he's dressed in black fatigues like the rest of them, he's not showcasing his rifle. I'm sure he has a weapon somewhere, but I'm thankful he's not shoving it in my face.

"Morning, Yan," Jeremy says absentmindedly, as he gathers some of his toy soldiers. He's sitting so close to me that his thigh touches mine and his feet are dangling off the bench.

"Morning," Yan replies, nodding his head in my direction.

"Morning," I blurt out, not sure how I should talk to him.

Now that he's not being overshadowed by Kolya and Adrian and I can watch him up close, I see how beautiful Yan actually is. His build is leaner than both Adrian's and Kolya's, his features are softer, less guarded, and he has thick eyelashes that are almost girly. That and his long hair make him somehow more approachable than the other two.

He also doesn't have a permanent scowl like the rest of them. His expression isn't welcoming either, just neutral. All those combined make Yan the one person I think I could get the closest to here. For some reason, I feel like I need allies aside from the angel sitting beside me.

"Do you watch over Jeremy all the time?" I ask.

"Yes."

"Yan plays with me sometimes," Jeremy informs me. "It's okay, Yan. I have Mommy now."

I smile at that, and even though Yan doesn't return it, his expression softens.

"Have you been here long?" I ask Yan.

"Since I was three." I notice that as he speaks, Yan doesn't make eye contact with me, choosing to focus on Jeremy, so I do the same while picking up a couple of his toys, no clue why.

"That's a long time."

"You could say that."

"Did you…know Lia?" I murmur, not wanting Jeremy to hear. "I mean, *me* before I…you know…"

"Kolya and I got you from that parking garage, Mrs. Volkov. We know."

Right. They did. So along with Adrian, Kolya and Yan also know I'm an imposter. That makes me feel closer and more at ease with Yan. "Please don't call me Mrs. Volkov."

"You are."

"You know I'm not."

He widens his stance but says nothing, so I repeat, "So did you know her?"

"Yes." His answer is short but not clipped, which means he's not opposed to other questions.

"How old was she?"

"It hasn't been long since she turned thirty."

"How long was she married to Adrian?"

"Since she was twenty-four."

That's six years—a long time to spend in the devil's company. I've been here for just two days and they feel like an eternity.

"How old is Adrian?"

"Thirty-six—and that's the only question I'll answer about him."

His meaning is obvious. Yan will satisfy my curiosity about Lia, but not Adrian. It's an admirable type of loyalty, even if that leaves me in the dark about my fake husband.

I should start calling him my captor and dehumanize him a little.

"Were you close with Lia?"

"I was her guard when the boss didn't need me."

"Let me guess. Now, you're stuck with me?"

"It's my duty." His voice is quiet with a hint of hesitation, as if he wants to say something else.

My gaze slides to him so that I can read his expression, but he shakes his head the slightest bit, still staring at Jeremy.

I lower my eyes and brush my fingers through the boy's hair as he struggles with an endless Lego-like game.

"How did she die?" I murmur.

"She just died." Now his voice *is* clipped, closed off, not offering any room for more.

The message is clear—*question time is over.*

But a multitude of them keep multiplying in my head. Like what type of woman was she? Mother? Wife? Did Adrian love her?

I scoff internally at that question. That devil isn't capable of emotions, let alone something that requires giving more than taking.

But he went to great lengths to replace her with me, so maybe he felt something for her.

Or maybe he was merely obsessed with her and he'll inflict that on me. He called me his *thing*, and people like Adrian don't like their property taken away.

It's not that they like them, but more that they crave the sense of power that comes with owning those things.

The things being Lia—and now, me.

Ghostly fingers scratch down my spine at that thought and I quickly shoo the feeling away, choosing to focus on Jeremy.

Apparently, he's trying to build a war zone for his toy soldiers by using Lego-like plastic thingies. Seems easy enough.

Wrong.

Assembling them is a lot harder than I anticipated and I have to cheat using YouTube. Yan catches me searching on my phone behind Jeremy's back, but says nothing, his attention quickly returning to stare into nowhere.

I want to ask him for help, but my pride stops me. Surely I can do it, no matter how complicated it is. What the hell are they selling to kids these days?

After unsuccessfully attempting to jam two incompatible parts together, Jeremy scowls at me as if I've kicked his puppy. "Not like that, Mommy."

"I'm trying, Jer." Even with YouTube, this thing is sophisticated as hell to assemble.

"You never do them right, Mommy." His little eyes judge me just like his father's. *Jesus.* Adrian gets an A+ for cloning himself.

I ruffle his hair. "Hey, are you saying I suck?"

"No, but Papa does them better."

"He plays with you?" I sound as unbelieving as I feel. I had the impression that Adrian barely pays attention to his son.

My focus slides to Yan, searching for some sort of

confirmation. But he shows no reaction, continuing to stand there like a pillar.

Jeremy lifts a shoulder. "Sometimes."

"I'm sorry, Jer."

"It's okay." He grins, showing me his teeth. "Papa is busy."

God. This little boy was brought up to be a man at a young age. No child should feel it's okay that his father spends more time with his work than with him. No child should be happy that he plays with him only *sometimes*.

If he couldn't raise a kid, why bring him into the world?

The back of my neck prickles as if Adrian is feeling my thoughts about him and will lash out his punishments for having them.

Jeremy picks two pieces and clicks them together. *Jesus.* The little rascal knows how to do this better than me. I really hope it's because he's seen it done countless times before and not because I suck.

"Don't you feel bad about him not being around more?" I ask.

"No."

"Why not?"

"Because Papa stayed with me when you were a ghost, Mommy."

SEVENTEEN

Winter

I FROWN. THAT'S THE SECOND TIME HE'S SAID THAT word. "Why do you say that I was a ghost, Jer?"

"Because you were," he says nonchalantly, his feet swinging back and forth. "I went to see you."

"You came to see me?"

"Uh-huh." He points to his right. "Over there."

My eyes follow the direction of his thumb. It's a small white building, separate from the house. It doesn't appear as well-kept as the main mansion. Cracks cover the exterior and vines of ivy grow on its walls, covering most of them.

The place instantly gives me a horrible feeling, like a bitter aftertaste mixed with vomit.

I realize this is the guest house Adrian told me to stay away from, and I have every intention to. But Jeremy's words about me—the real Lia—being a ghost throw me for a loop. What could be in there for a child to think of it as 'ghostly'?

I'm about to ask Yan, but my gaze shifts to the left and I freeze. In the main house, Adrian stares at me through a floor-to-ceiling window. He's behind a desk in what I assume is his office. Three monitors sit in front of him, but his attention is entirely on me as he taps his index finger on the wood surface.

He's watching me so intently, it feels like he's standing right over my head and sucking at my soul. I try to break eye contact, but the sheer intensity of his ashen gray eyes takes me hostage.

Adrian is merely observing me, but it strikes deeper, like a demand, a call—for what, I don't know.

What the hell do you want from me? I scream with my eyes, pursing my lips, but his focus doesn't shift.

I'm the first to avert my gaze, because looking into his eyes is still uncomfortable. It still resembles being choked by invisible hands. The act isn't real, but it's as palpable as the burn in my lungs and the contractions in my stomach.

That's one step further than when I first met him. Back then, it was only a sense of uneasiness. Now, I can decipher the reason behind that feeling—it's the terrifying awakening of a side of me I hate so much. Every time I see his eyes, all I can think about is how much depravity hides behind that calm. And how much I crave it, like nothing ever before.

After losing my mother and daughter, I thought I was done with this life. I was done wanting things.

Adrian has proved me wrong.

The man is married, or a widower, and I shamelessly came on his fingers. *Twice.*

I internally shake my head. It's not like I came to him or I can walk away from this. He's the one at fault for replacing his wife so soon.

I continue playing with Jeremy, trying to ignore the way Adrian's gaze digs into me like he's peeling off my damn skin, layer by each agonizing layer. I only release a breath when Kolya joins him and his attention is momentarily distracted from me.

Jeremy and I have lunch together and I ask Yan to come

with us. After living on the streets for so long, I've learned to share my meals, especially with people I feel at ease with. I wish Larry was around, and since I have no way to reach him, I somehow pretend that Yan is his replacement.

The guard shakes his head while Ogla fixes me with one of her judgmental stares for even suggesting it.

Adrian is still cooped up in his office and doesn't join us for lunch. Something that I want to ignore, but think about during the entire meal.

After I put Jeremy down for his nap, a sense of emptiness echoes in my chest.

Thus far, the little angel has been keeping me busy, but now that he's sleeping, nothing is able to.

Emptiness is bad as fuck in my case. If I don't occupy my mind, it'll occupy me, and that's the last thing I want in light of the damn nightmares I don't usually have.

I try searching for alcohol in the kitchen and come up empty-handed again. On my way out, Ogla startles me by appearing out of nowhere, standing in her rigid posture. The woman is everywhere, I swear.

I place a hand to my chest. "You scared me."

"Have you learned anything about the Bratva?"

"Yes, I've made some progress." While I was reading a story to Jeremy.

"What type of progress?"

"I know that the *Pakhan*'s name is Sergei Sorlov."

"It's Sokolov."

"Same thing."

"It is not the same thing," she scolds with stiff seriousness. "If you say the *Pakhan*'s last name wrong, Mr. Volkov will pay the price."

"Isn't Adrian high-ranked?"

"That doesn't make him bulletproof. If anything, he's more scrutinized than anyone else and his punishment would be the most brutal possible to set an example out of. So for everything that's holy, stop playing around and take this seriously."

I hate that she's making me feel like a petulant child, but at the same time, I can see the sincerity in her eyes. Her loyalty to Adrian is her incentive and no matter how much I hate the man, if something happens to him, Jeremy will be fatherless and this entire household will probably fall apart.

That's not what I want.

An idea pops into my head. Since my role is fairly important for Adrian, I can use that to my advantage.

"I understand, Ogla." I smoothen my tone. "Is Adrian coming out for a break anytime soon?"

"No."

"Doesn't he have to go to work or something?"

She narrows her eyes. "If you'd gotten past that first page in the document, you would've seen for yourself."

And with that, she turns and leaves, her heels clicking down the hall. I *really* don't want to call someone a bitch, but Ogla is heading in that direction with flying colors.

After I get the iPad, I wander around until I find Adrian's office. Since it's on the ground floor and I've seen it from the garden, it doesn't take me long to figure out where it's located.

The door is closed and Ogla said I'm not to disturb him when he's working, so I pace in front of it, then soon give up and choose to occupy my time until he comes out. It's not like I'm dying for another confrontation with the devil.

There's a small lounge area across from his office. I lie on my back on the sofa and kick my shoes away, sighing with contentment. One of my legs dangles from the armrest and I use my arm as a pillow as I read from the iPad.

Sure enough, as Ogla said, Adrian's duties are outlined on the second page of the document. His job consists of finding the right people to bribe for the brotherhood. His critical intelligence allows Sergei Sokolov's Bratva to be ahead of all other criminal organizations. Since he performs more of a background role, Adrian usually works from home and rarely appears in public.

Criminal. *Check, check, and check.*

Not that I expected anything different. After all, he did frame me for murder ever so easily.

I scowl at his picture at the top of the page. He's standing at some grand opening, wearing a tux and holding oversized scissors to cut a red ribbon. The asshole is too good-looking for his own good. He could be a bit shorter or have a beer belly. Hell, he could at least not be tatted. But no, he has to tick the boxes on all accounts.

The picture is mainly focused on him, but on his right, there's a blonde woman wearing a sharp pantsuit and a firm smile. She's stunning—so stunning that a weird feeling nudges in my gut at seeing her beside him.

I flip the pages to see if I can find her in the document. I don't have to search for long. There's a picture of her in a wedding dress, and an even stranger sense of relief hits me.

Rai Sokolov is the *Pakhan*'s grandniece and some hotshot in the brotherhood's company, V Corp. As I study her, a nagging sensation different from the one from earlier takes hold of me.

I feel like I know her, but from where? Was she perhaps in one of the charities from whom Larry and I were given food?

The door of the office opens and I stare ahead to be greeted by a frowning Kolya. Adrian follows soon after and stops short beside his guard, his eyes darkening so fast that I'm left breathless.

What?

I stare down at myself in case one of my shirt's buttons is undone or something.

"Get up," Adrian orders.

"Why? I'm reading the document you gave me. If I don't read it, I'm in trouble, and if I do, I'm also in trouble? Make up your mind."

Adrian reaches me in two steps and grabs me by the arm,

causing the iPad to fall onto the sofa. I squeal as he pulls me to my feet and undoes the knot of my shirt so that it blandly covers my ass.

I'm staring, speechless, when Kolya gives a curt nod and stalks down the hall.

"Don't dress like this again." Adrian's voice is laced with a threat.

"I don't like the wardrobe. It's boring."

He bunches my shirt in his fingers and pulls me against his chest. My hands land on his wall of muscles as my wide eyes clash with his cold ones. "I couldn't care less about it being boring. You do not dress that way in front of my men, and you sure as fuck don't lie down like you were just now. Is that clear?"

"I don't see what the big deal is."

"The big deal is that no one looks at you the way I do. No one gets a glimpse at what's mine."

There it is. The sense of ownership. The subtle obsession that he doesn't show openly but can be felt, nonetheless.

"I'm not your thing, Adrian."

"Is that a no, Lia?" His voice lowers and when I remain silent, he continues, "Did I or did I not say that you're to do as I tell you? Or is your ass in the mood for another whipping?"

I glare at him, then quickly soften my expression because what I have in mind is more important.

Sucking in a breath, I smooth an invisible wrinkle on his shirt, something for which he narrows his eyes, probably questioning my motives.

I really need to do this right. If I raise his alerts, he'll never grant me my wish.

"Fine," I tell him. "I'll do whatever you say."

"*Really?*" he drawls out the word, blatantly stating he doesn't believe me.

"Really. I don't want to be punished again."

"You don't want to be punished," he repeats, which I'm starting to think is his way of reading between the lines of my words.

"I don't."

"We will see."

"If…" I swallow. "If I'm good, shouldn't I be rewarded?"

"Rewarded. So that's what you want. How do you wish to be *rewarded*, Lia?"

"It's simple, really. For everything you're pleased with, I get something in return."

"You're already getting a roof over your head, free meals, and immunity from prison. You think you can ask for other things?"

"That was the original agreement. You didn't mention punishment back then, and yet you included them. I accepted them, so now, you should accept my suggestion."

"Did you, though?"

"Did I what?"

"Accept your punishments." His eyes are imploring mine so thoroughly that the feeling of being suffocated returns with a vengeance.

"Would it make a difference if I have?"

"Not really, no, but I'd like to know."

"If it doesn't make a difference, why would it matter if you know?"

"I'll be able to assert whether I should break you in further, Lenochka." His voice darkens with hidden intent. "So tell me, do I need to up my methods? Or have you smartened up to quit the habit of questioning me?"

I want to dig my nails into his chest, rip the surface open, and peer into his ribcage to see if he actually has a black heart. The more I talk to him, the surer I am that he feels no emotions. That he's a devil with psychopathic tendencies only meant to wreak havoc on everything that stands in his path.

While I hate bowing down to him this easily, I have a purpose, and antagonizing him is the surest way to prevent me from reaching my goal.

What I show on the outside doesn't matter anyway. On the inside, I completely abhor him, and that's enough for my self-worth.

"I am getting used to the punishments. It's only fair that rewards are included, too."

"I don't care about being fair."

"Adrian, please." I'm begging but saying it in an exasperated tone. "I promise not to ask for anything extravagant."

"Still no."

"Okay, let's do it this way."

"That's one for the day."

"What? Why?"

"What did I say about the word okay?"

Ugh. "Ok—I mean, fine. *Fine.* How about if I only ask for one reward a day?"

He shakes his head.

"Once every other day?"

"No."

"Twice a week?"

"Once a week and I'll judge whether or not it's reasonable."

I squeal. "Yes!"

In my delight that I won one against the devil himself, I catch myself on the verge of hugging him before I remember who he is.

No matter what he grants me, I will not be grateful. I will *not* humanize him.

Adrian stares down at me with what resembles approval, and I try not to get caught up in it.

Keyword being *try.*

Adrian's attention is like a powerful magnet I can't escape from. A black hole that swallows everything in its surroundings.

But the truth remains—he's only seeing Lia in me.

And I'm far from being her or her ghost. I'm a shell who needs to go back to her numb state before I become a danger to his and his son's life.

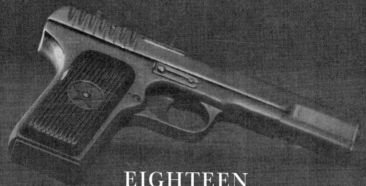

EIGHTEEN

Adrian

MY FINGERS TAP AGAINST THE WOOD OF MY DESK as I stare at the feed on my screen.

Kolya sits across from me, telling me about the latest reports from V Corp, but my concentration is scattered, and I'm hardly paying his words any attention.

Lia is hugging Jeremy, their legs wrapped around each other as they sleep on his bed. Her dress rides up her pale thigh, barely hiding the crack of her ass. Even through the monitor, I can see the red welts on the backs of her thighs from last night's punishment. I didn't hold back, and she writhed and squirmed more than the other times.

She almost screamed. *Almost.*

She's developed the habit of napping with Jeremy over the past couple of days. Something that makes my son ecstatic.

It's been a week since she became a part of his life, and he has no doubt in his mind that she's his mother.

During this short period of time, Lia has been doing weird things, like dressing him to match her and dancing with him in the hallways—things that Ogla does not like. His nanny has scarcely done any work, because Lia makes sure she's Jeremy's only caregiver, teacher, and playmate. In no time, they've become inseparable, their bond growing naturally, without the need for my interference.

However, her influence isn't exactly very positive. While I'm glad Jeremy is coming out of his shell, she's teaching him unnecessary things, like how to whistle or to run inside the house as they play hide-and-seek. I often bump into them, and she uses Jeremy's presence as a shield to escape my questioning.

At night, though, when Jeremy's fast asleep, she can't avoid me. At first, she tried to convince me that she's better off sleeping with him because he needs her more, but after that ended with her being punished, she started coming to the bedroom of her own volition.

Her movements remain hesitant with a slight twinge of fear in her light blue eyes. But the moment I touch her, she free-falls with no wings to hold her upright.

It's not due to her lack of resistance, because she does resist, fighting tooth and nail.

Lia still bites her lip or the pillow to muffle any sound she might make. She still stares at me with defiance after she orgasms. She still turns away from me when she sleeps and inches to the edge of the bed to keep as much distance from me as possible. She still stiffens like a board whenever I wrap an arm around her waist and flatten my chest against the delicate skin of her back.

I'm waiting for her to come around with time, but I'm not a patient man. Correction. I'm not a patient man when it comes to *her*.

In other parts of my life, I'm the epitome of steady decisions. I don't allow myself to get agitated or to lose my head; that will only lead me to rash decisions, and eventually, to my downfall.

When it comes to Lia, however, I seem to lose sight of my modus operandi. It doesn't help that she defies me every step of the way. Even when she's shattering all over my fingers.

She looks so compliant when asleep, her lips slightly parted and the soft lines of her face in eternal peace.

If only she were as docile while awake.

Maybe it's her sleeping face that stops me. Maybe it's her relationship with Jeremy.

But I've been holding off the inevitable for some time now. I need to take the next step with her before it's too late.

"Kirill didn't show any suspicious activity," Kolya says, tapping rapidly on his laptop.

When he received military training, Kolya excelled in both the intellectual and the physical departments. In a way, he's the most valuable second-in-command in the entire brotherhood. And he's smart enough to hide his actual worth so that the *Pakhan* doesn't take him for himself. Nikolai Sokolov came close once, but he died before he could fight me for him.

"Don't allow the men to slacken around Kirill," I say, still watching Lia. "He's most likely waiting for an opportunity to strike."

"They're my best men. They wouldn't disappoint you."

"We will see." I pause, tapping on the desk. "How about Vladimir?"

"We can't tell for sure." Kolya pauses and stares for a beat at his laptop screen before his brown eyes slide back to me. "He's keeping his cards close to his chest, but since the *Pakhan* hasn't said anything, he knows nothing."

"He knows nothing *yet*. That could change any second."

Kolya taps a few more things into his laptop. "Vladimir's movements have been normal. He's done nothing unusual except for going to the police station."

"He could be getting help."

"From whom?"

"Mikhail. Igor. *Rai*," I enunciate her name. "Keep an eye on the three of them and on her husband. He has killer friends and wouldn't hesitate to use their intel if he thinks it would benefit her."

"Not Damien and Kirill?"

"Kirill wouldn't have told me if he were going to choose the other side. His game is different than internal affairs. And Damien doesn't get involved in anything that won't allow him to use his fists."

"On it."

"And Kolya?"

"Yes?" He lifts his head.

"We need to have a meeting with the Italians."

His Adam's apple bobs up and down with a swallow. Nothing gets that reaction from my second-in-command. Not blood, not killing, and not even bombing a place just to get me out. When we were in our twenties, he single-handedly killed five men to save me from an attempted assassination.

He's the most courageous and loyal man I know, and it's been tested throughout the twenty-five years we've known each other. The fact that he's even showing a sliver of discomfort right now is for one reason, and one reason only.

He's worried for my life.

"I'm against it, sir."

"I didn't ask for your opinion. I only told you that it will happen."

"With all due respect, if Sergei or any of the others find out, it'll be the last strike. They will have every reason to question your loyalty."

"They already do. Might as well get things done."

"Suspecting you and having proof are entirely different. This will get you killed. You should stay away from the Italians for some time, until we at least know what Vladimir is up to."

"You know full well that I don't have time."

"You could carve some."

"Time is like a ticking bomb; the more I wait, the faster I'm heading to the end."

He sighs heavily, running his hand over his light hair.

"What is it, Kolya? If you have something to say, say it."

"Remember when that man tried to kill you some time ago? We ran after him, accompanied by Damien and Kirill, but then we found him dead?"

"Yes." I could never forget the only assassination attempt that my system failed to identify. Usually, I'd find the perpetrator and make an example out of them. Not that time, though. Not only the mercenary who was sent out to kill me was shot in the nape, but we also found evidence of someone removing the bullet from him.

"I have a premonition that the past will be repeated and the solution will be murdered before our eyes."

"Since when have you become superstitious?"

"Since then." His voice is hard, and while I know his concerns are genuine, I'm also certain that if I don't take a step now, everything will fall like a house of cards.

"We'll do the meeting on Igor's birthday." I tap my fingers on the table. "We'll make it seem normal. If I convince Lazlo Luciano to give us an in with his mayoral candidate, it'll appease Sergei."

"You can play your trump card."

"No," I say firmly.

"But it's desperate times."

"I said no, Kolya, and that's final."

He thins his lips but stops himself from spouting any more nonsense.

That's one of Kolya's best qualities. He knows when to stay quiet and when to talk.

My gaze slides back to the monitor as I notice some movement. Lia wraps her arms tightly around Jeremy to the point that he squirms awake. My entire body turns rigid and I'm about to go there until Jeremy breaks out in giggles as she tickles his stomach.

My body relaxes a little, but I keep watching them as she helps him put on his coat and wraps a scarf around his neck before she throws on her own coat and they head outside. I navigate through the hallway camera, then the stairs, following their every move.

Soon enough, they head to the gazebo in the garden. There's a camera there, but I watch them through the window instead. I see Yan, who's standing at a corner of the gazebo, posture relaxed but alert.

Jeremy and Lia are still struggling to build his war zone, or more like, *she's* struggling. It's the hundredth attempt, and Jeremy keeps bringing her one model after the other, wanting them all done.

Her brows draw together with concentration and she huffs a breath in frustration when it doesn't work. She has absolutely no patience, which is why she manages to get herself a punishment—or few—every night. She still talks back and spouts things, even when she knows full well that it will get her in trouble. Sometimes, I see the regret, but other times, her expression says without words, 'Fuck it, it'll happen anyway, so why delay it?'

After a few failed attempts, Lia calls for Yan, who joins them. She motions at the bench, probably inviting him to sit, but he shakes his head once.

So she stands up, grabs him by the hand, and drags him to the seat beside her. Yan's alert gaze meets mine through the window, and I'm about ready to go out there and beat him to a pulp.

I know it's not his fault, that she did it, but my brain can't look past her hand on his. *Her hand is on his.*

As if sensing my murderous plans, Yan swiftly pulls away, but that doesn't extinguish the fire that's burning holes in my chest.

Staring him down, I motion at him to get the fuck up, and he immediately starts to comply, but Lia places a hand on his knee, forcing him to stay.

That's it. I'm going to kill him.

I tilt my head to the side and motion at him to leave. In that moment, Lia turns around and faces me, her eyes narrowed and lips pursed, then she mouths, "Stop it."

Me, stop it?

I retrieve my phone and type her a text.

Adrian: Get in here.

She stares at her screen for a second, her lips pursing further before she types back at rapid-fire speed.

Lia: No. I'm playing with Jeremy.

Adrian: That's three, Lenochka.

Her eyes widen and she meets my gaze through the window.

Lia: I did nothing wrong today.

Adrian: You touched Yan twice and you just refused a direct order. Three.

Lia: You're impossible.

Adrian: I will show you how impossible I can truly become if you don't get in here in the next minute.

Lia glares at me through the window, her temper rising with every second before she types.

Lia: No.

Adrian: Then tell Yan to come.

A frown etches her delicate brow.

Lia: Why?

Adrian: So he can pay for touching you.

Lia: He didn't do it. I did.

Adrian: Doesn't matter.

The fact that she's defending him makes his case worse, and the more she takes Yan's side, the deeper his grave gets.

Lia: You need help, okay?

Adrian: And that's four.

Lia jerks upright, throwing her phone beside Jeremy. He stares up at her with unsure eyes, but soon smiles when she kisses his cheeks and probably tells him she won't be long.

Yan stands as well, but remains by Jeremy's side.

Kolya, who must've witnessed the entire thing, gets to his feet and grabs his laptop. "I'll be in the annex if you need me."

"What?" I ask when he doesn't attempt to go.

"Why do you keep Yan as her guard when you don't trust him around her?"

"I'm testing him."

"You're breaking him in."

"Same thing."

"Still."

"Stop spoiling him, Kolya. He's not a kid anymore. In fact, he's more cunning and works under the surface deeper than you're blinded to see."

"You're only saying that because he's close to Mrs. Volkov."

"And you're only defending him because you refuse to recognizes what he's turned into. Can't you see it?"

He frowns. "See what?"

"Yan is not the little kid who used to follow you around wherever you went."

He pauses as if he wants to say something, but thinks better of it, nods, and leaves.

I click my monitors shut and head to my minibar to pour myself a glass of cognac on ice. By the time I settle back into my chair, the door opens not so gently as a furious Lia barges inside and slams it shut behind her.

Taking my time, I drink her in. She removed the coat and is wearing a light pink dress that flattens against the curve of her breasts and waist before falling to her knees. Her cheeks are red, her lips pursed, accentuating the cut from when she bit them to the point of drawing blood.

That will change.

Sooner or later, that habit will disappear.

Sooner or later, she'll be completely mine. Literally. Figuratively. In every sense of the word.

I click on the remote, causing the curtains to fall closed, shielding us from the outside world.

"What the hell do you want?" she snaps.

"And that's five, Lenochka." I motion at her to move closer. "Now, come here."

NINETEEN

Winter

MY TEMPER IS ABOUT TO SNAP AND BREAK ALL hell loose.

I'm so tempted to get out of his office—to hell with his punishments every night. The sick bastard always finds a reason to spank me or whip me, anyway, so it's not like tonight will be any different.

He's making it his mission to not allow me to sit comfortably and to feel every lash of his punishment whenever I move. I constantly sense his presence with me, even when we don't see each other. It's a persistent reminder of my shameful orgasms and how my body responds to the pain as stimulation instead of discomfort.

The worst part is that I look forward to nighttime now. I look forward to all the things he'll do to me in the confinements of the bedroom's walls. Sometimes, I lie in still in the morning and feel like a slut for taking another woman's role and orgasming on the bed she slept in for years. I feel like an imposter and a horrible human being.

But come nightfall, all those thoughts vanish, except for the feel of his skin on mine. The scent of his cologne. The sheer power of his presence.

I tell myself to hate it, to loathe it, to rebel against it, but what's the point? I may muffle my orgasms and turn away from him, but he's a constant that's impossible to get rid of. He might have confiscated me from the streets, but he didn't force me to enjoy his ministrations. That was all on me. I chose to enjoy his brutality, his touch, and even crave it after a single taste.

Now that we're in his office, it feels different from the bedroom. There are no voices telling me it's wrong or that this place belonged to his wife.

Ever since the day I waited for him on the sofa outside, I've actively avoided this place, so this is the first time I've come in here. Like him, his office exudes an intense masculine vibe. The lounge area has a black high-back leather sofa and chairs. Even the glass on the coffee table is black. His dark brown wooden desk is topped by three monitors and he sits in a large chair that's dwarfed by his muscular frame. I'm surprised to find floor-to-ceiling shelves filled with endless books on either side of him.

They're probably for show.

He beckons me with a finger. "Come here."

My eyes widen when he lifts a glass to his mouth and the pieces of ice make a swirling sound, clinking tantalizingly.

Holy shit. *Alcohol.*

That liar Ogla told me there was none in the house. Adrian is obviously drinking some right now.

I've been trying my damnedest to not make mistakes so that I'll be rewarded and can ask for alcohol. However, my mouth usually gets me in trouble, because I can't stand Adrian's tyranny, so I end up being punished every night.

Or maybe you want to be punished every night.

I shove that idea in the black box at the back of my mind.

All this time, I've been holding on to the hope that I'll be able to get at least a little drunk.

Now, things have changed. Adrian has alcohol in this place. If I had known, I would've barged into his office before.

A plan immediately forms in my head as I slowly approach him. His calm façade doesn't fool me, because that's merely a layer of camouflage to hide his observant nature. I've lost count of the number of times I've caught him watching me, whether through his office window or while I'm sleeping.

It's creepy and causes my skin to crawl, but it's not only because of the act itself. It's because he really seems to be seeing through me sometimes. Due to that ability, he'll be able to figure out whether I'm being fake or genuine, so I conceal my anger while I gently sway my hips.

I'm wearing a soft pink dress that has a skater skirt instead of the straight ones Lia's closet is filled with. Needless to say, it took me a lot of digging to find it. I'm also wearing heels to add a bit of height to my short legs.

My hair is loose and I fixed my makeup after Jeremy and I woke up from our nap. So I have confidence in my looks. What I don't have confidence in is my ability to play a seduction game on someone like Adrian.

He's not only observant, but he also has the ability to barge into the soul of someone without armor.

I stop within an arm's length of him and inhale a drag of air into my lungs. The scent of cognac is almost enough to make me drunk. I would kill for a sip. *Just one, single sip.* But no matter how much I crave it, I force myself not to look at the glass nestled between his lean fingers.

If I do, Adrian will see right through me.

He tilts his head to the side as if he's trying to get past my skull and peer inside my head. "What did you think you were doing with Yan just now?"

"I was only inviting him to play with us. It's cold outside the gazebo."

"Yan does *not* play with you. Whether he's cold or freezes to death is none of your business."

"Are you always this heartless, even toward your own men?"

"Why?" He cocks his head further. "Are you offended on his behalf, Lenochka?"

"Of course I am. You don't deserve his loyalty to you."

"Do not touch him again. Do not invite him in again, and you do not even talk to him."

"It was innocent."

"Innocent," he repeats, as if the prospect is impossible.

"It was."

"Innocent or not. That will not happen again."

"Or what? You'll punish me?" I resist the urge to scoff, because that's part of his modus operandi.

"That goes without saying. However, that's not the only price. Anyone who dares to touch you will pay, too. In fact, if I catch anyone looking at you, they'll wish they were never born."

"Are you serious?" I know he is, so my question is rhetorical at best, but Adrian nods anyway.

"Go ahead and test me, Lenochka. If you prefer seeing that side of me sooner rather than later, if you'd like to witness Yan being beaten until a few bones are broken, you can keep up this attitude."

"You're crazy." My voice trembles as images of Yan being beaten slam into my head.

"You've seen nothing of my craziness, so do not provoke me."

"You're a fucking dictator. I don't know how the hell Lia stayed with you all this time. If I were her, I would've left long ago."

I regret the words as soon as I say them. Adrian is fully

believing that I'm Lia, and I just broke the spell he's accepted as truth for a whole week.

His expression darkens, and I'm tempted to bolt out of the room. Better yet, the whole damn house. But something keeps me rooted in place.

It must be the alcohol. No. It's definitely the alcohol that's making me stay here.

Adrian grabs me by the wrist and I squeal as my throbbing ass meets the edge of the desk. He rolls his chair forward and opens his legs, caging me between them.

The warmth of his skin captures me in its dark depths, pulling me under despite myself. We're separated by his pants and my dress, but it doesn't even matter. The hold he has on me is magnetic and it keeps getting worse, not better.

He wraps a possessive hand around my hip and I shiver as he speaks calmly, "You would have left?"

"Yes," I whisper truthfully, because there's no use in lying now. He'll see straight through it.

"But how would you have left when you're monitored?"

I lift my chin. "I would've found a way."

"Like…"

"Dressing as a maid or a delivery man or something."

His lips tilt in what resembles a smile, yet isn't. I've seen him every day for a whole week and I've never seen him smile, not even when he talks to his son. "How would you escape my guards and security?"

"I don't know. One of them would surely take pity on me and help me out."

"Take pity and help you out. Interesting." The way he mulls the words over makes it seem like this entire thing is a real situation, not a hypothetical one.

I shrug. "Not everyone is as heartless as you."

"And then?" he probes.

"Then, what?"

"Let's say you succeeded in escaping. How would you survive in the outside world?"

"I'd leave the state and go to the South and work as a waitress or something."

"And you think you'd get rid of me that easily?"

"I could try."

"What if I caught you? What if you failed?"

"I'd try again. I wouldn't stop trying until I succeeded."

His jaw clenches as if I've landed a punch to his face, and his fingers dig painfully into my side. "You will not succeed, Lia. Never."

"It's just a hypothetical situation." I squirm. "Ow. That hurts."

He loosens his grip on my hip, but he doesn't let me go. His face is still closed off and I'm lost as to why. Is it because Lia tried to escape before? I hope she succeeded.

An eerie feeling grabs hold of me at the thought that her escape could've only succeeded because she ended up dead.

The conversation has darkened his features, his cheekbones appear sharper, harder, like they're able to cut. I really don't want him in a sullen mood when I need that drink right now, so I clear my throat, motioning at the library. "Did you read any of these?"

"Why? Interested in reading one?"

"No, thanks. I'm barely finishing that thick as hell document."

"Not a reader?"

"Nope. I prefer music." I pause. "You're probably not a reader either and only keep them for show."

"I've read every book in this office."

"No way."

"Yes, I used to sit down and read as much as possible when my father was working here."

I recall the memos from the document that mentioned

his father, Georgy Volkov, who was a leader in the Bratva, too. His picture showed that he had grim, scary features, like he'd snap a person in two if they so much as spoke to him. Adrian shares some of his traits, but his looks and physique are more sophisticated than his father's. He can easily be considered an honorable gentleman in public, when he's actually a devil's minion.

Georgy passed away when Adrian was in his early twenties, and Adrian inherited everything, expanding his influence until he became who he is today.

There was no mention of his mother, though, so I ask, "Did your mother have an influence on your reading habits?"

He raises a brow as if he didn't expect that question. "Maybe."

"Is that a yes or a no?"

"Neither. That's why it's a maybe."

I narrow my eyes at him. Is he teasing me?

"Why wasn't your mother in the document?"

"Because she didn't exist."

"Oh. Did she die while you were young?"

"Something like that."

All his answers are vague at best. I can't figure out what he's trying to say or what he isn't, but at the same time, he's not completely refusing my questions. If anything, the small conversation has loosened him up a little to the point where his hold around my waist feels intimate. It's no longer to ensure his control on me, but more like he wants to touch me.

"Did you have a childhood like Jeremy's?" I ask.

"Like Jeremy's?"

"As in, your father was absent and your mother had to take care of you?"

"It was the other way around."

"Your mom was absent?"

He says nothing, his eyes looking at me but not seeming

like they're seeing me. I feel as if I'm losing hold of him, so I blurt, "If you had an absentee parent yourself, shouldn't you feel Jeremy's situation more?"

Some of the light goes back to his eyes at the mention of his son. "What about Jeremy's situation?"

"He barely sees you, even though you mostly work from home."

"We see each other fine."

"Have you ever read him a bedtime story?"

"He outgrew those."

"He's only five, Adrian. He didn't outgrow bedtime stories. Besides, he misses you."

"How would you know that?"

"Every time we do something, he never fails to mention when he did it with you or what you told him about it. He's looking at you all the time; why don't you look at him?" My voice chokes and I try to clear my throat.

He doesn't know how lucky he is to have an angel like Jeremy as a son. Adrian wipes a thumb under my eye, his expression warmer, almost like he doesn't want me to cry. The asshole doesn't seem to mind when I'm sobbing out my orgasms while he's punishing me.

"How about you?" he whispers.

"Me?"

"Do you look at me?"

"I have no reason to look at you."

"No?"

"No. I'm sorry if you think I'm your wife, but I'm not."

"Yes, you are, Lia."

"My name is Winter."

The darkness I thought was gone slams back into his eyes. "That's six."

"You can't erase my name. It's Winter. At least call me that when it's the two of us."

"Seven, Lia."

I squeeze my lips shut, feeling more tears barging to my eyes. I don't know why the fact that he refuses to call me by my name has this effect on me, why it feels like he's cutting me open more than any of his punishments would. It shouldn't, and yet, a morbid feeling gnaws at my insides, demanding I win this.

Because with each passing day, my real identity is disintegrating and I feel like I'll become Lia in no time.

"You can play your sick games all you want, Adrian, but you won't be able to wipe away who I am. *What* I am."

"Eight."

I should cut my losses and keep my mouth shut, but I don't. I can't. He has to know that I am my own person, that he can't transform me into his dead wife.

"My name is Winter Cavanaugh and I was born in Michigan. My father died when I was a toddler, and my mom relocated us to New York for work reasons."

"Shut up."

"No! You'll listen, because I'm not just some blow-up doll who's playing the sick role of your dead wife. I'm human. I have feelings. *I feel.*" I suck in a harsh breath before I continue, "After my mom relocated us here, I took ballet classes, even though they were expensive as fuck. When Mom couldn't afford to pay for them anymore, my teacher took me under her wing as a charity case and paid for them on my mom's behalf because she couldn't stand to see my talent go to waste. And you know what? I was a fucking brilliant ballerina. I made all my classmates green with envy because I had strong ankles and could stand on pointe from the time I was goddamn eleven. I was *that* good. But that was also when the rich kids started ganging up on me, calling me a charity case. Do you know what it feels like to grow up poor, Adrian? Of course, you don't. You had your rich mob father."

"Are you going to shut up?"

"No. You're going to listen. This time, you're going to fucking *listen*. I was recruited as a backup in the New York City Ballet when I was sixteen. I thought me and Mom's life would become rainbows. But no, the dancers there didn't like me and made it known. They bullied me, changed my broken-in shoes with new ones. They stole my Band-Aids, toe pads, and my elastic bandages and tore my leotards before important performances to stop me from going on stage. But I had a friend who helped me. She gave me a hand and protected me. She let me dance on her behalf sometimes. She had my back throughout the years, and even though her skills were no different from mine, she became a prima ballerina at the age of twenty. I didn't get very far. I only stayed there, in the background, like a nobody, but I didn't resent her for it. I was happy for her. I celebrated with her and was thankful I could keep a roof over our head.

"But do you know what happened next? I found out she was the one who'd kept me in the background. All her nice behavior was a ploy to keep me under her thumb. I was so stupid. So fucking *stupid*. I hated dancing so much after that, so I quit. I left that world and everything that came with it. But she never left my mind. She stayed at the back of it and in my nightmares. She was there when I was a nobody waitress seeing her posters on the streets. She said she wanted one last favor. She had the fucking nerve to ask for a favor. But I couldn't say no, and do you know why? Because my mom was dying, and I was knocked up by some fucking man whose name I don't remember and my daughter was born with weak lungs. I took the hotshot ballerina's offer, which included having my baby daughter ripped away from my hands soon after she was born. When I told my mom about what I was doing to ensure our future, she cursed me to hell, but I didn't stop. I didn't have the luxury of stopping.

"I didn't succeed, though. I had an accident where my head was nearly cracked open. When I woke up in the hospital, my mother was gone." I'm sobbing now, tears streaming down my cheeks. "My little girl's lungs gave up on her and she followed soon after. That's how I ended up on the streets. That's how I became a shadow of a person, homeless, a nobody. So no, Adrian. I'm *not* Lia. My name and identity are the last things I have, so don't you dare take those away, too."

I'm panting by the time I finish telling him my story. I never expected to blurt it out as if the words were burning my tongue. The only other person who knows about my history is Larry, and I only told him in batches. Not in one go like I just did.

If I expected sympathy from Adrian, he shows none. His expression remains the same. "What was the favor she asked of you?"

"What?"

"You said she asked you for a favor. What was it?"

"Why do you want to know?"

"Tell me."

"N-no."

He narrows his eyes. "Why not?"

"Because I'm not proud of it."

"You said it didn't succeed."

"I wanted it to. I guess that's what counts for me."

He's silent for a beat too long and I think he'll ask me another question, but he doesn't. His shoulders have visibly tensed beneath his light gray shirt and the subtle intensity in his eyes is sharpening by the second.

If I didn't know any better, I'd say he was angry. But for what? Because I didn't answer his question?

"Get on the table, Lia."

Any hope I had for him to call me by my name shatters and disperses in the background. It hurts worse than anything he's done to me. Worse than the lashes of his belt and the slap of his hands. Worse than him depriving me of alcohol.

Because at this moment, I realize that he'll never see me. That, just like in the ballet, I'm only a shadow of someone else.

An insignificant nobody.

TWENTY

Winter

WHEN IT TAKES ME MORE THAN A SECOND TO get on the desk, Adrian loops his hands around my waist, lifts me up, and sets me on it.

I'm now in direct view of his unforgiving gaze. I want to scream and yell, to hit and scratch. I can feel a tantrum or a meltdown—or both—building at the back of my brain, but I rein them in as I stare at the wall behind him.

"Lift your legs and open them," he orders.

I do as he says, my heels planted on the edge of the desk. My movements are mechanical at best and I'm thankful for it. I wait for the numbness to take me over, because that's what I need right now.

If I'm numb, I won't feel the sharp edges digging into my heart. If I'm numb, I won't hate a dead woman because she still lives through me. Because she's still alive for Adrian while I don't exist.

"Look at me."

I don't, my gaze stolen by the white wall behind him.

"Lia."

I'm not Lia. Stop calling me Lia. But I don't say that, because it doesn't matter. Not to Adrian.

"That's nine."

I remain silent. He can do whatever he likes with my body. He already thinks it's Lia's instead of mine, anyway.

"Ten." He stares at his watch. "The count will go up with every minute you don't fucking look at me."

My gaze slides to his, and I hope it's as dead as I feel. I hope he sees the cruelty of what he's doing to me, of the way he's erasing my identity. But would he even care if that were the case? Would he take a second of his precious time to think that the woman he brought from the street *feels*?

He doesn't.

Adrian brings the glass of cognac to his lips, and most of the ice has melted away. I want a sip of it more than anything in the world. It'll erase my feelings and make me numb again. If I'm drunk, it won't hurt that he's seeing another woman through me.

Seeming to notice my concentration on his drink, Adrian pauses before he stands. "Stay there and lift your dress up."

I do as he says, watching as he heads to a minibar and fills his glass with more ice and some alcohol.

By the time he returns, I'm holding the dress to my stomach, sitting on the table, half-naked, with only my white lace panties covering my pussy. He slides to his chair and takes another sip of his cognac as if he's taunting me. When he releases his lips from the glass, he rolls something in his mouth before he leans over and presses his cold lips to my inner thigh.

I gasp and brace myself back on one hand. He kisses his way up my thigh, running the tip of the ice over my heated skin. It melts in a matter of seconds, leaving chilling hot and cold trails in its wake. Adrian picks up another one, with his teeth this time, and paints a new trail, picking up from where the first one stopped.

I momentarily lose sight of the cognac, all my attention honed in on where the ice meets my skin, to how his lips slightly graze my thigh, his stubble creating unbearable friction.

My head rolls back and I bite my bottom lip as I try to close my legs.

"Keep them open," he orders, with the glass halfway to his mouth. "How many?"

"W-what?"

"You forgot how to count, Lenochka?"

Oh, so this is his sick version of punishment today. I prefer the searing pain. At least then I can think of him as a perverted psycho I should hate.

"Lia…"

"T-two." My voice trembles and I hate that name and him and the way he's making me feel invisible.

He wets his lips and glides two more ice cubes up my inner thigh before moving to the other one, giving it the same tormenting attention. I'm delirious by the eighth one. He always stops right before his lips or the ice cube touches the hem of my panties, as if he's doing it on purpose, torturing me on purpose, turning me into a version of myself I don't recognize *on purpose.*

I'm a panting mess, my heart beating in and out of synch, as he lowers my underwear down my legs, then throws them to the ground. He's deliberate, slow, like he knows exactly the effect of what he's doing to me.

"How many, Lia?"

"Eight…" I breathe out.

He takes a sip of the cognac and puts another cube of ice between his teeth. I suck in a sharp breath at the view of it wetting his lips, dripping down his stubbled chin. But that's all the view I get before he disappears between my legs. He places the ice against my soaking folds and I jerk on the rigid surface.

It doesn't matter how much I anticipated the contact, the moment it happens, it's like all the fireworks and explosions I never thought would be possible.

Adrian grabs hold of my thighs, imprisoning me in place as he thrusts the cube against my most sensitive spot. The cold temperature is supposed to drown my libido, but it only gets stronger. It could be because my hot temperature melts it in a second or because of Adrian's deliberate touch or his tongue against my clit.

As soon as the cube is gone, he takes another one and abandons his glass on the table. I should seize the chance and take a drink, but I can't move. I'm caged in place and it's not because of his fingers digging into my thighs. If I remove my hand, I feel like I'll somehow fall.

Adrian thrusts the ice against my entrance and I squeal before I bite my lip to hide the sound. He doesn't stop there, though.

His tongue nibbles on my clit as two of his fingers thrust the ice deep inside me. My back arches and the tip of my heel nearly falls off the edge of the table.

He laps at me roughly, diligently, as if he's punishing and rewarding me at the same time. As if he's worshipping my body and teaching it a lesson all at once.

I can feel the ice melting inside me, and that only heightens the pleasure I can feel through my clit. His teeth are sending electric shocks to my core. He sucks, nibbles, then flicks his tongue against that secret part of me he shouldn't know so well.

My head bumps against one of the curved monitors as I come with a muffled cry. Unable to hold the dress, I let it fall, covering his head as I ride the wave. My legs give up the fight of staying upright and fall down, shaking and dangling from the edge of the desk.

Adrian emerges from underneath my dress, licking his

lips. I stare away from him as I catch my breath. I don't want to look at him, at the arrogance etched across his face, at the way he's so smug about owning me. About how I'm his fucking Lenochka.

I'm *not*.

He grips my chin with both of his fingers and forces me to stare at him. "You didn't count."

"Nine. Ten." My voice is just above a murmur as I look down at his hand. He lifts the glass of cognac to his lips and my heart shatters.

He'll finish it and I'll gain nothing from all of this.

"Do you want this drink?" he asks nonchalantly, as if he's not seeing the eagerness on my face.

He's playing a sick game, but no matter how much I want that drink, I won't play into his hand.

"What's the point? You'll just say no."

"You can have a taste."

"Really?" I sound as distrustful as I feel.

"Come here." He pulls me by the arm and I stumble to my feet until I'm standing on shaky legs in front of him. He turns me around and sits me on his lap so I'm facing the desk.

My back is glued to his solid wall of muscles and my legs are tucked between his. A bulge pokes at my sore behind, and it takes everything in me to remain still, to not squirm or wiggle against it.

"Hook your feet on the chair, Lenochka. I want to have access to your pussy while you drink."

I do as I'm told and loop both of my feet around the chair, which naturally opens my legs farther apart. His free hand snakes underneath my dress until he cups me.

A shudder grips me and I try not to turn into a trembling leaf in his arms.

Adrian empties the glass, leaving only a sip behind. "Open your mouth."

I don't want to, I really don't want to, because my mouth is the place where all those embarrassing noises will come from, but he's not really stimulating me right now. It's about alcohol.

I slowly open my mouth. But instead of offering me the remaining droplets of cognac as I expect him to, Adrian downs it, and before I can protest, he lets the glass drop to the table as the fingers of his other hand wrap around my throat and lift my jaw up. His lips meet mine and I recognize the stringent taste of alcohol. It's slight, but it's enough to go to my head.

Actually, no. It's not the alcohol that goes to my head. It's a different taste altogether.

Adrian's.

He sucks on my tongue in an open-mouthed kiss, imploring, exploring, and robbing all of my common sense. It's tender but harsh. Passionate but demanding. Just like the way he ate me out not even a minute ago.

Adrian's never kissed me before, and yet, it feels like we've been kissing since we met. Like kissing has been the highlight of both of our existences. He's so into it, like he's attempting to lure something out of me by using my mouth. His vigor triggers mine and I can't help the need to kiss him back, to try and give as much as he does. I'm so in tune with him that my body feels like it's fusing with his.

I get drunk on him, not the alcohol.

He plunges two fingers inside me and I moan into his mouth. A groan slips out of him as if the sound is the best turn-on he's ever heard. I want to pull away from his mouth, to muffle my voice like I usually do, but Adrian keeps me in place as he thrusts his fingers in and out of me. I gasp when he adds a third one, filling me like never before.

Jesus.

Adrian devours my lips and my tongue as he pounds his fingers in and out of me. I wiggle my ass against his thigh, desperate for the release that only he can bring. He becomes rock-hard, his cock growing in size with every second. A tinge of fear mixed with anticipation rolls through me.

If his three fingers are stuffing me, how would his cock feel? I saw it a few times when he made me watch him get off with his own hands. I know it's massive when it's hard, and I really shouldn't be thinking about it inside me right now instead of his fingers.

But the mere thought is enough to send me over the edge.

I wrench away from his lips and bite on his arm that's holding my throat as I come. It must hurt like hell, but Adrian doesn't make a sound. If anything, he remains still, even his fingers halt as I ride the wave of my orgasm.

I'm breathing heavily, my teeth and lips still wrapped around his arm, when he asks quietly, "Are you ever going to let me hear your voice?"

I release his arm to stare up at him, at the slight furrow in his brow, at the disappointment I can taste off his posture.

"Are you ever going to call me Winter?" I murmur back.

He shakes his head once.

I want to cry. I want to fall off the chair and become one with the carpet. But instead, I say, "Then you'll never hear my voice, Adrian. Because it's mine, not Lia's."

There's a small knock on the door before he can say anything. I freeze, my heart thundering in my chest. I didn't lock it, and if anyone comes in, they'll see me sitting on Adrian's lap with his fingers deep inside me.

"Who is it?" Adrian asks in his strong voice, not attempting to let me go. He's so sure that no one will open the door, but then again, this is his castle. Why would anyone in their right mind defy him?

"Papa, is Mommy in there?"

I gasp at Jeremy's voice and I try to scramble from Adrian's hold, but he keeps me joined to him by the fingers inside me.

"Let me go. Your son is outside."

He's looking at me when he speaks to Jeremy, "Yes."

"Can I come in?" the little boy asks.

I shake my head frantically, but Adrian says, "Yes."

"Are you crazy?" I hiss under my breath.

"You said I don't spend much time with him."

"This isn't what I meant..." my words trail off when the door clicks open and Jeremy trots inside, carrying one of his toy soldiers. I drop my feet down and smooth the dress on my thighs to hide the position in which his father is holding me.

"What are you doing?" Jeremy stops at our right, his innocent eyes going from me to Adrian.

His father remains silent, leaving the ball in my court. Asshole. I plaster on a smile. "Your papa was showing me something."

"Really?"

Adrian wraps an arm around my waist and leans his chin on my shoulder. The gesture is new and feels intimate, even more than his fingers inside me, and that causes me to shudder. "Really."

"Can I see, too?"

"No!" I snap, then smile. "I mean, I was coming to you so we could play together."

"Can Papa come, too?" Jeremy asks slowly, almost shyly, and I want to punch Adrian for making him feel this way.

"I will, Malysh."

Jeremy's eyes jerk up at the same time as mine, and we both say, "You will?"

Adrian gives me an amused glance. "I will."

Jeremy takes my hand in his and tries to pull me with him. I elbow Adrian so he'll let me go and he does so, but not before he nibbles on the shell of my ear.

He takes a tissue and wipes his hand before swiftly picking my panties from the ground. My cheeks flame. I completely forgot they were there.

Instead of throwing them in the trash or hiding them in one of his drawers, Adrian shoves them in his pants pocket. I open my mouth to protest but then recall Jeremy's here.

He tucks his soldier in his pocket and places his hand in his father's—not the one that was inside me, thank God.

Adrian follows his son's lead as he walks us out of the office, talking about his soldiers. At least one of us is comfortable. I feel like my legs will stop holding me up from how much they're trembling.

"Hey, Papa." Jeremy stares up at his father.

"Yes?" I notice that Adrian's voice is gentler when he speaks to his son. It still has that intensity in it, but he doesn't direct it at Jeremy.

"Can I have Mommy?"

Adrian's ash eyes slide to me before he focuses on his son again. "You already do."

"Not now. At night. I want Mommy to sleep with me, but she said I have to ask you for it."

Flames creep up my cheeks. The kid took that suggestion seriously.

"She did, huh?" Adrian meets my gaze with a small smile that leaves me breathless. Holy shit. It's not even a full smile, but I feel like I'm being attacked.

"Uh-huh," Jeremy says, oblivious to the tension brewing in the air. "So, can I have her?"

"You already have her during the day, so no."

"Please, Papa."

"Do you want me to be all alone, Malysh?"

"No."

"Then you have to give me your mother during the night."

"Do you need Mommy too, Papa?"

Adrian pauses before he says calmly, assertively, "I do."

My heart lunges, thundering and squeezing against my ribcage as if wanting to escape its confinements. His words shouldn't have this effect on me. I should think that he only needs me because he wants his daily sick fix of punishing me, but the look in his eyes says something entirely different.

His eyes that I always thought were uncomfortable are now suffocating, trying to beat words into me that I don't want to listen to.

"All right, Papa." Jeremy grins at me. "We'll share Mommy then."

"Thank you, Malysh." Adrian smiles at his son, and I'm once again caught off guard by it.

What right does he have to smile like that?

Adrian helps me put my coat on and buttons it to the very top before he loops a scarf around my throat. Then he does the same for Jeremy and lifts him in his arms.

I don't want to focus on that, on how he can be a doting father, but the scene touches something inside me as we head outside.

The three of us sit in the gazebo, where Jeremy's war zone is still pathetically incomplete. The little angel settles between us with his feet swinging joyfully as his attention flits from me back to his father. Who knows how long it's been since he had both of his parents play with him?

"Mommy doesn't know how to do it, Papa."

Adrian's lips twitch a little.

"Hey, that's not true. I was taking it slowly, so he'd learn."

"Too slow, apparently." Adrian studies the wrong pieces jammed together. "Are you sure you're not the one who's learning?"

I flex my fingers. "Yes, I'm sure."

"You're an awful liar, Lenochka."

"I'm not lying."

"That's what all liars say."

I stare at him over Jeremy's head, and he stares right back, an easy, almost outgoing expression on his face. "How can you tell when someone is lying so easily?"

"So you admit you were lying?"

"No." I make a face and mouth, "Jeremy," so he doesn't label me as a liar in front of him.

Adrian's lips pull in a small smile. Holy hell. I'm glad he doesn't smile too often because I'd go into cardiac arrest or something. He seems to be in an awfully good mood right now and I wonder what triggered it. Was it inflicting my punishment in his office or simply being here with me and Jeremy? Knowing his controlling, dominant character, it's probably the first reason.

He takes a few pieces from Jeremy's game and assembles them without breaking eye contact with me. "Unless you're trained to lie, people have tells. The rub of a nose or a nape, fidgeting, or looking in a different direction to conjure a lie. The reason for that is because lying doesn't com naturally and takes a lot of energy, so most of the oxygen in the blood rushes to the brain, leaving the rest of the limbs either numb or cold. That's why you've been flexing your fingers."

I clench my fingers into the material of my coat and Adrian stares at me with utter amusement, no doubt finding fun in cornering me.

Jeremy gives me a disapproving glance. "Lying is bad, Mommy."

"I wasn't lying, Jer." I soften my tone even as I glare at Adrian.

"Okay," he agrees readily like the little angel he is. "Teach Mommy how to do my war zone, Papa."

"Hmm." Adrian's head tilts to the side in my direction. "I think I will."

I purse my lips at him, but he merely reaches to wrap the scarf around my neck before he gets to work. He literally finishes building the entire war zone in under fifteen minutes.

I try not to be impressed, but I am.

"Yay, Papa!" Jeremy kisses his father on the cheek, joy sparkling in his wide eyes.

Adrian faces me. "I think your mom should show appreciation, too, shouldn't she, Malysh?"

"Yes, Mommy! Kiss Papa."

I glare at Adrian for the way he's manipulating a kid, but I don't make a problem out of it as I lean in and press my lips to the stubble on his cheek.

For a fraction of a second, it feels normal, like we're actually a family who are out in the garden, doing family things.

I'm about to pull away when my gaze shifts upward. I don't know why I look in the direction of the guest house at a moment like this. I don't know why my eyes immediately go up.

All I know is that I shouldn't have. I really, *really* shouldn't have.

A figure stares at me from the window. Her face is as pale as her nightgown, but her eyes are a raging blue as she stares at me.

My eyes.

The ghost Jeremy mentioned is staring at me and she looks ready to kill me.

TWENTY-ONE

Winter

"LIFT YOUR ARMS."

I follow Adrian's command so he can slide the silky nightgown over my body. It feels soft, soothing, but it's still too much against my sensitive skin.

We've just finished another session of punishment. This time it was three successive orgasms for talking back to him three times today.

The number has been shortening over the past week. Maybe one day, it'll be zero and I'll be able to get my reward, but that doesn't seem like it will happen anytime soon.

It's been two weeks since I came into Adrian's house, and he always, without fail, finds something to punish me for. I guess I'm not being careful enough either, but he's not tolerant at all.

If I say 'okay', it's one.

If I ask why, it's two.

If I don't look at him while he's fucking me with his fingers or with his mouth, it's three.

If he calls me Lia and I don't answer immediately, it's four.

There's no winning with him, because he laid out all the circumstances, so they'd work in his favor.

Every evening, after Jeremy goes to sleep, I come to this bedroom with my heart in my throat in anticipation of what he'll do next. Sometimes, he doesn't wait until then and calls me to his office so he can extract his punishment. Then he'll restart the count to make sure his hands are busy during the night.

Hands that are currently buttoning the top of my nightgown. Big veiny hands with long, lean fingers that I couldn't stop staring at even if I wanted to.

Hands that can bring pleasure or pain—or both—depending on their owner's mood.

My eyes are droopy and I'm exhausted from the number of orgasms he gave me in one go, but I remain seated in front of the dresser while Adrian is kneeling before me.

He's fucking kneeling, and yet the movement doesn't deter anything from his power. From the hold he has on me—physically, at least.

Only physically.

He's just finished showering me. Since that day in his office, he's been open about caring for me. He lathered my whole body with soap and even washed my hair. At one point, my legs couldn't carry me and I sat on the floor of the shower. Adrian knelt behind me and finished with my hair. His hands were all over me—on my shoulders, my back, between my legs, and running over the birth scar.

It was too much. It still is. I don't want him to care for me that way. I don't like being cared for. It makes me feel weak—weaker than the situation I've been thrown in. And I sure as hell don't want Adrian to do it. Because he's not genuine. Or maybe he is, but not toward me.

It's toward his wife.

He's now in black sweatpants and no shirt. I study the hard ridges of his abdomen and the fine hairs on his masculine chest. I wonder why he doesn't have tattoos there.

His arms and hands are fully inked, but even as I watch them, I can't tell the meaning behind most of his tattoos. There's a compass on his forearm, but I don't think it indicates direction. There are birds escaping at the top of his shoulders. A bloody flower is inked in the middle of an intricate map that doesn't seem like one of the world. Maybe it's a map of Russia. I wonder what he was thinking when he got them.

But why would I wonder? I'm nothing to this man. Only a replacement.

I try engraving those words to memory so I don't get caught up in his gentle touch, in the way his fingers brush against the swell of my breasts every now and then.

He doesn't see you, Winter. He sees Lia.

My mind drifts back to the figure I saw at the windows that day when I was kissing his cheek.

The pale woman with raging eyes, who looked just like me.

When I blinked, she disappeared.

Either I was imagining things or Lia's ghost was actually there. I chose to go with the first option because the second one terrified me.

Whenever Jeremy and I play in the gazebo, I keep staring at that same window in case she reappears.

She never has.

I would probably have a better chance figuring out if my hallucinations are true or not if I go there, but Adrian's guards are keeping an eye on the garden—or us—all day long. Not to mention that the man himself is always watching us like a hawk from his office window.

Yan is constantly there, too.

The only time I would be able to go into the guest house

unnoticed is during the night. And that scares the shit out of me.

This house scares the shit out of me.

The man in front of me terrifies me more because he's the reason I feel like I'm crawling into some fucked-up territory.

Adrian stands up once he's finished and positions himself behind me, grabbing the blow-dryer. The slow humming of the machine fills the room as he removes the towel from around my head and dries my hair.

I shiver for a reason completely different from my wet hair meeting my neck. I keep my eyes downcast because I don't want to look in the mirror to see him caring for me and blow-drying my hair. I don't want to get caught up in these moments that aren't meant for me.

Lia was one lucky woman. Or maybe it was the opposite, considering the savage ways he touches me—*her*.

I wonder how it felt to have a man as hard as Adrian care for her like this, as if she was his world. Was she tingling like me, or did she consider it suffocating as I should?

I wonder if he also made her wait before he fucked her. I internally shake my head. Why the hell am I thinking about him fucking her? Or me?

It's just that it doesn't make sense for him to keep coming all over my stomach, my breasts or even my ass. His hard-ons seem painful, but he still refuses to fuck me.

I refuse to let him hear me moan or scream, so I guess it won't happen in the near future.

Is that what he did with Lia, too?

"How was your marriage with Lia?" I ask before I can stop myself.

My voice is quiet compared to the blow-dryer, so I pray to all the stars above that he didn't hear me.

But then he says, "It was a marriage."

My mortification at being heard disappears at his answer.

He has this infuriating way of avoiding questions. He doesn't exactly refuse to respond, but he gives something vague or re-phrases the original question.

"How did you guys meet?"

"Why do you want to know?"

Why do I want to know, really? Why am I interested to know about him and his wife?

Clinking my nails together, I keep staring at them. "I thought I should know in case anyone asks."

"The official version is that we met at a party."

My head slowly lifts and I stare at him through the mirror. "There's an unofficial version?"

He's preoccupied with my hair as he speaks, "Correct."

"What is it?"

"It's a secret between Lia and me."

"I thought I was Lia."

"I thought you didn't like being called Lia." He threads his fingers through my fast-drying hair.

"You still make me play her role."

"You still don't think you're her and that doesn't make you privy to my secrets with her."

I open my mouth to say something but choose not to, be-cause whatever I spout will backfire in my face.

The sick asshole is trying to completely erase me so I'll be-come his wife. If I let my guard down, there will be nothing left of me.

"You'll accompany me to a birthday party in a few days," he announces out of the blue, shutting off the blow-dryer and brushing my hair.

"Whose birthday party?"

"Igor's."

I squint. "Igor Petrov?"

He nods. "What do you know about him?"

I pause, feeling attacked by a quiz all of a sudden. I try

to recall the details I read about him. "He's higher up in the brotherhood. Not as high up as you, but he has a notable position."

"And?"

"And, what?"

"His family. How many members are there?"

"I...don't remember."

He glares at me through the mirror.

"What? There are too many people in your organization and I'm super bad with names. I'm sure I'll be fine when I meet them."

He wraps his hand around my hair and tugs back, tilting my head to peer down into my eyes. "You'll learn all about them before the birthday. You are not allowed, under any circumstances, to make any mistakes. Is that clear?"

"Ok—I mean, fine. Fine!" *Jeez.* He has a weird way of flipping from gentle to harsh in a fraction of a second. It's like he has a split personality or something.

"Ogla will ask you questions until she makes sure you've learned everything."

"Lovely," I mutter under my breath.

"What was that, Lenochka?"

"Nothing."

His grip tightens on my hair, but he lets it and the subject go.

"Let's sleep." He extends his palm, and I want to refuse it. I want to pretend it doesn't exist, but that will only result in more punishment and I really want to sleep.

As per every night, I try to scoot to the edge of the bed, facing away from him. Adrian doesn't stop me, as usual, but he spoons me from behind, his knee pushing between my thighs and his chin resting on my shoulder. He smells like woods and shower gel. Clean and strong like everything about him.

His hand slips under my arm and wraps around my

stomach. Sometimes, he grabs my breast and absentmindedly teases a nipple until it's sensitive and aching.

I stare at the soft light on the nightstand, attempting to erase his existence from my surroundings, to pretend that his skin isn't covering mine.

That I'm not a hostage in my own body.

If I at least had a drink, I wouldn't be feeling so victimized right now. I would've numbed it—everything about it.

Fourteen days without alcohol—aside from that slight taste that preceded Adrian's first and only kiss.

I don't think I was that much of an alcoholic if I've managed to go two weeks without a drop of it. Maybe I merely convinced myself I was one.

My cravings are somehow gone, but my yearning for that state of mind alcohol provided me is definitely real and ever-present.

Adrian traces an invisible line over the cloth on my stomach and it's hypnotizing—like his touch. I fall asleep almost immediately.

I shouldn't feel safe enough to fall asleep in the embrace of a monster like Adrian, but it just happens.

A small sound makes me open my eyes. I'm still sleeping on my side, Adrian wrapped all around me.

I blink the sleep away as the sound comes again. It's almost like the footsteps of a child, but they're heavier than Jeremy's.

Something jams against the doorknob. It turns but rolls back into place because of the lock.

Who the hell would attempt to come into the master bedroom at night? Adrian's guards don't step inside, except for Kolya and Yan sometimes, but never at night. Ogla never bothers us during this time either.

All sounds disappear and I think I'm imagining things, but the doorknob is jammed again, rattling harder this time.

I gasp, sitting up in bed and pulling the sheet to my chest.

Adrian's arms drop from around me and I shake his shoulder, tentative at first, but it becomes more urgent with every passing second. "Adrian…wake up…"

The doorknob is still twisting and turning with supersonic speed.

"Adrian!" I hiss, but he's not moving.

The door bursts open, and I suck in a sharp breath at the view.

The ghost I saw from the window is standing in the doorway. Her plain white gown falls to below her knees. Her hair is tied back and her face is pale, but other than that, she's a replica of me. Even her dark-circled eyes and hollow cheeks look like mine from when I was living on the streets.

"L-Lia…?" I whisper.

"So you know who I am, yet you still dare to steal my husband as if it were your God-given right."

I shake my head frantically. "No…I didn't…"

"Home-wrecking cunt."

I shake my head again. "I didn't want to…Adrian…" I extend a hand to wake him up, but I'm stopped by her harsh voice.

"Don't touch him! Leave!"

"I can't…" I'm crying now, my voice hoarse with how much I'm trying to form into words that I never wanted this. I never thought about taking her place or her name or her husband.

She lunges toward me and I cross my hands in front of my face to protect it. But she doesn't reach me. Instead, a gurgling sound emerges in the silence.

I peek from between my fingers and gasp as a patch of blood explodes on Lia's nightgown, something sharp protruding from her abdomen—a knife.

A large body stands behind her, the one who stabbed her, and I think it's one of the guards, but his face is shadowed.

Lia's neck lolls in an unnatural position, but her eyes

remain on me, watching me, following me, creeping me out of my damn skin.

It's like she wants to drag me with her to whatever place she's going.

I slam a palm over my mouth to muffle a gasp, but a harsh metal thing hits my lips.

Confused, I stare down at my hand and find my fingers wrapped around a gun.

What the...?

"Pull the trigger," the shadow behind Lia whispers. His voice is monotone, almost robotic. "You have one mission."

"Pull the trigger on who?" No clue why that question escapes me, because it doesn't matter. I won't do it.

"I killed this bitch for you. Pull. The. Trigger."

I shake my head violently, but then sinister laughter escapes the shadow. It's long and grates on my nerves like fingernails scratching on the walls of my brain.

"Stop it," I hiss.

"You already took a life. What's one more?"

"No..."

"But can't you see? It's already done."

"What?"

"Your gun."

I stare at my hand and watch with horror as my gun aims and my finger presses the trigger.

Straight into Adrian's chest.

He doesn't even stir as a blotch of blood covers his shoulder and chest, then forms a pool around him, soaking the sheets.

"Nooo!" I shriek and my world goes black.

TWENTY-TWO

Adrian

THUD.

Thud.

Thud.

A gurgling sound echoes in the air as if someone is choking on their own blood.

Or vomit.

My eyes snap open. I'm immediately alert, my heart beating loudly as the scene materializes in front of me.

Lia is thrashing in her sleep, her feet kicking in the air, and her body is heavy like a rock being thrown to the bottom of an ocean.

Both of her hands are fisted so tightly that there's a cut on her palm from her nails and droplets of blood color the white sheets in red.

But that's not what woke me up. It was the sound.

The gurgling.

The choking on her own saliva.

Two lines of drool cascade down her chin and neck, a foam rapidly forming at her mouth.

"Lia!"

She doesn't show any sign of hearing me and continues thrashing, squirming. *Gurgling.*

I shove two fingers into her mouth and open it wide in an attempt to help her breathe.

She doesn't.

It's like she's blocking her own trachea with an imaginary gag.

"Lia! Wake up!" I place a hand under her head, carefully lifting her up. She drags the sheets in her fisted hand, her body still snapped rigid like a board.

Her head moves sideways, then rolls so far back, the position would've snapped her neck if she were on her own. I support her nape and keep probing her mouth open with my other hand.

Her lips are turning blue and her face is reddening. She's not breathing, and hasn't in at least a fucking minute.

"Lia!" I shake her, but that brings me no result.

She's lost somewhere I can't reach. Somewhere that she can keep herself hidden away from me under lock and key.

Nothing will bring her out.

Except maybe…

"Winter," I call cautiously, to which she sucks in a deep breath, gasping and coughing as the air hits her lungs. I release her mouth so she can breathe properly.

As I watch her inhaling oxygen into her lungs, allowing life back in, I should be relieved. I am. But barbed wires wind around my chest, pricking my skin, inch by each agonizing inch.

Her eyes slowly open, but their blue is blank, as if she doesn't know who or where she is.

I hold my breath as the seconds tick by and she remains like that, caught in a trance.

"Lenochka?"

She blinks once, twice, before her gaze meets mine.

Moisture gathers in her eyes and a tear slides down her cheek. I wipe it with the pad of my thumb as she shakes uncontrollably in my arms.

Seeming to be out of her trance, she bolts upright, kneeling in front of me on the bed. Her expression is frantic now as she clutches my bicep, moves her hand up, then checks my side, my chest, and even my back.

She's touching me everywhere, feeling, inspecting, completely oblivious to how hard I've become in the short span of her ministrations.

I've had blue balls since she first walked into this bedroom, but I can't fuck her just yet. Not when she's having all these nightmares and building her walls.

"You're not shot," she breathes out in a whisper.

"Do I look like I am?" I try to keep my voice calm, even though my jaw is clenching, and not only because of being hard, but because she responded to Winter and not Lia.

"No. But it felt so real, so visceral…" She palms my cheek and freezes when she feels my jaw tightening under her hold, then swiftly drops her hand to her side.

"Another nightmare?"

She nods once.

It's not the first time I've had to wake her up because of a nightmare. It's happened twice in the past week, but she didn't really open her eyes and talk. She just fell back to sleep, so I doubt she remembers them.

I do, though.

The gurgling, choking sounds she makes is like my custom-made hell. Sometimes, I hear it even when I'm awake and I have to check on the cameras in case it's happening in real time.

"Lia was there," she says quietly. "She wanted to kill me and then…then…"

I touch her arm gently. "You don't have to talk about it."

She stares up at me with those huge eyes. They're lost like she doesn't know who she's looking at and she's somehow still trapped inside the nightmare.

"Why did you bring me here, Adrian?" she murmurs, her voice pained.

"You know."

"Because I look like Lia?"

I nod.

"I'm not her. And the more you compare me to her, the more I feel myself being erased, forgotten. I don't want to be forgotten."

I grab her by the arm and try to put her under the sheet. "Sleep for now."

"No." She yanks her arm free. "I don't want to sleep."

"Then what do you want?"

"Winter. For once, just call me Winter. *Please*."

I did and I hated it. I hated it so much that I want to pour bleach down my fucking throat.

"No."

"Please…" Tears cascade down her cheeks. "Please don't erase me. Please, Adrian."

"Don't beg me for something like that. You're Lia. Get used to it."

A sob tears from her throat, and her lips purse, one of them battered and cut from how much she bites down on it.

That has to heal before she's ever seen in public. She needs to snap out of it, but I know it won't be easy to have her comply. That is, if it's possible at all.

This time, she doesn't resist as I tuck her under the covers. She willingly closes her eyes and whispers, "I wish I'd never met you."

My lips brush against her forehead. "I'll meet you over and over again if I have to."

TWENTY-THREE

Winter

THREE DAYS LATER, WE GO TO THE PARTY.

Though, judging by the number of armed guards present, I wouldn't exactly call it a party.

It's the first time I've been out of Adrian's house since I got there, and while I thought it would be liberating, it's somehow more suffocating.

Part of it is because of the number of guards who are accompanying us in a separate car. Five, aside from Kolya and Yan.

Part is because Jeremy cried when I told him I wouldn't be reading him a bedtime story tonight. His tears drew a black hole in my chest that still hasn't mended.

Tonight is just wrong on so many levels. Will I make a mistake? Will all of Adrian's and Ogla's warnings come true? I want to crawl back into Jeremy's room, kiss his soft cheeks, and pretend like the whole world only exists because of him.

But here I am, in the middle of a party, celebrating the birthday of a man I've never met before.

The *Pakhan*, Sergei, decided to host Igor's birthday at his mansion, which is apparently a great honor. The brotherhood's compound is massive, even larger than Adrian's house, and has a garden that goes on for miles. It's surrounded by high walls and cameras that blink in every corner.

It feels scarier than the place I left behind, emptier, *bigger*. Which is weird since I think Adrian's house is terrifying. Whenever I walk the halls, I feel like its walls will open their mouths wide and scream in my face—or drag me into nothingness. Its soul is as black as its owner's.

Sergei Sokolov's house is scary because of the unfamiliarity of it, the nerves that keep wracking me, the sheer pressure of somehow making a mistake. What if someone figures out I'm not Lia? What if I put Adrian in danger and cause Jeremy to lose his father?

"Relax." Adrian wraps his hand around my gloved one that's gripping his jacket. "You're fine."

His words immediately still my jittery insides. I don't know what it is about his voice that's soothing. It shouldn't be, considering how deep it is, but during unfathomable moments, it feels like his voice is the only anchor I need.

"All you have to do is remain quiet. Everyone is used to that from you." His hand drops from mine, and I want to grab it and put it back again. Even through the glove, his touch offered the right amount of comfort I needed.

But Adrian has been making it his mission to deprive me of what I need these past couple of days. Ever since the night I dreamt about Lia being killed by an unknown shadow and me shooting him, he's withdrawn from me.

He still tends to me—puts ointment on my cut lip, blow-dries my hair, wraps a scarf around my neck when he thinks it's cold. But he doesn't touch me sexually.

No punishment.

No orgasms.

Nothing.

I've even talked back to him during breakfast so much that Ogla's eyebrows met her hairline and she eventually told me to shut up.

I haven't. I've kept doing all the things I know Adrian hates. I've told him 'okay' more than I thought I could, but he's ignored me. I wear tank tops in front of Yan, and he just dismisses his guard from the house.

He still spoons me from behind every night, but his touch feels mechanical and distant. He's been so distant that I think I might never be able to reach him. That should delight me. After all, I want him to leave me alone. But do I?

The answer is no.

Ever since he's withdrawn, I've been baffled by how much I've gotten used to him, to his punishments. To his…closeness.

He's just plucked it away as if it never existed and I want to demand he tell me why. I want to put my foot down and make it stop.

It's crueler than if he'd never again laid his hands on me.

The touch from just now is the first time he's felt close to me in three days, and I want to fight tooth and nail to hold on to it.

I discreetly peek at him, drinking in as much of his appearance as possible. He's wearing a black tailored tuxedo. It makes him look taller—which shouldn't be possible with his height—sharper, and more like a businessman. His hair is styled back and his thick stubble adds to his majesty. The outfit hides his tattoos, giving him a gentleman's image, like someone you'd see on the cover of Forbes.

I picked a dress to match him. No idea why I did it, but I thought we'd look good together if I wore a black gown. It's one of those that are tight at the breasts and waist but falls loose to the ground, its train following after me with every move. I gathered my hair in a classy bun and wore dangling earrings. They match the small purse in my hand, containing my phone. I completed the look with elegant white gloves from Lia's closet and the highest pair of heels I could find. They hurt, but I didn't want my height to give me an inferiority complex.

The gathering is in full swing. Men and women are dressed for the occasion and chatting animatedly among each other. Classical music plays in the background, and somehow, the sound gives me a bit of serenity, a promise that everything will be okay.

Adrian leads me to where three old men are seated in a lounge area. They seem like they're in a league of their own even before we approach them. Tall, bulky men like Kolya stand behind their chairs like statues, and I know they won't hesitate to make use of the weapons peeking from under their jackets.

It's no surprise that they're separated from the rest of the crowd. The one in the middle is the *Pakhan* himself, Sergei. On his right is the man of the hour, Igor Petrov. The one on the left is Mikhail Kozlov. The three of them are around twice my age and they're the pillars of the Russian Mafia in New York, aside from Adrian's father and Sergei's brother, who are now dead.

To occupy my mind the past few days, I spent all my time on the damn document about the brotherhood and the spider web of other organized crime rings related to it.

Even Ogla was impressed with how much I learned, and that's saying something.

"Adrian." Sergei motions at him, speaking with a pronounced Russian accent. "Come. Come."

Adrian takes his hand, kisses it, and places it to his forehead. I do the same because that's what's expected when you're in the presence of the leader of a scary organization.

"Lia." Sergei's eyes roam over me as if he's checking for

something to be missing. "You look good for someone who was unwell."

"Thank you," I speak with a smile. "I couldn't miss Igor's birthday."

"Much appreciated," Igor says with a similar Russian accent, his tone unwelcoming.

"Happy birthday. I brought you something, though it's not much."

He raises a brow. "I already received Adrian's present."

Adrian's eyes meet mine for a brief second. Right. I didn't tell him about my gift for Igor. Was I being out of line? What if I insult him? But if I backtrack now, it'll seem even more suspicious.

"It's a separate one."

"A separate one?" It's Mikhail who asks, drawing out the words, and I immediately dislike him. "Since when does your wife bring a separate gift, Adrian?"

My fake husband remains silent, so I speak calmly, almost like I'm not deterred by what just happened. "I figured that since Igor would have a lot of sugary cake today, I should add one more special birthday cake."

"At his age, that's too much," Sergei says.

"He's right." Igor complies with distaste. "My wife wouldn't approve of that much sugar."

"That's what makes mine special. It has a type of sugar that won't hurt your health. Try it." I smile. "And if you don't like it, I'll make it up to you."

Igor nods, but the wrinkles don't ease around his eyes. He seems like he wants to strangle me, as if I offended him in a previous life.

"My, Adrian. I didn't know Lia could cook. She's always too unwell; I thought she'd be a corpse by now." Mikhail takes a sip of a transparent drink, watching me suspiciously.

Shit.

I don't know why I feel like one of them will pull a mask from over my head and expose me for being a fake.

"She's been doing better," Adrian says in his usual calm tone.

"Obviously. Happy to have you with us." Sergei's watching me in an unnerving way. I'm glad I'm wearing gloves, because my hands are so sweaty, they would shine under the light.

"The pleasure is all mine, *Pakhan*." I don't know how the hell I manage to speak in a semi-normal tone.

Sergei motions at an empty chair beside Igor. "Sit, Adrian."

I don't miss that he only mentions Adrian's name. My fake husband hesitates for a beat before he releases me and heads to the seat the boss designated for him. I know what this means, I need to go. But I don't want to. Where will I go in the middle of all these people I don't know?

However, I force my head to move in a small nod as I turn and leave. I want to think Adrian is watching my back, that Kolya and Yan are somewhere here and will come to my aid, but my legs are shaking as I head to the nearest balcony. I need fresh air and to go home to Jeremy. I'll even be happy with Adrian's distant spooning tonight.

"Lia!"

My feet come to a halt at the feminine voice calling my name. I want to pretend I didn't hear her, but she calls again and I'm forced to turn around.

A beautiful blonde with flawless makeup waves me over to join her circle. Rai Sokolov.

Sergei's grandniece and the only woman who can rival men in the brotherhood. She's standing with Damien Orlov and Kirill Morozov. Both of them are leaders. Another man, Aleksander, Kirill's closest guard, who's basically in Kolya's rank, stands with them, but a step back.

I walk to their circle with hesitant steps until I'm a few feet away. That's when I notice Rai's baby bump under her royal blue dress.

She kisses my cheeks and I return the gesture. "How have you been, Lia? It's been a long time since I last saw you."

"I'm fine, thank you."

"She's like a moon, this one." Damien tilts his head to the side, watching me closely. "Tell me the truth. Is Adrian fattening you to offer you as a sacrifice to his demonic ancestors?"

I part my lips to speak, then close them, not knowing if it's a joke or how to reply. Damien is good-looking, tall, broad, and with a furious gaze, but he's marked in the document as reckless and unpredictable.

"Shut up, Damien," Rai scolds him.

"I'm really curious." He leans over, watching me as if I'm some mannequin in a store. "Why is he hiding you like you're some fucked-up version of Sleeping Beauty? Does he do satanic rituals I need to know about?"

"Maybe she's the one who does the rituals?" Kirill says slowly, readjusting his black-framed glasses. Unlike the old men, these two barely have an accent.

Kirill looks like an accountant, all suited up and with the glasses, but the document mentioned a few things about his suspicious background and that he would stop at nothing for his agenda.

"What is that supposed to mean?" I ask with my chin held high.

"I don't know, Mrs. Volkov. Why don't you tell me?"

"Why don't you fuck off?" Rai says point-blank. "I just want Sasha around, not you."

"*Aleksander*," Kirill stresses, "is my guard, Rai. We come as a set. Get used to it."

"I'm sure the only reason he's with you is because you're holding something over his head." Rai pats Aleksander's hand. "Don't worry, Sasha. I will save you from this demon."

Sasha—*Aleksander*—a guard who's even prettier than Yan, lowers his head, awkwardly clearing his throat.

"How about me, Rai?" Damien takes her free hand in his and kisses the back of it. "When are you going to save me? All you have to do is divorce Kyle and then we can ride into the sunset—or the battlefield. Same result."

She swiftly pulls her hand from his. "Only Kyle gets to touch me. Do it again and I will kick you in the balls."

I expect Damien to get offended, but he grins. "Kinky. I love it."

"Speaking of kinky." Kirill faces me again. He hasn't stopped watching me since I joined them. "Has Adrian picked up anything new lately?"

"He'll fucking kill you if he hears you talking to his wife about kink." Damien squeezes Kirill's shoulder. "Rest in pieces, motherfucker."

Rai opens her mouth, probably to come to my defense. Is she used to doing that? Was Lia a doormat who let anyone walk all over her?

But I'm not Lia. I'm Winter.

Lifting my chin, I face Kirill. "That question is distasteful, Kirill. You don't see me asking you about your private affairs, because it's simply none of my business. I believe what my husband and I do in the privacy of our home doesn't concern you either."

My reply has the exact opposite effect of what I intend. Kirill smirks as if he's in the know about something.

"Who are you and what have you done to the mute Lia?" Damien watches me closely. "You've never spoken up when we've poked you."

"It was out of respect, but if you show me none, why should I?"

"That's my girl." Rai interlinks her arm with mine. "Come on, let's leave these assholes—aside from Sasha."

I gladly follow her, but I feel Kirill's gaze on me, even after we disappear to a quiet balcony. I release a breath into the breeze and Rai smiles.

"You did very well. I'm so proud of you, Lia."

"Thank you." I try not to feel inferior now that it's just the two of us. It's not only about her bombshell looks or her height—*tall people suck*—but also her character. I know Adrian considers her a worthy member of the brotherhood, or he wouldn't have included her in the first pages of that document.

Maybe someone like her, strong, fearless, is who Adrian needs by his side.

Rai leans in, watching her surroundings before she whispers, "You didn't follow up on what happened. I was worried."

"W-what?" I stare at her with parted lips.

"You asked me to help you escape, and then I learn you returned to Adrian's side as if nothing had happened. Do you know how confused I was?"

Wait. What?

Lia asked Rai to help her escape Adrian? When the hell was that?

But I can't ask those questions, because that will give me away as a fraud.

I clear my throat. "I couldn't escape him."

"But you were so hell-bent on it."

"Jeremy," I blurt. "I can't leave Jeremy."

"I understand, but you could've at least called or left me a hint." Her voice lowers some more. "Adrian has been after my neck. He suspects I have something to do with your attempted escape. I told you I don't want him as an enemy, Lia. That I was helping you because you were on the verge of a breakdown."

Lia was on the verge of a breakdown when she wanted to leave Adrian. Rai helped her, but she…what? Did she die?

"I'm sorry," I whisper.

"Just tell me if Adrian saw Ruslan that day."

Ruslan is her senior guard. He's the one who's standing at the entrance of the balcony to ward off anyone, I assume. It's the first time I've seen his face, aside from his picture in the document.

He must have helped Lia escape on Rai's behalf, but I have no damn clue if Adrian saw him.

"I don't remember clearly," I say vaguely.

Rai grabs me by the shoulder. "Think, Lia. When Adrian was chasing after you that night, you escaped Ruslan. But did Adrian see him?"

"No, I don't think so." I'm speaking out of logic alone here, because if Ruslan helped Lia escape and Adrian had seen him, he would be dead by now.

Adrian may be calm, but he's lethal. He wouldn't forgive anyone who tries to take his damn precious Lia. Even Rai will be in jeopardy if he finds out about her involvement.

"That's good." She releases a breath.

"I'm sorry I got you involved in this," I shouldn't be apologizing on behalf of Lia, but she was a selfish woman. Not only did she leave her son behind, but she also got other people involved, knowing full well that Adrian would eradicate them.

I wonder why she tried to escape him. It couldn't be because she was feeling invisible like me.

For some reason, the knowledge that their marriage wasn't as solid as I thought relaxes me a little.

I'm such a horrible person.

But even that small relaxation doesn't last. It doesn't matter that she tried to escape. Adrian still cares about her. He still dotes on me because he thinks I'm her.

"Let's go back inside." Rai smiles at me. "Sergei will call us for dinner any minute now."

"All right."

I'm about to leave when I feel eyes watching me. I pause at the balcony and peer down. There are a few guards stationed outside. One of them is Adrian's driver, who's smoking a cigarette and talking animatedly with another guard, probably in Russian. They all speak in Russian at the house. Even Adrian addresses them in Russian, unless I'm around. That's when he switches to English. Jeremy knows a few expressions, too, but I think he still has trouble with mixing both languages together.

I'm about to chalk the sensation I just felt up to paranoia, but my skin prickles again. The feeling is so strong, I visibly shudder.

I search the men standing downstairs for a few more seconds, then my eyes roam over the vehicles parked in the distance. That's when I see it. A shadow stalking silently between the cars. Only his back is visible as he disappears in the midst of the parking area.

Just like the shadow from my recent nightmare.

My legs shake and my breathing deepens until I'm aware of every inhale and exhale.

It's paranoia. Only paranoia.

The nightmare was just that. A nightmare. There's no way a shadow from my subconscious would jump into real life. That must've been one of the guards doing his rounds.

My phone vibrates in my small purse and I jump, my nerves getting the better of me.

Only Adrian ever texts me on this phone. Unless it's Ogla? I told her to call me if something happens to Jeremy.

I retrieve the phone so fast, I nearly drop it.

It's not Ogla.

A text from an unknown number lights the screen. I click on it, the sense of dread from a few seconds ago gripping me by the throat.

My purse hits the ground as I read the text.

Unknown Number: You have one mission. Pull the fucking trigger.

TWENTY-FOUR

Adrian

Lia hasn't been herself since we sat down for dinner.

Her body is rigid, and every now and then, a shudder grips her and she drops her fork. Then she picks it up again to drag it through her food. Her hands are moving, but she rarely brings anything to her mouth. Since she came from the streets, meals have been sacred for her.

Not this one.

I knew bringing her here wouldn't go completely without problems. When I saw her talking with Damien and Kirill earlier, I fantasized about the million ways I wanted to cut both those fuckers' throats, but I settled with tapping my fingers against my thigh to not show disrespect to Sergei. Or worse, give him an incentive to attack.

He's been focused on me more than usual tonight, and the last thing I want is to confirm whatever is going on through his head.

Vladimir, who's now sitting across from me, hasn't

addressed me the entire night. He's huge, bulky, and has a beard that gives him a scary appearance to the outside world. The only time he speaks more than needed is when Rai is in sight. He pledged to protect her and the Sokolov last name from a young age. That's basically his driving force, which means he doesn't concern himself about other matters.

While I haven't figured out his angle about me, I know his loyalty runs deep for Sergei because of his last name. If the *Pakhan* gives an order to eliminate me, Vladimir will be the first to make it happen.

At the dining table, there's an easy chatter in which he doesn't participate and just nods when Rai whispers something to him. Kyle quickly steals her attention because he doesn't like her talking to anyone but him.

A small sigh leaves Lia, and even though I make it my mission not to look at her in public, I'm tempted to sneak a peek. It'd be a break in my pattern, something that Vladimir, Rai, and especially that fucker Kirill would notice.

My high alertness about this night is turning me into a paranoid dick, like Mikhail.

In the six years I've been married to Lia, I've treated her like a stranger in public. Everyone in the brotherhood thinks she means nothing to me, and that the only reason I have a sickly doll-faced woman by my side is because of an unplanned pregnancy.

Sergei didn't shy away from suggesting that I should leave her—even to her face. That's why I made use of every chance I had to not bring her here. Sergei and the other elders, Igor and Mikhail, never approved of her unknown origins or her 'nobody' status. They preferred I marry Igor's daughter and procreate to produce a 'pure' Russian bloodline.

Their aggression toward her is tangible, that's why I didn't want to give them more tangible reasons to act against her. She's not to draw their attention to herself. *At all.*

Lia releases a second sigh and I lean in, pretending to grab a piece of bread as I whisper, "What is wrong with you?"

She flinches, her hand fisting around her fork as she meets my gaze with her wide one. "Why are you asking?"

"You haven't been paying attention or eating."

"It's n-nothing."

"Lia," I warn under my breath.

"It's Jeremy," she blurts. "I'm worried about him."

I don't believe her, not because she's not concerned about Jeremy, but her tone suggests it's only an excuse.

She secretly touches the side of my jacket, her nails digging softly, almost hesitantly, into the material. "Can we go home?"

I don't miss the way she calls my place 'home' or how her voice shakes around the word.

She probably considers it one because of Jeremy, but I still take a moment to let that word sink in as I stare at her. At her desperation and the way she's breathing heavily. There's definitely something wrong with her, and I'll figure it out, but that's for later.

Shaking my head once, I say, "I have a business meeting to attend."

She drops her hand from my side and focuses back on her food, shoving a forkful in her mouth. I force myself to look away from her because she's had my attention more than I like to show.

I catch Kirill's smirk from my peripheral vision. He's sitting on my left, licking his fork and wearing a cunning smile. *The motherfucker.*

For the rest of the dinner, I don't glance in her direction again, even when I catch her stealing glimpses at me, begging me with her eyes to take her and leave.

There's nothing I want to do more than that, but Sergei has called for a meeting after dinner. Not only for the elite members of the brotherhood, but he also asked the heads of the other crime organizations to join us. As a show of respect to Igor's rank, he invited Lazlo, the Don of the Luciano family, and his underboss. There's also Kai, the second-in-command of the Yakuza branch in New York, and his leader, Abe, an old man who has the temper of a silent mountain. Yet he's been actively bugging Damien during the entire dinner, something for which our own black bull is about to shred the table to pieces. He has absolutely no patience whatsoever when it comes to using diplomatic methods.

A few other members from the Triads are also seated at Sergei's table. I need to be at that meeting tonight. Which means I have to leave Lia again. Under the circumstances, that's the last thing I want, but at least Kirill and Damien will be there with me and I won't have to worry about them.

Yan has been given clear orders to keep an eye on her from afar.

As soon as dinner ends, everyone stands. When Lia gets up and starts to follow me, I say, "Stay here," without turning toward her.

If I see her, if I get caught in her soft features and those sad blue eyes, I'll be tempted to touch her. It doesn't help that I haven't gotten my fill of her over the past few days so she won't cut her lip anymore.

"Adrian…" she murmurs.

"What?" I say harshly, still not looking at her, because now both Sergei and Kirill are standing there watching me instead of heading to the meeting.

"I want to tell you something."

"Not now."

"But…"

"Not now, Lia." My tone is low and firm, offering no room for negotiation.

I don't see her, but I can feel her going rigid behind me.

When I make a move to leave, Kirill and Sergei finally turn around and go upstairs to his office, where the meeting will be held.

I follow after but stop at the base of the stairs to glance at Lia and make sure she's in Yan's full view. Rai is linking her arms with her, leading her to a buffet section. I don't want that woman anywhere near Lia, but at the same time, I can't interfere and make myself noticeable.

Yan is standing about ten feet behind and nods at me when I meet his gaze. While he's been a pain in the ass lately, I can at least trust he'll keep her safe.

Kolya stops next to me and whispers in my ear in Russian, "Lazlo is coming, sir."

"Go before me."

My guard does as he's told and I synchronize my steps so that Lazlo and I are the last ascending the stairs. His guard and underboss are one step ahead of us after having gotten the message from Kolya. We strategically planned this so that our talk can take place on the stairs with no one suspecting us.

Lazlo Luciano is around the same age as Sergei, but not as sickly. His hair is completely white and he has a scar over his cheek from when someone wanted to carve his face with a knife.

No one knows the fate of that person or why he did it, but there's a rumor that Lazlo let them go. A rumor that meant weakness, and the Italians did all they could to prove it wrong.

"Long time no see, Adrian," he speaks with an Italian accent.

"Indeed," I counter with a Russian one, to highlight my roots.

"Are my clubs and house beneath you now?"

"Of course not, Don. I've been busy."

"Busy." He raises a brow. "Busy with what, Volkov?"

"Bratva business."

"That didn't stop you from paying me a visit before." He gives me a sideways glance. "Are we falling from each other's grace?"

"No, but I might be falling from Sergei's grace."

He pauses, weighing the severity of the statement. "How come?"

"You already know, Don. Richard Green's death serves you, not the brotherhood."

"Yes, yes. But we can make it work, no? The ball doesn't always need to be in your court, Adrian."

"If you don't pass it, you won't have an ally in me anymore, Don."

"Are you threatening me, Volkov?"

"I'm laying down the facts so you can choose wisely. If you don't give us a share in your new candidate, Sergei will suspect I'm betraying the brotherhood. That means my death."

"He wouldn't kill you over something like this."

"He would. He's already searching for my replacement. Igor's eldest son, Alexei, is the prime candidate." He's not actually, but it's an incentive to convince Lazlo of how serious this is. Igor doesn't like Lazlo because of an old grudge, and Alexei follows in his father's footsteps. If Lazlo loses his strongest ally within the brotherhood—me—he will have no one to fall back on.

He's gearing up for a new venture with one of the most notorious cartels in Columbia. The last thing he needs is a strained relationship with us or a domestic war. I use all the facts I know about him and his business plans to my advantage.

"Are you expecting me to share my cake, Volkov? We worked so hard to finally expand our reach, and now you're telling me I need to give it up?"

"Not give it up. Use it wisely." I pull back when Damien ascends the stairs behind us, accompanied by the Japanese.

He doesn't pay attention to these things, but Kai does. His dark eyes roam over me and the small meeting I just had with Lazlo before he nods in a show of respect.

He's also Rai's ally, in a way, and for that reason alone, I don't trust him. Sergei, Rai, Vladimir, and Kyle are all one package. If they put their minds into destroying me, it'll have more impact than anticipated.

If it were any other time, I would've taken them all on and taught each and every one of them a lesson. I would've used my system to destroy them before they were able to touch me.

However, this isn't only about me anymore.

The meeting goes well for the most part. The reason behind it is nothing but the strengthening of the brotherhood's allies with the Luciano family, the Yakuza, and the Triads. It's the same washed-up talk that Mikhail, Sergei, and Igor lead. Kirill speaks up, too, because he likes to appear to be a good sport. Damien spends most of the time smoking and pushing away Abe's advances to pour him a drink. Vladimir is watching me. He's being discreet about it, but I was taught by my mother to know when someone is a threat, even when I don't see them.

I remain silent, as usual, unless Sergei asks for my opinion. Tonight, he's out to throw jabs at me. I would've dismissed them any other time, but my unease about this night is once again filling with paranoia. A feeling I usually squash before it creeps into me.

"Adrian has the best relations with the Italians," Sergei states. "How did that come about again?"

He knows, but he wants me to say it. "I helped the Don once."

"What type of help?" It's Vladimir who asks this time.

"He saved my life," Lazlo says proudly. "The night of an attack on my club, I was swarmed by the fucking Rozettis and nearly died, but Adrian, who happened to be there by chance, saved me."

"By chance." Vladimir's eyes slide to me. "You don't believe in coincidences, though, do you, Volkov?"

"Coincidences happen." Kirill throws his hands dismissively. "If it weren't for coincidence, I wouldn't have been born."

"I'll drink to that. To Kirill's coincidental fucking existence." Damien raises his glass and everyone else follows.

The subject shifts from me to other crime-related topics that usually include drugs and shipments and customs.

Kirill gives me a look that says 'you're welcome' but I ignore him.

Once the meeting ends, I'm more than ready to take Lia and go the fuck home. On my way outside, Vladimir falls in step beside me and whispers in Russian so only I can hear, "I know you had something to do with Richard's death."

"Proof?" I remain calm.

"I will find it, and when I do, you'll count your fucking days, Adrian. I'll finish your life with my own hands."

"Good luck, Vladimir. I mean it."

And with that, Kolya and I storm down the stairs.

"Have you checked on Yan?" I ask.

"I just told him to take Mrs. Volkov to the car. They'll be there before us."

I hasten my footsteps until I reach the parking lot. Kolya hesitates behind me, staring at his phone.

"What?"

His brow furrows. "The car is moving."

"What do you mean, it's moving?" I stare at the GPS on his phone and, sure enough, our main car has already left the mansion.

I retrieve my phone and call Yan. The ringing on the other end of the line are the longest, most excruciating I've ever heard.

When the call is finally answered, there's rustling, panting, but it's not Yan's voice that greets me. It's Lia's, soft and in a small whisper-shout. "Yan! Yan, open your eyes!"

I don't speak, because I don't think she's alone. I don't want to give her away for talking to me.

"Yan!" she shrieks. "Adrian and Kolya will be here. They will help."

"Shut up, bitch," a voice says in the background and then she screams.

The line goes dead.

I grab it in a tight hold, my jaw clenching so hard, it's about to snap.

"What happened?" Kolya asks in an unsure tone.

"Lia's been kidnapped."

TWENTY-FIVE

Winter

IT HAPPENED SO FAST.

One second, Yan was ushering me inside the car, and the next, he was shot. It was silent, swift, and I wouldn't have noticed it if he hadn't jerked back, slamming into me.

Blood covered his shoulder, but he still reached out to push me away.

It was too late, though.

While I was preoccupied with trying to stop the bleeding in his shoulder, unyielding hands pulled me into the car as it revved forward.

Yan held on to me with all his might. They shot him again in the same shoulder. I put my chest to his so they wouldn't be able to kill him and used all my energy to pull him inside with me.

I can tell they don't want me dead or they would've shot me, too, so I used my body as a shield against Yan. It's clear they didn't want him to join us, and I probably should've let him fall outside the car for the others to find and help him, but

I couldn't trust that they wouldn't run him over on their way out, just to make sure he was dead.

My body is still covering his after one of the men in the front cut off my conversation with Adrian. Here's to hoping the small bits of information I got to my fake husband will enable him and his men to find us soon. Not only because I have a horrible feeling about where they're taking us, but also because Yan has lost a lot of blood. My white gloves have turned red from how much I've pressed on the two holes in his shoulder, but the blood won't stop oozing out.

His lips are pale and he keeps trying to push me off with his good hand, but I refuse to budge. If I do, the man from the front who's holding a damn rifle won't hesitate to shoot him.

I haven't paid attention to where we're going, but the roads are secluded, silent and dark. There are two men in the front. The one who's driving is wearing a leather jacket, hair hidden by a hat, and a black mask covers everything but his mouth and nose. He's the silent one, the one who hasn't talked since we got in here. The other man is nestling a rifle as if it's his pet. He's the one who shot Yan, the second time, at least, and cut off my phone call with Adrian.

They're not talking, so I can't tell what nationality they are, but Rifle Man spoke with an accented English just now.

I have no idea what this is, but I'm almost sure it has to do with Adrian. Are they kidnapping me to force him into doing something? I don't think it's because of a ransom, or they would've made their demands by now.

In that document, it was mentioned that Adrian was the target of many assassination attempts. Because of his position, he knows more than he should and uses it for the brotherhood's benefits. Whether it's to seize power, to order a hit, or to steal deals. His control over critical information has made him a target for numerous crime organizations and cartels—including the Bratva's classic allies.

Ogla mentioned once that he works from home for his own safety, and that the *Pakhan* prefers it because it keeps the brotherhood's most valuable asset, Adrian, from danger.

"Let me go," Yan groans.

I shake my head against his shoulder. I'm straddling his lap, both of my hands pressing on his wound. "They'll kill you."

He raises a brow. "If they don't, the boss will."

I scowl. "This is not the time to think about Adrian's stupid possessiveness."

"He'll really murder me for touching you."

"You're not touching. I am." I stare behind me at the silent men. "Who are they?"

Yan shakes his head, and I'm not sure if it means he doesn't know or that I shouldn't talk about them when they can hear us. Probably both.

All I know is that these men are dangerous—professional, even. They managed to slip under the heavy security at tonight's party and even leave unnoticed. The car does have tinted windows, which helped, but still. Yan and I were completely taken off guard.

"Why are you so calm?" Adrian's guard asks me, sweat trickling down his temples.

I stare at my steady hands. Even my breathing is calm. I didn't panic, not even when Yan was shot. My immediate thought was to get him safe and sound from that predicament. It still is.

But ever since I got that text, I've had a premonition that something bad would happen. That's why I practically begged Adrian to take us home.

"Panic won't do us any good, Yan."

"You're so different." He grabs my hand with his non-injured one and tries to pry me off him.

I swat it away as gently as possible. "Stop worrying about Adrian's reaction when you're about to bleed to death."

"Not possible. We exist for him."

"Jesus. That's some warped sense of loyalty."

"He's so blinded, though…" he trails off, his voice weakening. "He's lost sight of what's important…"

I press harder on his wound and he grunts, pursing his lips to stifle a moan of pain. I can feel my strength waning and Yan still won't stop bleeding.

It doesn't take him long to lose consciousness. He tries to fight it, I'll give him that. He keeps attempting to open his lids when I call his name, but then he's out cold.

"Yan! Don't faint. Think of your stupid boss and Kolya and Jeremy." My voice is urgent, hysterical almost. He's the only semblance of a friend I've had ever since I stepped into Lia's shoes.

His dry lips twitch, but he doesn't attempt to open his eyes. "Yan!"

"Shut the fuck up, bitch!" Rifle Man turns around and hits me across the face with the tip of his rifle. Pain explodes over my temple and I taste metal from my lips.

Tears fill my eyes from the stinging pain, but I don't let them out. I don't release Yan's inert, cold body either.

The car comes to a halt and I shrink further into Yan. If they throw him in the middle of nowhere, he won't be able to survive.

"It's time you deal with this bitch." Rifle Man retrieves a cigarette. "I'm so tired of her annoying voice—"

His cigarette falls from his fingers when the driver shoots him between the eyes. His head lolls to the side, face contorted in surprise.

I gasp, my whole body going rigid. He just shot his partner.

The driver tips his head down, and the black hat hides his expression. His hand, covered by a black leather glove, rests on the steering wheel, and his other one that's holding the gun is on his lap. His posture is relaxed, nonchalant.

"Noisy fucker," he mutters casually.

My lips part as the realization slams into me. It's the same voice from my nightmare.

The same tone.

The same tenor.

You have one mission. Pull the fucking trigger.

The shadow. The shadow is here.

"Long time no see, Duchess," he says without turning around. "Miss me?"

I try to wiggle sideways to see him, but the hat and the mask still camouflage his face.

"Who are you?" My voice is calm but cautious.

"Who am I is an interesting way of putting it. Who are you, Duchess? What's your mission?"

"I have no mission."

"Yes, you do." He twirls the gun in his hand, his forefinger pressing on the trigger. "You know it. I know it. If you don't make it happen, you'll pay the price."

"I don't know what the hell you're talking about," my lips tremble as the words leave them.

"Finding openings to talk to you is tedious as fuck, Duchess. Stop wasting my time and make it happen. I'll check on you soon." He gets out of the car, and before I can release a breath, he yanks my door open and wrenches me out.

I hold on to Yan and we both tumble to the ground. It's dark outside. So dark that I can barely see the contours of Yan's face.

The shadow stands in front of me, but there's no way of making out who he is. He's tall, lean, and smells like…bleach.

Bleach…why does he smell like that and why is it familiar?

"I'm not a patient man, Duchess. So don't test my limits."

And with that, he climbs in the car. The tires screech on the gravel and dirt before it shoots into the distance.

He's leaving us here?

I don't even have my phone to call Adrian or at least use it as a flashlight.

A groan comes from Yan and I feel in front of me until I catch something warm. His hand. Thank God it's his hand and not another organ.

"Yan! Open your eyes."

There's no response, and when I touch his shoulder, I can feel the blood still oozing. If I don't do something, he'll undoubtedly die.

I strain to place him on his stomach, then I crouch in front of him, hook his good arm around my neck and grab the hem of his jacket with my other hand.

Standing up, I attempt to carry him. He's heavier, taller, and bulkier than me, so that mission is an epic fail from the start. But I don't let go of him, even when his entire weight falls on me.

I don't stop.

I kick my heels off and walk barefoot to improve my balance. Pebbles dig into the soles of my feet like tiny needles. At first, I feel like my back will be broken into two, but after a few steps, an adrenaline wave rushes through my limbs.

I recall those times when I spent all-nighters in the studio, dancing and torturing my feet. I practiced again and again to perfect my posture, my technique, and my performance. If I could survive that, I can survive this. Because there's no way in hell I'd leave Yan behind. He took those bullets for me. He's dying because of *me*.

The night is calm and dark. There isn't even a moon to help give me direction. A chill covers me from head to toe and my muscles scream in pain.

I walk for so long that I start losing feeling in my feet. I need to find a place to call for help, and I need to find it soon.

My toes touch a solid surface and I smile, even as I strain to hold him up. "I found a road, Yan. I'm going to get us to safety."

He doesn't release a sound. His pulse under my fingers is becoming weaker, his body heavier.

"Come on. Stay with me, Yan."

Headlights shine in the distance and I attempt to make it to the road. I halt mid-step, jerking back when the car speeds past us. Fuck. That was close. If I had been on the road, it would've hit us.

The car stops up ahead, its red lights shining before it reverses at full speed, stopping right in front of us.

I nearly cry with joy when the passenger door opens and Adrian barges out. I stare up at his tightened features and his drawn gun. At the way he looks like a warlord ready to start a battle—and win it.

He found us.

No clue how he managed to do it so fast, but I'm so glad that he's here. He grabs me by the shoulders. "Are you okay?"

I manage a slight nod, then motion at Yan. "He was shot. Twice. Help him."

The words aren't fully out before Kolya takes Yan from me and carries him. I don't sag in relief that his weight is gone, though. If anything, my fingers shake as pessimistic thoughts rush in. At least when he was leaning on my back, I could feel his heartbeat, as low as it was, and tell myself he was alive. Now, it feels like he's closer to death than life.

A second car stops behind this one and Kolya carefully places Yan inside.

"Lia."

"What?" I answer absentmindedly, still watching Yan's lifeless body.

"Lia!"

"What?" I snap at Adrian.

He's wiping under my eyes. I taste salt and that's when I realize I've been crying. For how long, I have no idea, but it's been long enough that I'm sniffling and shaking.

Adrian checks my hands, my dress, and my coat.

"It's not mine. It's Yan's," I say to explain the blood.

Adrian's thumb swipes under my cheek and I wince as he touches my cut lip. "Where's the fucker who did this?"

"He died."

"Died?"

"His partner killed him."

"And where's his partner?"

"He left in the car." I stare up at him as the vehicle carrying Yan revs in the distance. "Is he going to be okay?"

I can sense the hesitation in Adrian. He saw him. He saw the blood. He knows that his second closest guard might not survive.

"Let's leave." He ushers me to the back seat and two of his guards get in the front.

Adrian keeps his arms around me during the entire ride home. The stupid tears won't stop coming and I keep shivering like a leaf in winter.

He removes his jacket and wraps it over my bloodied coat, but that doesn't ease the ache I'm feeling deep in my chest.

I'm crying, but it's not only about Yan. I'm also crying because I think I know that man, the shadow, the one who said I had a mission.

And something tells me this mission is more dangerous than I could ever imagine.

TWENTY-SIX

Winter

ISUCK IN MY FIRST REAL BREATH WHEN THE DOCTOR says that Yan will survive.

He lost a lot of blood and he's still unconscious, but there's no immediate threat to his life.

Those words tear into my chest and lodge against my heart with a force that robs me of balance. I grab Adrian's arm and anchor myself as we stand in the middle of Yan's room that's located in the guest house, the place Adrian never allowed me in before now.

He's on his back, chest bandaged, no more blood leaving his body, but he's not opening his eyes either. His pretty model face is pasty pale and his lips are chapped.

Kolya is by his side, checking his temperature just as the doctor showed him. I don't miss that they have an onsite doctor, or that he didn't ask any questions about why he had to treat a gunshot patient in Adrian's house.

He just nodded and left as if this were an everyday occurrence.

It probably is.

"How is his temperature?" I ask Kolya as he stares at the device in his hand.

The room is plain, with a bed in the middle and a closet in the corner. The only light comes from the lamp on the nightstand, casting dark shadows across Yan's pale face.

"It's high, but not alarming." Kolya straightens, and even though his usual scowl is strapped in place, there's a subtle wariness in his posture. "I'll make sure it goes down through the night."

I take a step forward. "I'll stay, too."

"No." Adrian grabs me by the elbow and pulls me back. "You did your part. Leave it to Kolya now."

"He's right, Mrs. Volkov. Thank you for everything you've done. If you hadn't carried him or tried to stop his bleeding, he wouldn't have made it." Kolya offers what resembles a smile. He's just like his boss in that department. They could use a lesson or two from the lively Yan.

"It was nothing."

I want to stay and watch over Yan, but Adrian carries me in his arms and leaves the guest house, heading to the main one. He's been doing it since earlier because I have no shoes on, and I'm thankful because my legs can't carry me properly. My hands inside my bloodied gloves rest on my lap and I try not to get caught up in the sight of them and recall what happened to Yan.

"Hold on to me, Lia," Adrian says sternly.

"They're bloodied."

"Do I look like I care?"

He doesn't, but I do. Even as I wrap my arms around his neck, I try to keep the gloves away. I don't want to get blood on him.

There shouldn't be any blood near him.

As soon as we're inside the room, I squirm so he'll let me

go. In the bright light, I can see the crimson on my gloves, all over my coat, and down my dress. It's everywhere, like a second skin.

Adrian lowers me to my feet and I scoot away. He clicks the door shut, and when he advances toward me, his eyes are hooded, dark, as if they're brewing a storm or a volcano or both.

His white tuxedo shirt has smudges of blood on it. There's some on his forehead, too. I don't like it. I don't want it on him and I hate that I'm the reason it's there.

There really shouldn't be blood on him.

I frown. That's the second time I've had that thought in a few seconds. I have no clue why I'm plagued by that, but I know that I can't see the crimson color on him. It tugs on a dark part of me where that black box I was trapped in exists.

"I… I'm going to take a shower." I slip past him to the door. "I'll do it in one of the other rooms."

My hand is on the doorknob when his body flattens mine from behind, his hard muscles and tall build dwarfing my smaller frame. His palm covers my bloodied gloves over the doorknob as he whispers against the shell of my ear, "Where do you think you're going?"

"Shower…" My voice is low, breathy, and sounds insincere because showering is actually the last thing I want to do right now.

"Do you have any idea how worried I was?" He rubs his chin against the side of my head as his fingers undo the clips holding my hair. The strands fall to my back and he nuzzles his nose against it, inhaling me in. "I thought I'd lost you again, Lia."

My eyes close, soaking in the deep, low tenor of his voice and the feel of him behind me. It's safe and so damn familiar. I shouldn't be having these thoughts right now, not when he's speaking about another woman, but I'm unable to think past his presence. His touch. His words.

I've become addicted to him instead of alcohol. His brutal punishments and my overwhelming orgasms have become my new fix, but he took it away and that hurt more than not drinking. At least with the lack of alcohol, it was a headache. With him, my whole body has been going through withdrawal.

I've been starved for so long—an eternity it seems—and tonight's events only added to my hunger.

Adrian's lips brush against the curve of my jaw and trail down to the hollow of my throat, nibbling, sucking.

My muscles lose their rigidity from earlier and I relax into his grasp, my fingers releasing the doorknob. Adrian holds my jaw with two fingers, lifting it so he can kiss my neck, then my collarbone, before moving back to my jaw.

The blood doesn't deter him. It's as if it doesn't exist.

He whirls me around and I stare up at him as my behind meets the solid surface of the door.

He stares back as he removes his jacket and follows with my coat. I'm silent, as one item of clothing follows the other, pooling around me.

Adrian threads the fingers of one hand through my hair as the other finds my zipper, undoing it in one swift move. The material slides down my arms before it joins the rest of the clothes scattered on the floor. I'm standing in nothing but a strapless bra and black lace panties.

I'm half-naked, and yet I don't feel vulnerable, because the way Adrian watches me is heated, burning, unlike all the robotic looks he's given me over the past couple of days.

"I'm so proud of what you did to help Yan, Lenochka," he murmurs against my face as he hooks his fingers around the edge of my panties.

"You're proud of me?" I grab the sides of his shirt for balance.

"I've always been proud of you." He pauses. "Let's change that to *mostly*."

I want to ask if 'mostly' includes me or Lia, but I choose not to ruin the moment. I don't care what he sees me as right now, because I'm the one here.

It's not Lia.

Me.

Adrian unbuckles his belt and I stare with bated breath as he lets his pants and boxers fall to his feet. He's always a sight to behold, something that I can't take my eyes off of, even when my instincts tell me he's dangerous.

Despite that danger, or more like *because* of it, I've been caught in his orbit with no way of escaping.

He lifts one of my legs and loops it around his waist. I keep it there, unable to look away from his cock. It's hard, thick, and so ready that my insides flutter with a carnal type of desire.

Adrian enters me slowly, and even with my slick core, his cock forces its way into my body, filling me without being all the way in. As he takes his time, I realize it's not only desire that's gripping me, tearing through my flesh and finding refuge in my bones. It's something deeper, darker, and more sinister. At this moment, I want to watch the way he's owning me, inch by each agonizing inch. I want to watch how our bodies are joined.

A throaty moan fills the air and I realize it's mine.

Adrian pauses and a pleased groan spills from his lips. "Fuck, Lenochka… Do you know how many times I've thought about hearing your sexy throaty voice?"

I want to bite my lip, to end this, to not allow him to hear my voice when he's still calling me by another woman's name, but the look in his eyes stops me. The gray is intense, but not harsh. It's like being trapped in a bright dream and knowing that I'll wake up soon, so I should enjoy every second of it.

"You're so beautiful," he rasps, rolling his hips until his cock is all the way inside me. "You're fucking home."

I gasp at both his words and the way he's filling me to the point of stretching me in the most delicious way possible.

Home.

He called me home.

My arms circle his neck as I climb up his body so that both of my legs are looped around his waist. I don't care about the blood or how this is possibly my worst appearance yet.

The only thing that keeps ringing in my head is the word 'home.' I've never actually had one, not really, and the fact that Adrian is calling me his is triggering a dormant part of me I didn't think existed.

The part who also wants a home and wants him to show me how much I'm *his* home.

Adrian drives slowly into me, the new position giving him a depth that allows him to hit me in a sensitive spot with each unhurried thrust.

"You're so tight, Lenochka. Come on, open up to me."

I realize then that he's only taking it slow so he won't hurt me. Despite his ruthless nature and his merciless punishments, Adrian sometimes treats me as if I'm a crystal glass that will break if he presses hard enough.

That might be true since he is, in fact, huge. He's so big that I feel a burn every time he pounds inside, even though I'm soaking wet. But it's the exquisite type. The type that moths wouldn't mind being burned alive in as long as they get to taste it.

I dig my heels into his ass, urging him silently. Adrian's lips capture mine as his rhythm increases. His kiss matches the ferocity of his thrusts. First, they're deep and unhurried. Then, they're fast and merciless, robbing me of any sense of reason.

It's impossible to keep up, even if I try. My back hits the door, sliding over it and bumping against it to match the sharp power of his hips, of his kiss, of his whole body.

I'm a marionette in his hands, but he's not taking my logic away. He's engraving himself under my skin. He's stealing my common sense and my breath. He's opening doors inside me I didn't realize existed.

Since he started kissing me, I haven't longed for air. He's my oxygen now. The reason I'm fighting tooth and nail to hold on to life.

The orgasm hits me so hard, I don't see it coming until it blasts in my face. I roll my head back, my lips momentarily leaving his. "Aaaah… Adrian! Adrian!"

"Fuck, fuck."

Hearing him curse only strengthens my orgasm. He's not the type to curse usually, but he seems to have lost some of his iron control ever since he got me in his arms.

He powers into me with animalistic force, fucking me against the door with deep, furious strokes. "Repeat that. Repeat my name."

"Adrian," I whisper, then moan. "Adrian!"

For a moment in time, I feel like I'm suspended in mid-air. My head and heart are lightheaded. My scar doesn't tingle, my chest doesn't ache.

I'm free.

In Adrian's arms, I'm free of everything and everyone. I'm just me.

Those thoughts expand the wave of my orgasm as it swallows me whole. It's nothing like I've ever felt before and it scares me, but I ride it, anyway. My fingers dig into Adrian's shoulders as a long whimper mixed with a moan spills from my lips.

Adrian comes then. I feel his cum warming my insides as his shoulders tighten beneath my fingers.

"Fuck," he breathes out against the hollow of my neck.

But he doesn't even pause as he steps out of his pants and boxers and carries me to the bathroom while he's still inside me. He removes my gloves and my bra, throwing them behind him. My hands are bloodied, but Adrian doesn't look at them with disgust, more like with pride.

I'm proud of you, he said.

You're my home, he also said.

Am I still over the moon because of the orgasm or is this something entirely different?

He puts me on my feet, and I'm a bit unsteady, so he keeps a hand on my arm as he eases out of me. I shiver at the loss of him, then my eyes droop when his cum trickles down my legs.

Jesus. Is that supposed to be a turn-on?

Adrian watches the evidence of his thorough fucking as he shrugs off his shirt, revealing his hard muscles and the ethereal ink decorating his arms.

I want to touch them, to hold him, but it always feels like it's not my place to do that. Like I have absolutely no claim on him to be able to study his tattoos.

Adrian hits the button and the water soaks us in a second. He slowly rubs the blood off my hands and uses a brush to remove it from under my nails. Then he moves on to my face, my neck, and my arms.

I'm about to melt from the way he touches me. The care in his eyes. The softness that doesn't suit his character that he shows only to me.

When he's done, he wraps his arms around my waist and lifts me up, digging his fingertips into my ass. Then he rams inside me in one ruthless stroke.

I come. Just like that.

I wasn't even that aroused, but I think the way he washed me was so stimulating that all he had to do was enter me for me to orgasm.

It's not even the physical stimulation, it's the meaning behind it, the tenderness, the concern in his gray eyes that he's only ever dedicated to me.

I don't bother to muffle my moans, my screams, and my utter joy as he fucks me under the shower. I hold onto him with both hands, not wanting to let him go.

Not now, not ever.

He doesn't stop fucking me, owning me, changing position every so often. His hands are everywhere, cupping my breasts, pinching my nipples, pulling my hair so he can nibble on a sensitive spot on my throat. He kisses me, then bites my tongue. He sucks on my nipple, then tugs on it. He powers into me slowly, then takes it to an irregular, maddening level.

It's like he can't get enough of me and wants to deepen our connection with each touch. He fucks like he talks, with apparent calm yet subtle darkness.

I'm so stimulated, I feel like one orgasm keeps bleeding into the other.

My front is now against the transparent shower stall as he powers into me from behind while caging both of my wrists in one hand on the glass above me.

My mouth is open in an 'O' as I take every delicious thrust and every sting of pain that comes with it.

"Ahhh…Adrian…I'm coming…"

He increases his rhythm, pinching my nipples with his other hand until they're sore and I scream in pain. "So sensitive."

"Adrian!" I fall down without any landing. I keep falling and rolling, finding a pause just so I can fall again.

If I knew this was how it would feel, I would've let him hear my voice so he would've fucked me a long time ago.

Adrian still hasn't come. If anything, my orgasm has made him grow harder inside me. His lips meet my ear as he whispers, "Thank you for welcoming me home."

And then he comes inside me again. I close my eyes to memorize the sensation and his words.

Thank you for being my home, I'm about to whisper in

response, but his head falls into the space between my neck and shoulder and he kisses the skin there. "Fuck, I missed you, Lia."

My whole body goes slack against him. Everything that happened tonight. His worry, his unbound passion, and even the way he's nibbling on my skin and slightly rocking his hips were never meant for me.

He doesn't *see* me. He's only seeing Lia.

That thought cuts me open so deep, a tear slides down my cheek, mixing with the water and falling down the drain.

Because I know, I just know that he'll never see me as Winter.

I'll always be Lia.

TWENTY-SEVEN

Adrian

I CAN'T STOP.

I say I will after one more time as I lift her up and lay her down on her stomach, opening her legs wide and thrusting into her from behind.

I said I would stop after I took her one more time in bed last night.

I said I would stop after I woke her up, my teeth nibbling on her neck and fingers teasing her clit.

But I'm a fucking liar.

I have no will or plan to stop. The more I taste her and inhale the tangible scent of her arousal, the more I'm tempted to feast on it. To eat her out, swallow her down so deep that she'll never think about finding a way out. I come up with method after method to wrench one orgasm after the other from her.

Usually, I'm the type who knows the exact moment to stop. You can't overdo or underdo things. Finding that balance is impossible for most people, but not for me. I've always excelled at being the 'right amount' type of person.

I've never cared too much or too little. Never gone overboard, never pushed boundaries. Never had addictions or things I couldn't easily get rid of.

Lia is the exception to all of those.

She's the addiction I didn't see coming, and when I finally noticed her, she was already streaming in my blood.

She's the one whose boundaries were supposed to be pushed, but I ended up being the one in a clusterfuck of problems.

This woman is intoxicating. She crept under my skin and injected her black magic into my bones. Now, she's the reason I breathe. I feel like if I stop touching her, if I let her go, she'll disappear again.

I'll never have her again.

My thrusts become profound, sharp, and animalistic at the thought. I've never been as hard as I was last night and this morning. My dick is in a constant need to claim her, own her, and teach her that she'll never go anywhere—willingly or unwillingly.

Lia's body jerks, her fingers fisting into the belt that I looped around her wrists and attached to the hook in the bedpost. She looks so beautiful and so fucking mine.

Her frame is petite, breakable, and so fragile that it hurts to think what could've happened to her last night. Cuts mark the soles of her feet and there's a bruise forming under her eye. The moment I saw her panting, crying, and in a mild state of shock, I swore to find whoever touched her and snap his fucking neck with my bare hands.

At the same time, when I saw her struggling to hold Yan upright and knowing she'd probably carried him for a long time, judging by the scratches on her feet, I felt a deep sense of pride. Because even though Yan was supposed to protect her, they found themselves in a reversed position and she didn't leave a man behind.

This tiny fucking woman carried a large man on her back as if that were normal.

Those thoughts only fill me with more desire for her, more need to engrave myself under her skin and into her blood.

I dig my fingers into her ass cheek as my other hand lifts her stomach the slightest bit. With one of my knees firmly planted between her open thighs, this position gives me more room to power into her.

Lia bites the pillow, muffling her sounds again. She's been doing that since I carried her out of the shower last night. I release her ass and lean over so my chest covers her back.

Her muscles bend under my touch, caving in the slightest bit as her walls clench around my dick. I thrust two fingers into her mouth, opening it. "Don't hide from me, Lia. Let me hear your voice."

Her eyes meet mine, moisture gathering in them. They're quiet, but defiant. Determined, yet sad, like a natural disaster that doesn't want to ruin people's lives but knows that it has to happen, anyway.

"Lia. *Open.*"

She wraps her lips around my fingers and bites down hard as her insides strangle me. I come at the same time, my balls aching from the intensity of my release.

Lia's knees buckle and she collapses the mattress. I want to fall over her, too, to kiss her throat and nibble on her rosy erect nipples. I want to worship her entire body just so I can do it all over again.

But I pull out of her and hold myself in a push-up position so as not to crush her with my weight. She's so tiny, it aches to imagine hurting her that way.

Lia stops biting my fingers and releases them, leaving a trail of saliva and her teeth marks. She tries to look away, but I drop one of my knees between her legs and grab her by the hair, forcing her to stay in place.

I run the tips of my index and middle fingers—the ones she just bit—over her lips. "If you like something, own up to it."

She stares at my fingers, pursing her lips shut as I glide the tip of my tongue over her throat before I find her ear. Her whole body shudders and I can feel her lust, even without touching between her legs. Her eyes get wide, her breathing shatters, and her skin becomes hot to the touch, a bit sweaty, a bit messy, and so fucking perfect.

"Why are you muting yourself again, hmm?" I whisper in low words, trying my hardest not to let my temper loose.

"Ask yourself," she says, breathless.

"I'm asking you. Answer me."

She purses her lips again.

"Are you in the mood for some punishment, Lia? It's been some time, so maybe your body is craving that lash of pain."

She scoffs.

"That's one, Lia."

Her glare meets mine and I think it's because of the punishment, but she grits out from between clenched teeth, "I'm *not* Lia."

"Two. And you are."

Fresh tears fill her eyes as she bucks off the bed, trying to push me away. I can easily overpower her, especially with her tied and bound for the taking, but the tears stop me. They're not tears of pleasure like when she was sobbing through her orgasm while being whipped.

They're tears of pain.

I give her room, sitting on my knees to undo the belt from around her hands. I'm attempting to massage her wrists, but she yanks them back and points a thumb at herself. "Winter! My name is Winter. Stop calling me Lia. Just stop!"

My jaw clenches. "Three."

"Make it a hundred. I don't fucking care." She hits my chest with a closed fist. "You're erasing me, Adrian. You're wiping me from existence."

I wrap a hand around her head and pull her to me, forcing an end to her tantrum. She struggles against me some more, her tiny hands pushing at me, her teeth biting the ridges of my chest, but her energy wanes as a sob tears from her throat. It's raw, but it bounces right against my ribcage and disappears.

I couldn't give a fuck about the reason she's crying.

Soon after, her breathing levels even out, though her fists are still bunched against my chest. I think she's fallen asleep until she murmurs, "Winter. My name is Winter…"

And then she's out cold.

I place her on the bed, go to the bathroom, and return with a wet towel to clean her up. I lift her, remove the sheets that are wet with my cum and her arousal, and wrap her up in the thick duvet.

There are still tears in her eyes and I wipe them with the back of my fingers. She leans into my touch because, even in her sleep, her body is attuned to me.

After I make sure she's comfortable, I take a quick shower, get dressed, and join my men downstairs. It's a little early, but no time is too early for what we have to do. They're all up and about, and I've already received reports from my hackers.

My eyes narrow as I read the email from one of the hackers I asked to force entry into my car's GPS after it disappeared last night. He replied back that they found it down a cliff, not far from where we picked up Lia and Yan.

I send two of my guards to investigate before the police show up at the site of the accident. If there's anything to clean up, they'll do that as well.

But most of all, I need to know who the fuck dared to kidnap my wife.

My. *Wife.*

It didn't even happen on the streets or in an insignificant place. They dared to take her from an event held by Sergei in his own house. They have balls, I'll give them that, but I'll enjoy every second of cutting them.

I send a few more guards to investigate Sergei's house in case anyone knows about the incident. After I received the phone call from Lia, my men and I were careful enough not to alert the others. Any security hazard in the presence of the other crime families would reflect badly on the brotherhood and Sergei. I didn't want to give him one more reason to dig into me or force me to throw Lia out. He'd probably think I staged the whole fucking kidnapping and sacrificed Yan to make myself look innocent about the Italians' fiasco.

That's something his fucker-in-law, Kyle, would do, not me. Rai's husband wouldn't hesitate to put himself in danger as long as he gets to move ahead. I'm not like that. I would never sacrifice my people or put Lia in danger for my own benefit.

Sergei doesn't have many cameras in the parking lot, so I need my men to tell me if anything was caught on footage, and then I'll worry about it.

After I make sure all my men are where they should be, I head to Yan's room in the guest house.

I take a second to suck in a breath. As much as the fucker has been getting on my nerves, I don't like entertaining the idea of Yan's death. Kolya always used to joke that he's like our kid with how much we've doted on him, and he is, in a way. Seeing him shot was equivalent to seeing Jeremy choke a few months ago.

After a moment, I push the door open. Kolya's sitting on a chair beside Yan's bed and clutching a wet towel. His eyes are bloodshot but alert. He most definitely didn't sleep a wink last night because he has a weakness for the reckless bastard lying on the bed.

My second-in-command tries to stand up, but I motion at him to stay and ask in Russian, "How is he?"

"The fever went down," Kolya answers in the same language. "But he hasn't woken up yet."

"He will."

"I know." He hesitates. "Did you find out anything?"

"The other men say they hadn't received the order to move to the car yet, so they witnessed nothing of what happened."

"Yan probably wanted to get Mrs. Volkov to the car first."

"Yes." I stare at Yan's bandaged chest, finger tapping against my thigh. "Remember when Kyle got shot pretending to protect Sergei, when he was the one behind the attack?"

Kolya frowns, probably not knowing where I'm going with this, but nods.

My attention remains on Yan as I speak. "Do you know why he did it?"

"To get in Sergei's good graces."

"Which was basically his camouflage. His cover-up. He took a non-fatal bullet as a form of sacrifice."

Kolya's eyes widen, finally getting my point. "You can't mean…you're not accusing Yan of the same, are you?"

My tapping halts as Yan's eyes twitch. "Hmm. Who knows?"

"With all due respect, sir, Yan has served you since he was a toddler. He's not some unnamed assassin like Kyle, who's trying to get in anyone's good graces. He took two bullets for your wife!"

"Watch your tone, Kolya."

He purses his lips, but he doesn't apologize. After a moment, he swallows. "All I'm saying is that Yan wouldn't do that to you."

"You're saying that because you've known him his entire life. You find it hard to suspect him because of your bond."

"Apparently, you have no problem with that. Congratulations."

"I said to watch your tone, and no, Kolya, I have no problem distrusting people."

"So what now? Are you going to kill him?"

"I'm not that cruel. I wouldn't kill him without questioning him first."

I can tell by Kolya's expression that he's enraged, disappointed, and probably wants to punch me in the face. We might have been brought up together, but he knows me to be cold and calculative toward other people, not my own. So the fact that I'm directing those traits inward, at Yan, is pissing him off like nothing before.

"Am I next?" he asks quietly. "After Yan, is it my turn?"

"Don't give me a reason." I turn around. "Tell me when he wakes up."

"You know," he speaks from behind me. "As much as you hated your parents, you're a replica of them."

I'm not under the implication to answer him, so I don't as I click the door shut behind me.

A replica of them.

Possibly.

After all, monsters can only birth monsters.

TWENTY-EIGHT

Winter

I CAN'T DO THIS ANYMORE.

I just *can't*.

Today, I woke up sweating and in tears. My whole body was shaking so hard that I scared Jeremy when he came into my room.

Sometimes, I don't remember my nightmares, but I recall this one. I recall how Adrian was fucking me on the bed, my arms and legs looped around him as Lia barged through the door with a knife. However, this time, no shadow saved me from her as she slit my throat.

Adrian didn't look at me twice when she was in the room. As I was clutching my bleeding neck, he pulled out of me and went to her.

He hugged her from the front in a way that he's never hugged me. He breathed in her scent and kissed her temples.

"I've missed you, Lenochka," he whispered to her while she was holding the bloodied knife that slit my throat.

"You're finally home," he murmured between kisses to

her cheek, her mouth, and her throat as I lay there, gurgling, thrashing, *crying*.

Help! I screamed in my head. *Adrian, help me!*

He didn't.

All of his attention was on Lia, on her face, her cheeks, her throat, her mouth. She looked at me, though. Her eyes met my identical ones, and she smirked as she hugged Adrian back and mouthed, "Mine."

That's when I died.

But then I was shoved into another nightmare, where a man wrapped his hand around mine and forced me to pull the trigger. Blood covered my skin as I shrieked at the top of my lungs.

Then it was over.

Jeremy was the one trying to wake me, standing by my bed, holding one of his toy soldiers. He jerked back when I startled into a sitting position.

He's now standing near the dresser, his face pale and his lips trembling. "Are you a ghost, Mommy?"

My breathing immediately calms and a different type of worry takes over me. Jeremy seems like he's scared of me and that hurts more than I like to admit.

I extend a hand toward him. "I'm so sorry, Jer. Mommy just had a nightmare. It's over now."

"Really?" he doesn't seem convinced, even as he stares at my hand.

"Really."

"You're not gonna be Ghost Mommy?"

"Of course not, my angel."

He cautiously takes a step forward and places his tiny hand in mine. I smile and he grins back. "You're my mommy."

"I am."

He climbs on top of the bed and wraps his small arms around me. "Can you always be my mommy?"

The desperation and exasperation from earlier sticks to my throat as I think of what to tell him.

I'm not staying here anymore.

I don't care if the police lock me up. I just can't, under any circumstances, remain in a house that gives me the creeps with a man who's erasing me from existence.

It's been a week since the attack. A whole seven days since he first fucked me.

He's done it again and again since. Sometimes twice a day. Sometimes as a form of punishment. Last night, it was because he figured out that I'd spent most of the day taking care of Yan—a fact he doesn't like.

He was harsh, unyielding, and didn't pull out of me until my lips bled from how much I bit down on them. I'm glad he cleaned me up and covered my body with a nightgown, because the last thing I want is for Jeremy to see me in that state.

But then again, Adrian provides the best aftercare I've ever witnessed. I've only ever known selfish men who paid attention to their own pleasure and to hell with mine. Adrian doesn't only make sure I come first—and multiple times—he also never leaves me dirty and walks away. He always bathes me, dresses me, brushes my hair, tucks me in, and even tells Ogla to bring me meals in bed when he feels I'm too sore to move.

I want to convince myself that I don't like any of that. That I have no choice but to go with it. But is that the case if my body always comes undone? If I crave him as soon as his hand is on me?

It's not his touch that I hate. It's him and the way he's never called me by my name.

I stopped asking for it, because not only is it useless, but I always get punished for it. Hard, with more pain than pleasure, as if he wants to erase that thought from my brain.

And that's why I need to escape. My heart bleeds at

leaving Jeremy, who's staring up at me expectantly, his gray eyes huge. Unless…

My heart jolts as a crazy idea forms in my head.

"Mommy?"

"Yes?"

"You didn't answer me."

I scoff. He's definitely taking on his father's demanding personality.

"I'll always be your mommy, Jer. Nothing will change that."

"Can we play together today?"

"Yes, but we have to pay a visit to Yan first."

"Is he still sick because he saved you, Mommy?"

"Yeah."

"I'm gonna give him one of my toys then."

"You're such a good boy, Jer. Come on. Let's get ready."

After we get dressed, I take Jeremy downstairs to have breakfast. Ogla watches me peculiarly but says nothing. I'm packing some toast and jam when she finally speaks, "Where are you taking those, Mrs. Volkov?"

"To Yan and Kolya. They barely have real breakfast nowadays." While I've hardly seen them—or the other guards—eat before, I know Ogla usually takes their meals to some back building where they live and have their food.

"You're not allowed to visit Yan."

I lift my head, pausing my task. "What?"

"Before he went out this morning, Mr. Volkov gave specific orders that you're not allowed to visit Yan."

"Oh, fuck him and his *specific* orders."

Ogla's bland eyes widen as if not believing I just said that. I made her speechless for once.

Jeremy giggles as he tugs on my dress. "Bad word, Mommy."

"Sorry, angel." I smile, then direct my stare at Ogla. "Tell your boss that he can't stop me from tending to a patient."

And with that, I take the food and tell Jeremy to come with me.

We go into the guest house. Unlike the other guards, Kolya and Yan apparently live here. As usual, there are two soldiers with drawn weapons in front of the building. I'm prepared to give them a piece of my mind if they try to stop me, but they don't.

When we go into Yan's room, we find him sleeping. He woke up a few days ago, but the doctor put him on pain medication that causes him to sleep more.

He's covered by a gray duvet that's been pulled up to his chin, a slight stubble growing on his jaw, but he's not as pale as those first few days.

Kolya sits by his side, tapping on his laptop. I'm surprised to find him here, because he's usually Adrian's shadow, and since Ogla told me Adrian has outside business today, I thought Kolya would be with him.

But then again, there's been simmering tension between the two of them since Yan's injury. They barely address each other, even in Russian. Adrian has been going out a lot during the day with the other men, and Kolya has hardly left Yan's side

When we enter, he closes his laptop and stands up.

"Is he better?" I offer Kolya food.

He takes it and places it on the nightstand. "Yes. I believe so."

Jeremy sits on the floor running his figurine over the sheet, but it's far enough from Yan so that it doesn't cause him discomfort.

"Mrs. Volkov."

My attention slides from Jeremy to Kolya. "Yes?"

"Please leave. Boss gave clear instructions about not welcoming you here anymore."

I grit my teeth. That fucking asshole.

"I'm not leaving." I cross my arms. "And if Adrian says anything, tell him I insisted."

Kolya's face remains stoic as he murmurs, "You're making Yan's case worse, not better, Mrs. Volkov."

"Surely he wouldn't hurt his injured man because I want to visit him."

"No, but he'll suspect him more."

I frown. "Suspect him?"

"Boss thinks Yan could've been behind your kidnapping."

"What the hell? He got shot. *Twice.*"

Kolya's jaw tightens. "He thinks Yan could've done that on purpose to get away with it."

"Holy shit. Your boss is a fucking dictator."

I can tell Kolya wants to defend Adrian, but something stops him. Or someone. Yan's inert body. So that's the reason behind the tension between them. Adrian suspects Yan, and the senior guard doesn't like it.

"Did you tell him your version of events, Mrs. Volkov?"

"Of course." The bastard made me repeat it again and again as if to make sure I wasn't making things up and that I was re-telling it as it happened.

I didn't mention the man shadow and what he said. I screwed some details up to make it seem like the kidnappers threw us out of the car and left. I heard Adrian talk to one of his men, who said that they found a disfigured corpse with the car that fell down the cliff. It must've been Rifle Man.

No one mentioned anything about the other man. The shadow, who said that I have a mission and called me Duchess. I doubted that would help Adrian in any way, and it would've been bad for me.

Because even I still don't understand what his words mean.

But I didn't think Adrian would believe Yan had betrayed him. He's such a bastard for suspecting his closest people.

"Mommy." Jeremy tugs on my dress.

"Yes, angel?"

"I want to bring my war zone here."

"Okay." I pause before complying. "Can you do it, Kolya?"

"I'm taking care of Yan."

"I'll do it."

"It's better if you don't. Boss doesn't like it."

"I told you, I don't care what he does or doesn't like."

Kolya remains there for a few seconds and when it's clear that I won't budge, he releases a small sigh. "Very well."

"I wanna come too! I wanna come too!" Jeremy releases me and goes to his father's closest guard. "Take me, Kolya."

"Keep an eye on him." Kolya tips his head in Yan's direction and I nod.

After the door closes behind them, I pull the covers up a little over his body. "I'm sorry your boss is a major fucking jerk, Yan."

His lips move in what resembles a smile before his eyes open. When he speaks, his voice is hoarse. "He always was. Are you only seeing it now?"

"Yan! Do you need anything? Should I get you water or food or—"

My words cut off when he lifts his hand and wraps it around mine. "Thank you for saving me."

"Sure..."

The look in his eyes coupled with his touch is throwing me off. There's something behind them, but what?

As if sensing my reaction, he pulls his hand from mine. "To show my gratitude, I want you to go somewhere."

"Somewhere?"

"Kolya is the only guard inside. So you won't have anyone to stop you now that he's not here."

"Stop me from what?"

"The second story, Mrs. Volkov. The one you've been looking at for weeks."

My heart leaps to my throat as his words register. *He noticed.*

I have contemplated going up there ever since I had the chance to come here and visit Yan, but Kolya always, without doubt, escorts me out after every visit.

And I haven't had the courage to come back during the night, especially with how often I pass out due to Adrian's thorough fucking.

"Kolya is Adrian's number one man and confidant," Yan says. "His loyalty lies with him and always will, no matter what the boss does. Make no mistake, if he finds you, he won't hesitate to sell you out, so you better hurry up."

"What about you, Yan? Wouldn't this get you in trouble?"

"I'm just a patient asleep. I'll pretend I know nothing." He winks, and my heart thunders.

Holy shit. I saw that wink before, but where? *Where?*

"Go," he whispers.

A part of me doesn't want to, a part of me wants to bury my head under the sand like little Miss Ostrich.

But that part doesn't win.

Because the biggest part of me wants to go up there and see what's going on. Maybe if I do, I can find a solution to the situation I'm in. Maybe I can finally get rid of the nightmares.

I squeeze Yan's arm as a message of thanks, then leave the room. I go up the stairs two at a time because I know Kolya won't take long to return. As soon as I'm on the second floor, a gloomy sensation crawls up my skin.

Marionette strings snap in my neck as I take mechanical steps down the hall. I shouldn't know where I'm going and yet, it feels like I do.

I don't open the first or the second door and, instead, stop in front of the last one to the right. The one with the window I saw that day.

My fingers tremble as I turn the doorknob. I expect it to snap shut and lock me out, but a soft click echoes in the air.

As it opens, the hinges make a small squeaky sound like the ones from horror movies and heart-pounding thrillers.

I don't know why I think a monster is waiting for me on the other side.

It's not.

It's way worse.

Someone lies on a simple bed.

Wires are hooked to the person's arm. They're still, unmoving, like they're dead. But the beeping machine to the right shows a normal beat.

Beep.

Beep.

Beep.

My sweaty fingers release the doorknob as I approach the bed slowly. My feet are about to fail me, my heart is thudding so loud, it would've broken the machine if it were attached to one.

My palms cover my mouth as I stare at the person lying there.

She's wearing a white nightgown like in the nightmare, her dark hair splaying all over the pillow and her skin is pasty white.

The woolen sheet covers her to the breasts and her hands are crossed on her stomach as if she's in a casket.

Lia Volkov.

The *real* Lia Volkov.

I thought she was dead. How could she be…? Why is she…?

My thoughts tumble over each other with no clear direction as a sickening feeling settles over my stomach, demanding I throw up my breakfast.

Her eyes snap open, their blue clashing with mine.

I stumble backward as my mouth opens in a shriek.

TWENTY-NINE

Winter

THIS IS A NIGHTMARE.

This could only be another nightmare. I didn't really wake up this morning and I'm having another nightmare.

I screw my eyes shut, then open them again.

Lia is still there, staring, but not at me. Her gaze didn't follow me when I stumbled.

I pinch myself in a desperate attempt to wake up, but only searing pain greets me.

My entire body trembles as I approach her again. She continues to stare, but nothing on her body moves. Not her hands, not her limbs.

It's like she's asleep with her eyes open.

"Lia," I whisper, afraid anything louder will make her leap out of the bed and slice my throat as she did in my most recent nightmare.

She shows no reaction to hearing me. Her eyes still staring up ahead, caught in a foreign land. I run a hand in front of her face, but she doesn't follow it.

She's not even blinking, completely in a trance. Now that I'm no longer in shock, I can see that her eyes are blank, lighter than mine, as if the feelings that made them bright have completely disappeared.

I slowly touch her shoulder, even though my body is facing away, ready to bolt out of here any second.

Lia doesn't move. Not even an inch.

Is she paralyzed? Braindead? What is it exactly that causes a person to stay in this state without making a single movement?

"Lia…" I murmur again.

Nothing.

But that doesn't give me relief. If anything, the dread and gloom from earlier slash against my ribcage and tighten a noose around my heart.

My leg vibrates and I gasp, thinking Lia's touched me.

It's the phone. *Just the phone.*

I retrieve it with shaky fingers. The text that greets me deepens my trembling state.

Unknown Number: Have you found your mission yet?

My gaze slides from the screen to Lia and then back again, my heart thundering in my throat.

Does he…does the shadow have something to do with this? I type a response.

Lia: Does it have something to do with Lia?

Unknown Number: You became Lia Volkov for a reason. Find it. Do it. I'm losing patience, Duchess.

"What the hell is that supposed to mean?" I mutter under my breath.

Lia's head rolls to the side in an unnatural angle as if it's about to snap. Her eyes blink rapidly and her mouth opens as a long moan of pain leaves it. It's raw, deep, and so damn haunting.

I bolt out of her room, slamming the door behind me. My

fingers shake around the phone as I run. I don't stop running until I'm outside.

My heart hammers in my throat and I'm almost sure the guards notice it, but if they do, they don't comment on it.

I force myself to walk at a moderate pace until I reach the main house. I sprint up the stairs, barge into the bedroom, and hide under the covers.

My hand is still wrapped tightly around the phone as if it's a safe line from the ghostly fingers I feel trying to peel the covers off me or the marionette strings attempting to direct me to a dark tunnel.

What if Lia followed me? What if she'll kill me now?

Sweat covers my brow and my fingers are stiff as I stare at the phone's light under the darkness of the covers.

The texts from the unknown number glare back at me. He knows something. He said I took her place for a reason. But what? Aside from being coerced by Adrian into this, I had no reason to be Lia. I don't *want* to be Lia.

Then the realization of what I saw hits me like a sledgehammer.

She's alive.

Lia Volkov is alive.

I was barely hanging by a thread before, but now that I know she's alive, I feel tenfold worse than I did this morning.

Everything Adrian did to me has been fucked-up, but I thought I was up against someone dead, someone who doesn't exist. But she *does* exist. She *breathes*. She's right there, in the same damn house while a homeless lookalike is fucking her husband day in and day out.

I took her life, her son, her husband. Everything.

I think I'm going to throw up.

No wonder I had nightmares about her killing me or attempting to. I would've done the same. If my husband, the man I love, brought another woman to fuck under my roof, I would murder him with my own hands.

I wouldn't care that he calls her by my name or that he only brought her as a replacement. She's not me.

It's cheating.

It's fucking *wrong*.

I might have stayed quiet about it before, but now that I know, I can't go on like this.

I'm not as sick as Adrian. I'm not a homewrecker.

The other woman.

Bringing out my conversation with the shadow, I know that he's the only one who can allow me an escape.

After all, he kidnapped me from that birthday party, in the midst of all that security, just for a talk. He can do it again if I lie and say I know the mission.

This time, I won't go back to Adrian's side and his sick, twisted games.

This time, I'll need to fucking leave.

THIRTY

Adrian

WHEN I STEP INTO OUR BEDROOM, THE FIRST THING I smell is…roses.

There are a few candles lit on the nightstand, their lights flickering in the otherwise dark room.

I pause at the entrance as I shrug off my jacket. Today has been tedious as fuck and the meeting at Sergei's table was all about throwing jabs. While I don't usually bat an eye at that, the visible threat Vladimir and Sergei are showing toward me have made me wary.

Thankfully, the cameras in Sergei's mansion caught nothing about that night's kidnapping. I watched them myself, pretending I'd lost my card, but that part was completely cut off from the footage. The last thing it showed was Yan ushering Lia inside my car before she grabbed his shoulder and pulled him in with her.

I watched the footage from the opposite cameras, then paused and zoomed in to see the faces of the attackers, but they both wore masks. The driver had a hat on and he never raised his head enough for me to get a glimpse at his face.

The other one wasn't so careful, and that makes sense since I assume he's the one we found at the bottom of the cliff. He was a Spetsnaz turned assassin. A mercenary through and through, without any actual alliances, and like most professional Spetsnaz, it's impossible to track how he got in contact with his clients.

I was—and still am—more interested in the motherfucker who hid his face the entire time, because he seemed like he held the reins of this entire operation. I watched all the footage from the parking lot that day and even took a week's worth with me. He didn't appear on the camera. At all. Which means he knew all about them and made sure to go in their blind spots.

He also knew how to shoot Yan in a way that wouldn't be caught on camera, then used roads that have no surveillance.

Now, that's the part that makes zero fucking sense. Why did he go through all that trouble just to let them go? He could've inflicted more damage on me if he'd threatened me with Lia's life.

If Yan isn't part of this, and I'm ninety nine percent sure he isn't, he could've simply killed my guard.

Why the fuck did he release them both?

Unless his goal was never about capturing them.

Yan said that he was unconscious most of the car ride and couldn't recall much. He's lying. I can tell when Yan lies. But I still can't figure out why he's lying, so I told him that his livelihood depends on whether or not he remembers what happened in that fucking car.

Kolya gave me a dirty look before he realized he shouldn't be glaring at me. My second-in-command is softhearted as fuck when it comes to Yan, so much so that even he was fooled by his performance. He only sees his pain, but I see way past that.

I see into the bond he's formed with Lia over the time he's

been watching her—as much as I hate it. I see how his loyalty to me is no longer absolute. It's split between me and her and that will only hurt him in the long run.

I close the bedroom door behind me. When Ogla and Kolya said that Lia openly defied my order to stay away from Yan, I was coming here bent on punishing her, but that was before I saw this view.

Lia sits at her dresser, brushing her hair over her slender, delicate shoulder. She's wearing a blue satin nightgown that matches the color of her sparkling eyes.

Its strap falls off the creamy curve of her shoulder and she doesn't bother holding it up. Her attention is on the mirror as she slowly brushes the shiny strands of her dark hair.

I abandon my jacket on the chair as my feet breeze toward her. I don't have a choice in wanting to be near her. It's engraved in the very marrow of my bones without an option to purge it.

The scent of roses fills my nostrils when I'm within touching distance. As if finally feeling my presence, Lia's fingers pause on the brush and she meets my gaze through the mirror, mouth parting.

Her lips are painted in a dark red lipstick that I want to glide my tongue over and smear on her rosy cheeks.

"You're back," she murmurs.

"I'm back," I speak quietly as I place my hands on her shoulders. Instead of lifting up the strap, I push the other one down her arm. The material slips, uncovering her pale tits and her soft pink nipples.

I release one of her shoulders and grab a breast in my palm. It fits so perfectly, like it was made for my hand. My thumb strokes her nipple and she sucks in a deep breath as both her hands rest on her lap.

"Candles?" I ask nonchalantly as if I'm not, in fact, thinking about fucking her on the floor right now. She looks so tantalizing, like my most screwed-up fantasy coming to reality.

I'm talking to distract the animal in me from acting on those carnal desires and to somehow calm my raging hard-on.

That strategy is failing as we speak.

"They smell nice." Her voice is breathy, erotic as fuck, and it's not helping my mission. "Don't you think?"

"They do." I flick strands of her hair and lift it to my nose, inhaling it deeply. "But no more than you."

"Really?"

"Really."

"What do I smell like?"

"Like roses and fucking addictions."

"How do you know what addictions smell like?"

"I didn't. Until you."

"*Me?*" she drawls the word.

"Yes, you. Hmm. If I didn't know any better, I'd say you're seducing me, Lenochka." I pinch her nipple and she gasps before biting her lower lip.

The fact that she's muting herself should be a turn-off, but I'm too far gone for this woman to register that.

I release her hair and jam two of my fingers in her mouth, expecting her to bite me. At least I can feel how much she wants me that way. The harder her bite, the more she's gone for me as much as I am for her.

It's a fucked-up sense of self-affirmation. Something that keeps me afloat. I'm fully aware that she'll withdraw from me after we're done. That she'll turn to her side and give me her back, erasing me from her world. But right now, while I'm touching her, she's mine for the taking.

Mine to own.

Mine to fucking possess.

Instead of biting, though, Lia laps her tongue around my fingers. Her eyes meet mine through the mirror, a thousand sparkles going through them all at once.

I pinch her nipple, tugging on the tight rosy bud and she

gasps around my fingers. I pull them out before shoving them in again. She sucks on them, diligently and with renowned energy, her eyes never leaving mine.

"Fuck this." I lift her up, one arm wrapping around her waist. She's so tiny that she snuggles against me, even with one hand.

I knock whatever's on her dresser off with my other hand and she gasps as her fingers dig into my shoulders. Some bottles crash to the ground and other things fall over. Thankfully, none of the candles are here, because I would've started a fire.

The better option would've been to carry her to bed, to be a fucking human being, but I have no patience to reach the bed right now. The small distance seems like a light-year away. My steel-like control is null and void when it comes to this woman.

That's why I keep her away from the brotherhood. That's why I'd rather we don't go out in public. I'm always tempted to go on a killing spree if anyone so much as looks in her direction, let alone talks to her. I'm always tempted to lock us both in a place no one can find us.

I unbuckle my pants and yank them down with my boxer briefs to free my engorged dick. Lia watches me, unblinking, unmoving. She even stops breathing for a second.

She's usually watched my erection with a half-stunned, half-excited expression, and I'm praying for the excited part to win, because I'm on the verge of blowing up.

"I'm going to fuck you hard and fast tonight, Lia. I won't be gentle. I *can't* be gentle, but if I hurt you, if it becomes unbearable, tell me."

Her chest rises and falls heavily, her rosy-tipped breasts pushing up and down with every movement.

"Is that clear, Lia?"

She nods once, her gaze sliding to mine.

"Use your words. I want to hear you."

"Hear me?"

"Your voice. I want to hear it, Lia. So when I fuck you, don't mute yourself from me."

"Why is that so important to you?" she whispers.

"Because it's all of you." *And because she'll be my Lia. Wholly. Fully.*

My arm is still wrapped around her waist as I use my other hand to part her thighs and rip her underwear. It comes undone in one go, coupled with her gasp, as I slam inside her wet heat.

She welcomes me into her warmth, walls clenching and legs trembling. Her body caves into mine and her arms wind around my shoulders, nails clawing at my skin with every roll of my hips.

As promised, I take her hard and fast. Her back hits the mirror with each of my thrusts. I can feel her tightening around me in preparation of her orgasm.

But not yet.

I pull out of her and she releases a sound that's caught between a gasp and a whine. I bite her lip into my mouth before releasing it and flipping her around so she's facing the mirror.

Her eyes widen when she sees herself, half-naked, the nightgown bunched around her waist. She quickly bows her head when I thrust inside her. I clutch her jaw, fingers digging into her flesh, and tip her head in the direction of the mirror. "Look at your face when I fuck you. Look at how your body responds to me."

She tries to break eye contact again, seemingly ashamed of what she's seeing, but I keep my firm hold around her jaw, immobilizing her.

"Look at me, Lia."

She doesn't, so I roll my hips, pounding deeper into her, my fingertips sinking into her leg. "Look at me."

Her eyes meet mine through the mirror, hesitantly, almost as if she's afraid of what she'll find on my face. I'm not sure what she sees—it could be my animalistic need for her, my dark obsession with her, or the secrets and lies that wind our lives together.

Whatever it is keeps her rooted in place as I fuck her harder, powering into her with a maddening urgency. I place a protective hand around her stomach so she doesn't hit the dresser's edge with each of my raw thrusts.

Her small, perky breasts bounce and her legs tremble with the power of my hips.

"Adrian…" she moans, her voice the sweetest, most erotic, throaty sound I've ever heard.

She doesn't bite her lip, doesn't even attempt to look away from me.

Lia's moans rise in the air like the time I fucked her after she was kidnapped. They're raw and hungry, leaving the corners of her soul and slamming straight into mine.

That only manages to get me harder, my pace rising and my rhythm spiraling out of fucking control.

The fact that she's letting me hear her voice, unbound, unmodified, fills both my groin and my chest with an unmatched sense of lust, of ownership, and something else entirely different.

I've always been meant to ruin this woman, but I also get to own her.

To confiscate her.

To have her all for myself.

Lia comes with a hoarse cry, her fingers gripping the edge of the dresser. I join her soon after, spilling my seed into her and staking my claim.

Harsh breathing fills the air as we both slowly descend from our high. Lia still doesn't look away from me, as if her enchanting eyes are caught in a trance.

I brush my lips against her shoulders. A sheen of sweat covers her skin, but I couldn't give a fuck about that. Everything about her is perfection.

"Adrian?" she whispers.

"Hmm?" I mumble, continuing my slow nibbling on her skin. I'm only giving her some downtime before I carry her to bed and fuck her again. Slower this time. Though I'm sure that when I'm inside her, I won't be able to control myself.

Again.

"Have I been good?"

"Very, Lenochka."

"Do I deserve a reward?"

"Hmm." I slide my tongue up her throat before my lips meet her ear. "What do you want?"

"I want to go outside with Jeremy."

"You do, every day." I resume nibbling on her neck, fingers fondling her breasts and nipples, making her gasp.

"N-not to the garden."

"Then where?"

"The park. A place with actual children and people he can see."

"Security hazard. No."

"Adrian, please." She turns around to face me, so that she's caged between me and the dresser, and places a soft hand on my chest. "Kids his age need to go outside and meet other children. It'll just be for a few hours, and I'm sure your guards will keep an eye on us."

I don't like them outside, not even when my guards are with them. But I know that she's been stressed. I've sensed it in her absentminded gestures lately and the rising intensity of her nightmares. If she doesn't release that tension, she could—and will—start acting out soon.

While I'm not sure about the extent of what happens, patterns don't lie, and she's developing one.

But instead of agreeing readily, I raise a brow. "One condition."

Her eyes light up. "What?"

"From now on, you'll let me hear your voice."

She swallows, hesitating before she nods. I don't like that moment of hesitation, how she wants to say no but knows she has to say yes to get what she wants.

That doesn't mean I won't hold her to it, though.

I lift her chin. "Starting tonight."

"Does that mean you'll let us?"

"I'll make arrangements."

"Thank you." She smiles wide, and I kiss that smile. I feast on it, thrusting my tongue inside, and kissing her with a violence that leaves her gasping for air.

I love making her happy. I love how she melts in my arms and I intend to show her how much I love it all night long.

But even I know that this phase will come to an end. That we both need to face our demons.

I carry her in my arms toward the bed.

I'll worry about it when it happens, because right now, my wife is the only one who matters.

THIRTY-ONE

Winter

I NEVER THOUGHT ADRIAN WOULD ACTUALLY LET US out.

When I came up with this plan, the only variable was Adrian. He always keeps me in an ivory tower that he's somehow blocked from the outside world.

So when I asked him to let me and Jeremy outside, I thought he'd refuse, even though I used my body to relax him a little. Well, *used* is an exaggeration. I enjoyed every second of last night's sex. In fact, I enjoyed it so much that I was a little terrified by the pure want I saw on my face in the mirror.

But I also used it to my advantage.

Adrian becomes more open to me when he's inside me. I wouldn't say he lets his guard down, but he's more attuned to me. And for that, I had to completely let go, to sacrifice my fight so he'd fall more into me. I couldn't have managed to do it if I'd faked it or resisted him. He's too perceptive, so methodical that I held my breath the entire night thinking he'd catch onto me.

I'm still holding my breath.

Jeremy is playing with his toy car as we sit on the bench in a nearby park. Two of Adrian's guards stand not far from us, but I convinced them to give us some room. They're both bulky, scowly, and scary as hell. They would draw more attention instead of warding it off.

The sky is cloudy, the air chilly, and the wind is a constant reminder of the cold season each time it blows my hair back.

The park's busy, though, as I'd hoped. Kids are playing with their toys and adults are jogging or cycling. It's the type of chaos that's keeping the guards on their toes and will work in my favor.

The unknown phone number—or 'shadow,' as I like to call him—said he'll make contact. I sent him a text that I would be in this park today before I deleted the entire conversation.

I'm not sure if Adrian is going through my phone, so I couldn't take any risks.

Waiting for the shadow to make contact is a whole new concept of nerve-wracking. I've been watching my surroundings for the past half an hour like a junkie searching for her next fix. I forced myself to remain still so I wouldn't alert the guards. They're neither Kolya nor Yan, but they're Adrian's men all the same. They're alert and won't hesitate to inform their boss if they notice something sketchy.

My phone vibrates in my purse.

My heart thunders as I retrieve it. Adrian. Although I should feel disappointed that it's not the shadow, my pulse sky-rockets even more.

I wish there was a way to stop myself from having this reaction whenever Adrian is involved. I wish I wasn't lusting after a married man.

Fuck.

It's not only lust. It's something more, and that's what brought tears to my eyes this morning in the shower.

It doesn't matter, though. He's not mine and never will be. That's why I need to leave.

He doesn't call me usually—but then again, *usually* he has me under his watch at home.

Clearing my throat, I answer, "Hey."

"Are you and Jeremy having fun?" His calm, sophisticated voice comes through. I can imagine him sitting behind his desk and tapping his finger on the table.

"Yeah." I glance at Jeremy, who's now preoccupied with watching an army of ants disappearing behind the bench.

"It's cold."

"We wore coats, scarves, and gloves. You made sure of it, remember?"

"I do."

"We're fine, Adrian. We really are."

"I like that." His voice drops in range.

"You like what?"

"You two being fine."

You mean Lia and Jeremy. But I don't say that, choosing to remain silent.

"Have a date with me tonight."

"A d-date?"

"Yes. It's when two people have one-on-one time together."

"I know what a date is. I'm just not sure why you want it."

"You're already having a date with Jeremy. Why not with me?"

"Are you jealous of your own son?"

"Sometimes. What do you say?"

"About what?"

"The date."

"Do I even get to refuse?"

"You do, but it's more fun if you don't."

"Fine."

"I'll see you later, Lenochka."

"Go see your fucking comatose wife," I mutter to the dead line as I release a harsh breath.

I know all this is acting, but it's getting tedious and I want out of this whole charade. I want to erase the day that I first met Adrian. I want to go back to being the nobody on the streets, thinking about my next meal with Larry.

I wonder if I will find my old friend now.

"Mommy, look!" Jeremy exclaims, pointing at a mini passing circus.

A few clowns walk by with large balloons in their hands. A man on tall stilts throws balls in the air and another man with painted white and black eyes plays the harmonica. The crowd's attention shifts to them. The children—including Jeremy—are completely captivated by the show.

They stop near us, the clowns dancing and taking children by their hands. One of them perches over to Jeremy and gives him a balloon.

My little angel takes it with a huge grin on his face. Adrian's guards start to cross the distance between us, probably seeing the clowns as a threat.

My spine jerks upright, but for a different reason entirely. The mini circus is enveloping Jeremy. He dances with them, laughing and calling me over. I try to get to him, but they keep me out while smiling and juggling balls in the air.

I shove through them, my palms turning sweaty. "Jeremy!"

A heavy grip closes around my wrist and I shriek as I'm pulled back, but the sound is drowned by a hand against my mouth.

All I can breathe in is leather as he drags me away from the crowd. I attempt to kick him, but he grabs me by the hair. "Stay fucking still, Duchess. We don't want to snap your beautiful neck now, do we?"

"Jeremy!" I mumble against his hand, but it barely comes out as a word.

He doesn't release me until we're in an alleyway with my back pressed against a wall. I'm breathing harshly as I stare up at him. He's wearing a black hat and a mask that covers his nose and mouth. Only his eyes are visible, they're brown, deep, and so familiar.

"I told you I'm taking Jeremy with me," I say, panting.

He chuckles, the sound condescending. "You think Adrian will let his only son leave his sight? He'll flip the world upside down for him."

"Still—"

"Shut the fuck up with your whining, Duchess. You said you have something for me."

"I won't tell you until you take me and Jeremy away."

"*Away?* Your mission is here. Why the fuck should you go away?"

"But—"

"You don't remember, do you?" He expels an exaggerated sigh. "You're a pain in the fucking ass, Duchess. Always were."

"What?"

He removes his mask and I gasp. His face, the one with the slight stubble and the straight nose. It's the same from my nightmare. The man who was holding my hand as I grabbed the gun and pulled the trigger. "You!"

"Yes, me. Your one and only—or what-the-fuck-ever."

"But you're not real. It was a nightmare."

He pinches my cheek. Hard.

"Ow. What was that for?"

"It's how you differentiate between reality and a hallucination, Duchess. Pain means it's real. Lack of pain means it's a sick game playing in your head."

My mouth drops open. "How...how do you know that?"

"I know a lot of things about you, but most important of all, I know you didn't get your mission done, Lia."

"I'm not Lia," I mutter. For the first time, the words feeling insincere.

"Yes, you are, Duchess."

"No. The real Lia is lying in bed, staring at nowhere."

He raises a brow. "Is she real, though? Did you test your pain?"

My tongue sticks to the roof of my mouth and I force it down as I murmur, "No. I'm not Lia. I'm *Winter*."

"You really believe that shit, don't you? Just how far have you gone this time?"

"It is real," I snap. "I'm not Lia."

He leans over to whisper, "Then how did you help me with Adrian's assassination attempt a year ago? The nightmare you saw me in? Yeah, that was a memory, Duchess."

I shake my head frantically, not wanting to hear this, not wanting to let the influx of energy that's flowing through my veins hit my head.

My limbs tremble and I'm terrified of what that influx will bring.

"I'm Winter. My name is Winter Cavanaugh and—"

A flashback hits me so hard, my words die in my throat.

I'm standing in the middle of a church, murmuring "I do" as I stare up at Adrian. He's in a tux that makes him tenfold more handsome while I'm wearing a white wedding dress.

His strong hand wraps around my nape as he pulls me against his chest. "You're mine now, Mrs. Volkov."

His lips meet mine in all consuming kiss that robs my breaths. I don't kiss him back.

All I think about is how to finish his life.

I gasp as I'm thrust back to the present.

"Do you remember now?" Luca asks. That's his name. Luca. My partner in all of this.

And I do remember.

It's true.

My name is Lia. Lia Volkov.

TO BE CONTINUED

Adrian and Lia's story continues in the following book of the Deception Trilogy, *Tempted by Deception*.

Curious about Rai and Kyle who appeared in this book? You can read their completed story in *Throne of Power*.

For a sneak peek into Adrian's past, you can download the free prequel, Dark Deception at:
bookhip.com/RZJCDQG.

WHAT'S NEXT?

Thank you so much for reading *Vow of Deception*! If you liked it, please leave a review.
Your support means the world to me.

If you're thirsty for more discussions with other readers of the series, you can join the Facebook group, Rina's Spoilers Room at www.facebook.com/groups/RinaSpoilers

Next up is the continuation of the Deception Trilogy, *Tempted by Deception.*

Blurb

My husband. My villain.

We started with death and blood.
We started with games and carnal pleasure.
Adrian and I shouldn't have been together.
He's wrong.
I'm wrong.
What we have is the epitome disaster.
Yet, it's impossible to stop.
My husband will either destroy me or I'll destroy him.

ALSO BY RINA KENT

For more books by the author and a reading order, please visit:

www.rinakent.com/books

ABOUT THE AUTHOR

Rina Kent is a *USA Today*, international, and #1 Amazon bestselling author of everything enemies to lovers romance.

She's known to write unapologetic anti-heroes and villains because she often fell in love with men no one roots for. Her books are sprinkled with a touch of darkness, a pinch of angst, and an unhealthy dose of intensity.

She spends her private days in London laughing like an evil mastermind about adding mayhem to her expanding universe. When she's not writing, Rina travels, hikes, and spoils cats in a pure Cat Lady fashion.

Find Rina Below:

Website: www.rinakent.com

Neswsletter: www.subscribepage.com/rinakent

BookBub: www.bookbub.com/profile/rina-kent

Amazon: www.amazon.com/Rina-Kent/e/B07MM54G22

Goodreads: www.goodreads.com/author/show/18697906.
Rina_Kent

Instagram: www.instagram.com/author_rina

Facebook: www.facebook.com/rinaakent

Reader Group: www.facebook.com/groups/rinakent.club

Pinterest: www.pinterest.co.uk/AuthorRina/boards

Tiktok: www.tiktok.com/@rina.kent

Twitter: twitter.com/AuthorRina

Made in United States
North Haven, CT
12 December 2023

45741335R00178